The Accidental Yogini

By Tracey L. Ulshafer

Nicole -
I think
you'll enjoy + appreciate
the journey
Tracey

ISBN-10: 1985197545

ISBN-13: 978-1985197541

This book is dedicated to my husband, Scott. Thank you for challenging me to be a better person, even though you sometimes drive me crazy doing it.

Acknowledgments

As a writer it is sometimes easy to feel that I have done all the work on a book or project. The truth of the matter is that without many people, this book simply wouldn't have manifested. It is often challenging to share my vision with people and I am always put at ease when it is received well. Thankfully, to everyone who took the time to edit or peruse it, *The Accidental Yogini* was received very well!

First I wish to thank both Mary Procacci and Suzy Fenton, who both edited the book from different perspectives and validated many facets of the storyline. To Pamela Barricklow, I wish to extend my unending gratitude for the professional critique and proofs — those darn Em Dashes! And to Dustin E. Mascione, illustrator extraordinaire, for the beautiful job on co-creating the cover art of our Accidental Yogini.

To all of my students, both past and present, I continue to learn from you daily. Thank you for continually renewing my love of yoga as I see it through your eyes, anew all the time.

And to my family and friends who always support my quirky stories and books. I am forever grateful to you all.

I hope that this book speaks to you all in some way, for there is surely a little piece of you in it somewhere.

Namaste.

Tracey

yogini

[yoh-*guh*-nee]

noun

1.   a woman who practices yoga

1880-85; < Sanskrit *yogini*, feminine derivative of yogin yogi

Dictionary.com Unabridged

Based on the Random House Dictionary, © Random House, Inc. 2017

Chapters:

Chapter 1

The Nectar of Life

"Look past your thoughts, so you may drink the pure nectar of This Moment." ~ Rumi

Kristin shook one final hand, thanked him for attending her presentation, then clasped her hands together and took a huge sigh. As the breath comfortably released from her mouth, she felt her shoulders melt and her body glide into a state of perfect being. Years of working on her kids' yoga project was finally completed and she had just spent the last couple of hours discussing the benefits of teaching yoga to children at an ivy league university to an audience of educators and parents. Both the presentation, and she, had been well received and now that it was complete, she felt relief.

As she gathered her personal belongings, she nodded to the organizer of the event and slipped out the side door. She had noticed earlier a lovely courtyard on the side of the building, and felt a need to go there and kick off her high-heeled shoes and run her toes through the grass. She was a stranger to heels anymore, having given up office attire for her more preferred bare-footed yogini life. And yet, there were times when it was called for, and this was one.

Kristin found a bench and put her purse, bag and sweater down. She slipped off her shoes and stepped into the grass eagerly. She took a deep breath and lifted her arms over her head, gently bending to one side, taking several deep breaths before bending to the other. Her body mimicked the half moon that hung in the spring night sky. The temperature was a perfect seventy-eight degrees and there seemed to be a million stars out tonight. As she waved her arms from side to side, she gazed upward to appreciate the beauty above — the vastness and unlimited potential that the night sky offered a glimpse of. And then there was the moon: the light in the otherwise dark night, softly guiding the way. She loved the energy of the waning moon. Most people focus on the energy of the full moon, which can be rather intense. She preferred the softer, gentler moon as it quietly recedes into darkness. At these times the sweetness of the nectar of life could be felt, without the over-stimulated and, often, manic energies felt when the moon was full. No, this was a her kind of evening and she felt with humility her place in it.

Kristin sat down on the bench and folded her feet underneath her body, in a traditional yogic posture. She took another few deep breaths with her eyes closed. A well-known buzz came from her purse. Kristin smiled. She knew it was Joshua, checking in on her to find out how it went. He had wanted to be with her today, but obligations with his own children kept him at home. And that was just one of the qualities that she loved about this man: his deep commitment to his family. She felt happy to now be a part of it. As she was thinking about Joshua she felt another well-known buzz. She snorted out loud. *That* would be her mother. She didn't even have to look — she just knew. One of the surprising benefits to being connected more through body, mind and soul had been the awakening of her intuition. Her purse buzzed again and she laughed out loud, not caring what the students and faculty passing by might think of her.

As she sat on the bench laughing, she felt the presence of her uncle there with her, also laughing. He had been a bright light in her life, always trying to make her smile and keep her happy during difficult times. She loved him for how he went out of his way to be there for her after her father died. And she felt him present with her, laughing at all the buzzing going on in her purse. She could visualize all of his funny faces, and that made her laugh even more.

Kristin didn't feel a pressing need to check her phone or call them back. Maybe another time in her life she would have. But right now what she wanted — needed — most was to just be in the moment. This beautiful, amazing moment had been given to her where the stars had all aligned perfectly, and she wanted to bask in it and enjoy. She soon found herself crying sweet tears of joy. If she had felt a need to post on social media how she felt at that moment she would have used the word "blessed." And in that context it might have sounded trite or self-serving. But as she put her hands over her heart, softly cried and just felt herself in the moment, she knew that blessed was simply the only word that would describe how she was feeling. And, this feeling was only meant for her and her alone. She sat with it for some time.

Eventually, when it felt right, Kristin opened her eyes and started to stretch and put her heels back on. Her feet cringed as she squeezed them back into the confined space of the shoes. She stood up and fixed her blouse and gathered her things. Today she looked much more like the office employee she had once been. But even though she might look the part, she thought for a moment how different her life was today from those days way back when. She had found purpose in her life. She had found love. She had found herself. Somehow and somewhere along the way, by the grace of the universe, her life had aligned and she was finally in the flow of this expressive life-force energy and connected in such a way that even the little things that she would have obsessed over and worried about in the past, no longer affected her energy or life today. Of course there are always interesting turns of events in life and sometimes, she learned, one just had to let go and trust.

Kristin began walking to her car, listening to her heels click on the pavement. She remembered when she had first started working in an office after school how that sound made her feel important in some way. As if to say, "Here I come, world," the sound of her heels clicking on the floor was a warning to others that she was on the move. Then sometime several years in, she would try to hide the same sound of her heels clicking so that nobody heard her or knew that she was around. At some point she realized she would rather blend in to the cubicles of the office than draw attention to herself. Attention either meant more work or work-related conversations, and back then her work was not anything that lifted her spirit or left her feeling thriving or purposeful at all. No, back then, work was just that — work. Back then, her mind was underused, her body falling apart, and her spirit in the dumps. Today, she could hardly see much of that person. Today, her life was much sweeter.

Soma, she thought to herself, pulling her car out of the parking lot and glancing up at the moon one more time before driving away. Soma is the Sanskrit word for the sweet, divine nectar of life. And as she drove off from a successful evening of sharing her life's work with others and being in the pregnant pause before it erupted into a full state-wide program, that particular word was the only one that seemed to describe this moment.

Kristin smiled because, well, because it was simply all that she could do.

Chapter 2

FML

"Happy people find a way to live with their problems, and miserable people let their problems stop them from living."
~ Sonya Parker

There it was again — that sharp pain digging into Kristin's right hip. She gasped and clutched her lower back in an all-too familiar way. Leaning back in her office chair she closed her eyes, tightened her muscles and held her breath until the pain began to somewhat subside. Finally that agonizing, initial pain went away. Opening her eyes, Kristin reconnected to the computer screen that sat in front of her. Unfortunately she was still at work. A quick glance at the corner of the screen revealed that it was merely 3:15 pm, which indicated nearly another two hours of this same grim situation. She honestly didn't know if she could hang in there that long. But what were her choices, really? This was her life. And Kristin felt as though she was running through the same sad cycle day after day.

Holding her breath again, Kristin pushed her arms into her chair and lifted herself up. It took her a moment to stand fully upright due to the pain, but she managed to do it. Although she couldn't see many of her co-workers hiding in their cubicle confines, it was easy to hear the rattling of keyboards and the occasional phone ringing across the long, open workroom. It was the late-day drive when most of her colleagues sat quietly pushing out as much work as they could in an effort to make the beginning of the next workday a little less stressful — as if these efforts had any real ability to do such a thing. Kristin rolled her eyes and took a few cautionary steps out into the hallway, heading towards the bathroom. While it seemed like the company was slowly taking away every right or privilege that the workers had, Kristin mused that until artificial intelligence replaced the workforce entirely that the powers that be would still have to manage allowing their workers to take bathroom breaks. They were also allowed two government appointed ten-minute breaks each day as well. The second of which Kristin realized she had not taken yet today. So, she quickly skipped back to her cubicle to retrieve her purse. For that moment she forgot about the pain in her lower back. With purse in hand, Kristin smiled and made her way down the long hallway in the back of the room, then followed a small stairway downward to a level below. She noticed in the quiet stairwell that her footsteps sounded louder than usual today. Was she more tired? Or perhaps she was having more trouble walking than she usually did. The reason hardly mattered. And Kristin thought, *It is what it is...*

At the bottom of the stairway Kristin took a sharp right and then another right behind some old file cabinets. The lights above the old filing system hissed and blinked as if they might give out at any moment. Like a victim in a horror movie, she glanced back over her shoulder, almost ready to see something she would have to outrun. Of course, nothing was there that she could see. And Kristin was almost to her destination. Another one hundred yards and she clutched the handle of the outside door and thrust it open to a gathering of a loud bunch of co-workers huddled around the smokers' patio. She nodded at a few of them and they nodded back. There were no chairs in this special area so she rifled through her purse and pulled out her pack of cigarettes and popped one in her mouth while she fiddled around some more looking for her lighter. While Kristin was looking, a lighter was presented to her from her left. She looked up to see Brian grinning at her. She smiled back and let him light her up. After one big, long drag she finally exhaled slowly. Suddenly she was feeling more herself or more normal. She felt momentarily intoxicated.

"The first drag is the best, isn't it?" said Brian taking another puff of his nearly finished cigarette.

"Absolutely," she responded, then clutching her lower back, grimaced in pain.

"Back still bothering you?" he asked.

"Always. What else is new?" she sarcastically responded.

"You do that physical therapy?" he asked, looking mildly encouraging.

She laughed and shook her head, taking another long drag before answering. "Yea, I tried it. Felt worse on the days when I went there than when I just went home and drank a couple of glasses of wine and rested."

That statement was not entirely true. The truth was that she hardly gave it a chance. She went three times and just felt defeated each time and gave up. The therapists expected her to do some exercises that were difficult for her and she didn't see where that was going to help. She hated doing anything physical anyway. It was certainly much easier to sit on her couch and relax the muscles that were aching rather than use them. But she didn't quite feel like sharing all of that with Brian, or with anyone else for that matter. She knew that most people might have pushed her to try it some more and she was tired of that conversation. She had made up her mind. Brian probably wouldn't have pressed her like that, however. She was aware that he had a "thing" for her since the last office Christmas party when he gave her an uncomfortably long hug. She broke out of it before he had a chance to go for what she assumed would be an attempt at a kiss. She thought of an old adage of not "dipping the pen in the company ink." It was something she had heard her favorite uncle say once...or twice. She always tried to keep work and pleasure separate — and usually there was no issue doing that, since there literally was nothing at all pleasurable about her work.

"You doing anything good this weekend?" Brian asked, this time snuffing out the remaining portion of his cigarette, and jamming his hands into his pockets, fiddling around nervously with what sounded like change.

Kristin shook her head no, then decided to give a longer answer: "My sister has this thing for her kid — my niece. I will probably go over there for a little while. My friend and I had talked about going somewhere to get away, but I've used up most of my sick days, so..." As she trailed off, she took another drag of her cigarette, rolled her eyes and then lifted her shoulders up and down as if to say, "whatever."

Brian nodded his head without any retort, then pulled his hand out of his pants pocket and checked his watch. "Well, I better get back. They started making us clock out in IT for our breaks."

"Really?" Kristin reacted, surprised.

"Yup, and it's rolling out company-wide next month once we work out the kinks, so enjoy your extra few minutes of break time while you can or else you're going to start seeing time coming off your paycheck," Brian said. She rolled her eyes and took another drag of her cigarette. Brian tapped her awkwardly on the upper arm and walked away with his head down.

Clocking out for breaks? Kristin felt as though another piece of her died a little bit more in that moment. She tried to focus on and enjoy what she could of the last of her cigarette but angry thoughts about her company kept creeping into her mind instead. She felt hopeless. There was nothing that she could do about it. Nobody cared. The big guns still made their money and got their bonuses every year. She guessed taking a few more pennies out of the pockets of employees like her would only line their own pockets more. She could feel her rage boiling and consuming her. She squinted again in pain and grabbed her lower back. There was that pain again. And she just didn't know what to do about that either.

Not feeling like conversing with anyone else she snuffed out her cigarette early and headed inside, walking passed the flickering lights, up the lonely staircase, and down the long hallway. Just before her desk she darted off to the left and to the bathroom where she sat and stared blankly at the stall walls for several minutes, leaning forward with her arms resting on her thighs. Somehow that seemed to relieve something in her back. So even though she didn't really have to use the toilet, she sat there for a while. She wasn't sure how long she was there, but was brought back to the present moment when the bathroom door banged open again. And even though she didn't actually use the toilet, she pulled off some paper, threw it in the bowl, and flushed. She had no idea why she carried the lie out to that extent, but she somehow felt obligated to do that and to wash her hands before going back to her cubicle. Of course the soap dispenser was almost empty when she went to wash her hands, and there were never enough paper towels this late in the workday. She waved her hands and air-dried them for a moment before finding a creative way to open the door with wet hands.

On the way back to her desk Kristin ran into Betty, who almost seemed to be looking for her. She smiled weakly at Betty and dropped her purse onto her chair.

"What's up, Betty?" Kristin asked, faking concern and sincerity.

"Hey, Kristin. Tom wants to know if you have those reports ready yet? He said you would have them by noon today, but I didn't want to bother you about it earlier." Betty looked at her watch, grimaced, and opened her eyes widely as if to report to Kristin that the deadline was long gone.

Kristin had been waiting for Betty to come to her since noon. She had anticipated this conversation a few hours ago, yet it hadn't made a difference in the actualization of the material being completed. "Yea, I would have finished them by noon if my computer hadn't locked up three times this morning. I don't know what happened. I called IT and they just kept telling me to reboot the system. Every time I did I lost the work I had done before." Kristin looked at Betty waiting for a response, but soon saw that there would be none to receive. "Anyway," she continued, "I will do my best to get them to him before I leave today."

Betty shook her head. "You know, if you don't he's going to want you to come in tomorrow."

Yes, Kristin was fully aware that she might have to come in on Saturday to finish the reports. But what did that matter? It wasn't like she had anything else to do with her Saturday. She smiled and nodded at Betty and waited for the response. Finally Betty nodded and made a faint indefinable noise before walking away from her.

"FML," Kristin grunted under her breath.

The rest of the afternoon went just about as expected. Her computer locked up two more times, creating entire reboots that took nearly twenty minutes each time to get her back online. Each time Kristin held her breath and cursed in her head, lest she actually let out how she really felt. Of course when everyone else started heading out at 5 p.m., she knew that she would have to wait out Betty and Tom leaving before she could sneak out herself...only to return early tomorrow morning. So, she cowered down in her cubicle until it was completely quiet in the office.

FML, indeed, she thought.

* * *

The cool water felt great between her toes. Kristin smiled as the warm sun cascaded down her face while she waded her feet through the pool water. She lifted a piña colada up and took a sip. It was yummy. No, it was yummier than yummy. That was *the best* piña colada that she had ever had! While she was smiling, two strong hands began to massage her shoulders. She sighed and looked up only to receive a warm, hot kiss from her masseur. Now *this* was the life!

As she continued smiling the weather abruptly changed and in another moment she was in the midst of a downpour. Her man was suddenly nowhere in sight and the deluge was about to ruin her hair and her phone. She got up to run under an umbrella for cover, but instead found herself back at her desk staring at a black computer screen. Oh yes, that's right, the damn thing had locked up again, and on a Saturday when there was no IT there to help her. Not that they had helped the previous day either, but this situation was certainly not getting her any closer to finishing her reports.

Kristin sat back in her office chair and assessed her options. First of all, was this report necessary? Well, that didn't matter much since it was her job to hand it in. Her boss needed it and she was supposed to do it. There was obviously something wrong with her computer. Nobody else seemed to have the same issues that she did with it locking up all the time, or if they did, they rebooted it and went about their day without complaining. Regardless, she really didn't have a choice. She had to get it done, but, how? She tapped her fingers on her desk until a light went off in her brain.

She sat up quickly and smiled. She had a thought — perhaps she could get it done on a co-worker's computer. She decided to text Janice to see if she could access her computer. Janice sat just two desks down from her so it would be minimal back and forth.

She sent Janice a text and crossed her fingers. "Come on, Janice, just answer me back!"

Kristin grew impatient. She tapped her fingers on her desk. She bit her upper lip. She checked Facebook from her phone. She even went to the bathroom. And, just for good measure, she rebooted her computer...again.

Almost as soon as she logged into Facebook she regretted the decision. Most of her high school friends who were married with children had posts of their amazing family days in the park or in their fabulous backyards. She scrolled down and checked out some of her sister's posts from the past week. Right, tomorrow was her niece's piano recital picnic. An eight-year-old's piano recital could probably be missed, but not her sister's eight-year-old's. She had already said she was going to the "event," but she clicked into it anyway. There was a post of her niece practicing. Kristin giggled. At eight years old the kid was already better than she was. Granted, she had never taken any lessons, but still, the kid was a better piano player than she would ever be.

Her phone flashed a text from Janice. She gave her the thumbs-up emoji. That was it — no questions, no actual words, just an emoji indicating that it was fine to use her system. So, why waste any more time? With that, Kristin grabbed her data folders and hopped up to get to Janice's computer. And then it happened again — that stabbing pain in her lower back and hip area.

She let out a number of profanities loud enough for the staff to hear the echo through the office walls Monday morning. Then she held her breath, put one hand on her body and limped over to Janice's desk. With the concentration of a monk she banged out the report and emailed it to her boss. Finally, something had gone her way this week. Granted, it was a work-related victory, but she had to be thankful for something. Didn't she?

Kristin turned her non-working computer back off, shut off her cubicle light, and gathered her personal belongings. For a moment, she thought about smoking at the desk. She gazed up and saw the smoke detector just a cubicle over and realized that smoking at the desk would probably be quite a poor decision. But she was feeling so good about completing the job, she thought that maybe this one time nobody would mind. She really did. And just as she was pulling her pack out of her purse her phone went off. This startled and halted her, fortunately. It was her sister calling. She always had a knack of calling Kristin when she was just about to do something very stupid. She often wondered how her sister could know?

"Yo, what's up?" Kristin said, jamming her cigarettes back into her purse and getting up and heading towards the door.

"Wow, you actually sound a little cheery," said Sandy, surprised, as this was not her sister's "normal."

Kristin smiled, pushed the office door open and stepped outside to finally enjoy her weekend. "Well, I finished my report and I am now off for the weekend. So, I am happy."

"Well good. I'm glad to hear that. You're coming to Brenda's recital tomorrow, right? You said you were. Brenda is expecting you to be there."

Kristin rolled her eyes. Brenda surely was not expecting her to be there. That was just her sister's way of guilting her for her own reasons. That's what her sister did. It was her way of controlling people without taking responsibility for it. There's a name for that type of personality trait, but Kristin couldn't remember it right now. It didn't matter. It was what it was.

"Of course I am. I said I was, didn't I? I'll be there."

The rest of the conversation went on with Kristin listening to Sandy discuss all of the things she had to accomplish between now and tomorrow night, and how she would be hosting their family and friends and other kids from the recital and their parents after the recital. So, as the only aunt, that Kristin should bring this and do that.

Her sister was still talking when she got into her car and turned it on. She hit the Bluetooth button and Sandy's voice screamed through the car speakers as if she were right in the car with her talking through a megaphone. Kristin forgot that she herself had been singing rather loudly to some aggressive lyrics on the way to work this morning and had left the volume up pretty high. She quickly remedied that and continued to listen to her sister talk as she drove home. This affected Sandy in no way at all.

By the time Kristin hung up with Sandy it was 1:25 p.m. She hadn't had lunch yet and had the rest of the day and night open. She thought about calling one of her friends to go out, but while walking to her car her back started shouting at her again. And even though she could have really used a good dose of girl talk, wine and Seafood Grill, she decided to head inside for Advil, pasta and the couch. It was a lovely day outside, but she just didn't have it in her to do anything. She felt like crap physically. And the momentary mental ease that she felt from finishing her report had quickly receded. The reality of her thirty-four-year-old body failing her began to bring her right back down to the energy of despair.

She walked into her townhouse and dropped her purse on the table. Clicking the light switch on Kristin went into the kitchen to put on a pot of hot water. Spaghetti and marinara sauce it was — again. She would make the whole pound so that she could warm it up for dinner too. While in the kitchen, she noticed the spider plant Sandy had given her sitting on the kitchen counter, away from any light that would have helped it grow. It was looking pretty sad. She stuck her finger in it and found it to be bone dry. Several thoughts came to her:

> *When was the last time that you watered it?*
> *Have you ever watered it?*
> *How do you manage to kill everything?*

Out of pity she picked it up and held it under the faucet until water started pouring out of the bottom. She let it drain and then plopped it back on the counter, thinking she may never remember to water it again, poor, pathetic thing. She had warned her sister when she'd given it to her that the chances of it making it were slim. It was just too much trouble remembering to water it just the right amount and give it sunlight. The truth was, she wasn't good at keeping anything alive. The fish tank her friend Melissa had given her lasted about six months. Two of those months actually had live fish in it. After that, however, something happened and all the fish died. Then she just walked past the dirty water for another four months until Sandy came over one weekend and tossed it all out. That was the end of the fish and the fish tank. She had managed to kill a cactus that a co-worker had given her for her birthday three years ago, too. That's right, a cactus! She just couldn't do it. That's why she didn't want kids. The thought of that responsibility was just too much to bear. She imagined, instead of it being a little spider plant, that it was a little two-year-old, sitting there in its high chair, forgotten. Then she imagined the two-year-old screaming and crying and realized the other reasons she didn't want children. They were loud, noisy, messy, and needy. She certainly couldn't even consider caring for another human being until she figured out her own self-care, which wasn't going very well thus far.

As the water boiled, Kristin went into the bathroom and grabbed her Advil. She took out two pills and popped them into her mouth, chasing them down with a big gulp of Coca-Cola. She took another swig of Coke and walked back into the kitchen. The pot was warmer, but still not ready. So she went into the living room and turned on the TV. Nothing of value was on. She flipped through several reality shows, pausing momentarily to consider watching a few before ultimately moving on. HBO, Showtime, Cinemax and Stars all had the same tired movies playing. She continue looking through the lesser known cable channels looking for something remotely interesting, and somewhere in that meandering she could hear sizzling sounds coming from the stovetop, indicating that the pot of water had started to boil and was now overflowing. Even after tending to the next phase of the pasta and going back surfing through more channels, she was still no closer to deciding what to watch.

An hour later with a half pound of pasta, two Advil, and a glass of wine in her stomach, Kristin fell asleep on the couch. It was barely 3 p.m. An old episode of *I Dream of Jeanie* was playing while she slept.

Sometime in the middle of the night she awoke from the gunfire of *M.A.S.H.* and thought of going to bed. Then Kristin realized, *what does it matter*? She was as comfortable as she was going to get right there on the couch. Why not stay until morning? She decided to leave the television on for companionship, hit the "Do Not Disturb" button on her phone and was just about to fall back into a deep sleep when she rolled over and felt that gripping pain in her low back and hip. "*FML*...," she thought, dozing off. That seemed to be her life's theme. And it was difficult to imagine any other reality.

Chapter 3

Leave Me in My Misery

"Joy is a natural phenomenon. Misery is your creation."
~ Sadguru

If there was one thing for certain it was that Sandy could certainly throw a party. Sandy and her husband, Sam, had a great house in which to host special events. Kids ran around outside swinging from play sets while parents gathered on the patio and drank wine spritzers and beer with little citrus wedges inside the bottles. Every one of Sandy's friends seemed sincerely happy. Kristin sometimes wondered if they were putting on a show or if this happiness was actually true. As an outsider, watching families together often left her feeling that every one of them was happier in their family lives than she was in hers. She often equated her general malaise with living alone and not being married. She hadn't yet reconciled in herself how to work this out since she presently felt strongly against having children and being married. So instead of thinking about her future or navigating her feelings, she chose to ignore and run from them. She realized that everyone has his or her issues, but for some reason it appeared that Sandy and her friends had a lot fewer issues than she did. She decided, in her infinite wisdom, that her judgment was correct and went about engaging in more self-loathing.

Kristin witnessed their mother flirting with one of Sandy's friend's husbands. Well, her mother wouldn't call it that, of course. She observed her mom flip her hair, drop her head, lift her gaze coyly and even giggle. No, that woman knew what she was doing. She'd watched her mother behave that way for a very long time now. It had been nearly thirty years since her father died and she watched her mother date a lot of men throughout the years. Mom never managed to settle down again though. Admitting that their father was the love of her life, Kristin's mother said that nobody else would ever come close to comparing to him. But that did not stop her from flirting, dating, and even holding a string of monogamous relationships that would each ultimately fail because she would not commit to the relationship in the way that the man wanted. This behavior did not seem so strange to Kristin. According to all her female friends, men were the ones who were supposed to play hard to get and not want to commit. However, that was not exactly her personal experience. Although Kristin didn't deem herself a natural flirt like her mother, she had learned from her to keep men at a distance, emotionally. She had dated before and had even been in a couple of more serious relationships, but just when things started to get more serious, Kristin would withdraw, as she had watched her mother do so many times. In fact, her love life was kind of like that spider plant — she just didn't give it much energy to grow. And she didn't know if she even wanted to. She thought that maybe someday that she would find a way to be with someone fully and be happy. She wondered if she just hadn't met the right guy yet or if she hadn't matured enough? Maybe it was a little of both — along with some other things that hadn't yet been revealed to her. Or, there was always that possibility that she was meant to be alone. Kristin rolled her eyes at herself and at her mother's behavior.

She may have not had all of her own answers, but one thing was for sure, watching her mother flirt was exhausting. Kristin decided to walk away and went to get another beer. She shuffled over to the bounty of beverages, chose a bottle, popped off the top, and put it up to her mouth, taking a big guzzle.

"Hey, let me get you a piece of orange," said Sandy's husband. She hadn't even noticed Sam there.

"No, no, that's ok," said Kristin, wiping her mouth. "I like my beer tasting like, well, beer."

Sandy's husband nodded and walked away. She appreciated the fact that Sam cared enough to try, but never pushed her. He definitely hadn't learned that from Sandy. Kristin took another swig of her beer and felt it slide down her throat, coating it with a cooling, magical sizzle. Now, what she really wanted was a cigarette. But she had told her mom that she had quit smoking two years ago and had thus managed to keep that a little secret somehow. Her cigarettes were sitting in the car, but she decided not to chance sneaking one in the event that her mother had come looking for her. She dared not leave the pack in her purse because her mother would still sneak into it from time to time and check. It angered her that her mother did not trust her. Yet the irony that she was lying to her failed to come up when she thought about her mother's boundary issues. She took another big chug of beer, swallowing all those feelings, when her sister walked up with a male friend in tow.

"Hey, Kristin, I want you to meet Joshua. His son, Michael, was also in the recital tonight. He and Brenda are very good friends," Sandy said, swinging around to find the kids and pointing them out. Currently, they were at the chocolate fountain dipping potato chips in it. "Anyway, I thought that you and Joshua might like to talk since you're both single."

Kristin immediately flushed and flashed her sister the wild, "I can't believe you" eyes. Sandy smiled. She realized that this introduction had made her sister uncomfortable, but then, what didn't make her sister uncomfortable? Sandy realized that if she didn't push herself into her sister's life to help her get on with it, that she was going to be unhappy and alone even longer. And nobody, not even Kristin, really wanted that.

"Well, I'll leave you two alone. I better get the rest of the food out." And with that Sandy walked off without looking back, leaving Kristin and Joshua standing there awkwardly.

Silence hung over Kristin and Joshua with the intensity of a storm cloud just before cracking thunder and opening up a tremendous downpour. Kristin honestly didn't know what to say. She could hardly look at him. Instead, she decided to look down at her feet. This was not helpful. Now she found herself regretting not getting a pedicure before the party. She also realized that, in addition to having chipped toenails, her left shoe had begun to fray apart and was starting to look like a cat's toy. She decided to stop looking at herself because moving upward was only going to prove to be even more devastating to her already frail ego. As she took another swig of her beer, she wondered why it even mattered to her how she looked to Joshua.

He had a kid so who cared if he was single and available anyway? Sandy knew that she had no interest in dating a guy with kids. She was really going to kill her sister this time. Seriously, that wasn't just a series of words. She was actually thinking about how she could get away with murdering her sister when Joshua finally broke the ungodly long silence between them.

"Wow, this is AWK ward," he said, breaking it into two words to emphasize the discomfort he was feeling.

Kristin laughed. The way he said it was kind of funny. She had to respect a guy who didn't try to jump right in and make a move on her with compliments or impressive conversation. She rather enjoyed his unassuming dorkiness.

"You can say that again. Leave it to Sandy," she replied, smiling and rolling her eyes.

Joshua nodded and repeated "AWK ward" and then laughed in that same vein. Of course she hadn't meant for him to actually repeat what he had said. And yet, there it was coming out of his mouth. He took a drink and swallowed loudly. She nodded and looked back at her chipped toenails.

In the strange silence between them, Joshua found himself stealing glances at Kristin. She seemed like a tough nut, a little withdrawn and definitely uninterested in exploring a new relationship. And yet, there was something there inside her that he felt quite drawn to. She seemed familiar to him in some way. He thought at first that perhaps it was because she was Sandy's sister and that the family resemblance was what he was seeing. But the longer he stole a look or watched her move, the more he realized that there was something deeper to their acquaintance. Although he was secure in what he was feeling, he was also quite sure that Kristin was not at the same place that he was. She was looking at anything else that she could instead of him. If they had a connection in some way, she was not on the same page with it as he was. And yet, it seemed a shame not to at least try to see if he could bring what he was feeling out of her. His upbringing had taught him to never give up on people and to always see people in their best and highest light.

Naturally, then he began to ramble. "If I had known that she was going to dump me off and run like this, I wouldn't have followed her over. I'm sorry. She just yanked on my sleeve and told me to come with her over here. I didn't know she was going to pull a move like that. I hate when people do things like that to me. I'm a grown-ass man, I know how to have a basic conversation with a woman if I want to." Joshua took a big drink from his own beverage.

His awkwardness was obvious and Kristin wondered if he had meant to verbalize that last phrase out loud or if he had meant to keep it inside his head. She didn't want to respond in the event that he didn't realize that it had, in fact, come out. Could it actually be that he felt even weirder than she did at this moment? That small bit of information gave her a slight sense of confidence. She smiled and joked with him that he could feel free to walk away and she wouldn't feel bad about him doing so. He graciously offered to stay so that they could try to come up with a plan for vengeance against Sandy. She liked that idea, and flipped her hair, giggling. Instantaneously Kristin realized that she was performing like her mother, and quickly stifled her laughter. Joshua noted the spark, albeit a short and quick one. There was indeed something there between them. Perhaps polite conversation could bring it out.

So they talked about Sandy and Sam, the house and the recital. Joshua talked about his children, Michael and Gabriella, who Kristin had not yet met. He told her how his ex-wife, a devout Catholic, had named both of the children after Archangels. Michael was born on the winter solstice and as an infant dealt with serious respiratory issues. Kristin watched the smile in his eyes as he talked about never giving up hope and how he knew that his son would be able to heal himself and grow strong. When Michael and Brenda looped past them again as they were talking, Kristin could see that Michael was certainly faring well. She even found herself smiling and feeling what could only be the fatherly love that Joshua had for his children. It was a weird feeling for Kristin to acknowledge and she found herself quickly blinking her eyes and swigging her beer to ward it off. And then she grew silent again.

Kristin found the silence intolerable. Just when she was about to give up and excuse herself, Joshua came back with a new approach to keep her interested.

"See that guy over there with the orange shirt?" he asked her.

She followed his pointed finger and found a short, chunky, balding man shoving a hot dog in his mouth and talking to someone while chewing said hotdog. She nodded in affirmation, and in a little disgust, then swigged her beer.

"That is our security guy at work. He's a huge basketball fan. I'll make a bet with you. I will call him over here. If the first thing out of his mouth is about basketball, which he knows for a fact that I don't care a thing about, but will not stop him in any way from bringing it up, you owe me a beer," Josh offered.

Laughing, Kristin replied, "Well, since my sister is buying the beer, I will take that bet." She thought to herself, *what do I have to lose.*

Joshua and Kristin clinked their beer bottles together in a show of agreement, and then he whistled and called his co-worker over. He seemed happy to walk away form his current conversation and head over and talk to Joshua. It was easy for Kristin to see that Joshua's co-worker was a nice enough guy. And just as Joshua had predicted, his first statement was about the basketball game that evening and if Joshua was going to be watching it. And then, without waiting for an answer from Joshua, he went into a tirade about the two teams that were playing against each other and how he imagined it was all going to go down, even predicting citations and referee remarks. Kristin hung in for as long as she could take. It could have been only a minute or so, but that was it. Although she had enjoyed some of the conversation with Joshua and he seemed a genuinely good guy, she just had to make a break for it. She excused herself and ducked inside to use the bathroom. In the process, she ran into her mother.

Without hesitation, she started in on her. "Kristin, there you are. How are you feeling, honey? How is your back doing? Did you go to that acupuncturist I sent you the email about? I just worry about you all the time. I know you're not eating right, I can tell. You look pasty. Your skin is horrible..."

Before more insults came, Kristin jumped in. "No, Mom. I didn't have a chance to call him yet. And it isn't just my back. I told you, it's my hip or my back and my hip or something. I don't really know what it is. I think it's my hip. Anyway, I've been really busy at work. I even had to work yesterday..."

Kristin didn't finish.

"Well, honey, you only have one body, you know. You better do something and take care of it. I mean, you quit P.T., you canceled the personal trainer I got you for Christmas, you won't go back to the massage therapist..."

Rolling her eyes, Kristin, in turn, cut her mother off. "Mom, you don't understand. None of that stuff works. I have tried it all. It doesn't work. The last time I saw the doctor he said I could try some injections and you know I can't take any needles. I just have to manage it day by day. This is my life."

Her mother shook her head disapprovingly.

"Well, what does that mean? How do you manage something day by day? Come on, you need to heal yourself. You don't have to accept that this is your life, always being in pain. Here." She grabbed Kristin's hand and pulled her. "Come with me. I want to give you this Arnica cream that someone suggested for my tennis elbow. It really helps. I want you to try it."

"Mom..." Kristin whined as her mother pulled her into the living room where her purse was sitting.

Rummaging through the monstrosity that her mother considered a purse she came back at Kristin. "Don't 'Mom' me. You have to try everything. You have to try anything you can until you find what works."

"Advil works. Wine works," said Kristin, sarcastically. She was good at sarcasm. She even smiled thinking about it. She felt proud that she was good at that one thing for sure.

Her mother flashed her a disapproving look. "Advil and wine are Band-Aids. They don't actually fix the problem." She continued rummaging through her purse.

"Mom, I don't know if the problem can be fixed. I'm broken!" Kristin yelled, unsure if she wanted to cry or scream or run away.

Her mother, pulling the Arnica cream out of her purse and dropping said purse on the floor, took her daughter by a hand, and with compassion began, "You're not broken, you're just—"

"—I'm what?" Kristin interrupted her mother. Then waited. Although she knew that there was nothing really to wait for.

The stare down between them lasted at least forty seconds. Then, her mother retrieved her purse and dropped the Arnica cream back inside. Kristin took this as victory, albeit a sad one. The truth seemed to be that she was broken. But it wasn't just her body. Something inside her soul felt broken and her body seemed to just be displaying it. She didn't have anything else to say — not to her mother or anyone else really. She just wanted to be left alone in her misery. At least she knew how to manage that. Although at the moment she didn't even feel like finishing the beer she had been drinking. It seemed to have somehow lost its flavor.

With a big hug and a kiss her mother told her that she loved her and if she needed anything that all she had to do was call her. Of course, Kristin already knew that. Her mother would do anything for her. She always knew that. But she honestly didn't want to be bothered about it anymore today or at all. She just wanted one day without pain and without talking about the pain. She just wanted one day to pretend it did not exist. And now she really wanted that damn cigarette, too.

She walked out of the house and into the backyard and caught sight of Joshua still being cornered by the basketball fan. He waved her over, but she simply gave him a half smile and then turned abruptly and walked the other way, nearly walking into her friend Melissa.

"Damn, girl, where are you headed in such a rush?" Melissa said with a smile.

"Oh, I'm sorry. I'm trying to get away from my mom and then that guy over there is pretty annoying and I just can't take it right now," Kristin said.

Melissa looked over in the direction that she had just pointed. "Joshua? I thought he was pretty cute," she said, confused. "Did you know that he and his ex-wife are still very good friends? They're like the only divorced couple that I know who gets along better now that they are not together. I met her at another event — I think you were sick or something and didn't make it. Anyway, she is just great and they put the kids first. That little Gabriella is something too. I guess she is with her mom today, but man, she is just a little angel. She's like four years old and so sweet and happy. I'll tell you what, nothing is sexier than a man who knows how to be a father."

Melissa took a deep, sensual sigh and gazed towards Joshua. Kristin could clearly see how Melissa felt about Joshua. Had she seen all that? Or was her friend just a little buzzed up? She decided to get back to her point.

"No, not Joshua. The other guy."

Kristin paused as if the thought had just struck her to check to see if Joshua was actually cute. "Wait, is he cute?" she asked her friend.

"Of course he's cute. Check out that jawline," said Melissa, whirling around, checking him out. "I'll bet he has those six-pack abs under that polo shirt too."

Suddenly Kristin was picturing Joshua with a six-pack of abs and noticing his amazingly chiseled jawline. How had she missed all that before when they were talking? Was she too busy worrying about her own incompetency in procuring proper footwear and toenail polish?

"He has a kid," she said out loud, attempting to deflect from his handsomeness.

"And?" Melissa asked.

"And, he has a kid. That means he has an ex, that means he was married, that means he has this thing he has to manage and take care of and be responsible for..." Kristin stopped herself. She knew she sounded selfish and stupid. But then, she knew Melissa knew that about her already.

"Actually he has two kids," Melissa said nonchalantly, taking a sip of her wine.

Kristin closed her eyes. She felt it coming. In her usual response, she tightened all of her muscles and held her breath. Her hand went for her lower back and when she went to take a step and put her beer bottle down on the nearest table, she shrieked in pain, unable to move for a moment or so.

Having watched this painful episode come on, Melissa's face said it all: concern. Kristin noticed this once her pain subsided and she was able to breathe and move again. She shook her head and responded to her friend's uneasy look.

"I know. I know. It just sucks. I don't know what to do," Kristin admitted. "I feel like I'm almost out of options. They don't even know what's wrong with me. The last doctor thought it was in my head. According to him, there's nothing wrong with my bones."

"Well, there are more than bones in there, right?" Melissa made the comment in a very funny way. She was trying to bring levity to the situation. "I mean, or are you just like Skelator?"

It had worked. Kristin giggled. Then both women laughed, and took a seat in two nearby chairs. The truth was she had no idea what was inside her, but she knew that something was wrong because it hurt all the time now and not just when she was at work, miserable.

"Some days I just feel like giving up," admitted Kristin.

Melissa shook her head and reached out for her friend's hand, gently squeezing it. Melissa didn't want to push Kristin like her mother did, but she did want her friend to feel better.

"Maybe we should just shoot you and put you out to pasture," Melissa said, patting Kristin's arm, then retrieving her hand to take a drink.

"I was thinking about going skydiving and just not pulling the chute!"

Melissa winced. That path sounded particularly gruesome. She did have something that she wanted to bring up to Kristin, an idea that just might help. She was cautious in her approach, however, because she knew that her friend tended to react negatively to new ideas. But now was as good a time as ever to put it out there.

"Hey, I know that you won't want to do this. I know you probably will think it's stupid. But there's this new yoga place opening on Broad Street and I thought we could maybe go and check it out. There are a lot of good things I've heard about yoga. It even helps people going through cancer treatment..." Melissa began saying when Kristin, who's head had been shaking NO since Melissa started talking finally broke in.

"I am not doing yoga."

"Why not?" Melissa said, pouting.

Kristin had no real reason why. Yoga just sounded stupid. She said the only thing that she could think of in that moment.

"All I can think of is that song about piña coladas."

"Huh?" Melissa rebuffed.

"You know...'la la la...piña coladas...la la not into yoga...la la la have half a brain...'" sang Kristin, poorly.

Melissa laughed at her friend. "You cannot sing."

"I know." Kristin laughed.

"And what does that mean anyway? It is a stupid song. Who sings it?" Melissa asked.

Kristin really hadn't a clue who sang the song. The girls both started breaking out into random conversation to the melody of the song and laughing.

"If you like bread and mimosas...and walking down on the beach..." Melissa sang.

Kristin responded in tune, "If you like winning the lottery...and living life like a prince..."

They were having a great time when Sandy walked over.

"Hey, what are you two doing? What happened to Joshua?" Sandy asked.

Kristin pointed to the basketball man who still, unfortunately, had Joshua's ear. She had noticed Joshua looking over at her several times while she had been talking to Melissa, but had quickly looked away so that he wouldn't catch her looking his way. There was something about him that she felt drawn to. Now that Melissa had pointed it out, his handsome looks were undeniable, of course. But there was something else about him that did make her smile. She filled Sandy in on her escape from the basketball man. Then Melissa started filling Sandy in about the yoga plan.

"I am not going to yoga!" said Kristin, laughing. All joking aside, she for real did not want to do yoga.

"Why not? Someone in my neighborhood mom's club goes to hot yoga every week. She's thin as a rail and in great shape. She has three kids and you'd never know it. She says it keeps her flexible and strong and she even says it helps with her sex life. Maybe it will help. You never know, maybe you'll feel better and get a sex life!" Sandy offered.

Melissa laughed. Kristin shot her sister the usual disapproving, sisterly look. She should be changing the subject to the awkward way in which she dumped Joshua on her earlier in the day, but she had to determine if she wanted to defend her reasons not to go to yoga or her personal life...or lack of it. Melissa and Sandy continued to drop reasons why she should try yoga. In the background she watched Joshua politely deal with the Basketballer and in the foreground rapid-fire yoga healing was being forced on her. She imagined inviting the guys to come over and join them, then imaged in horror that the basketball guy might also advocate yoga because of a basketball team that uses it as part of their training. She didn't even know if that was true. But she couldn't take the thoughts in her head any longer, so she just blurted out the only thing she could.

"It's stupid."

"How do you know it's stupid, you haven't done it?" said Sandy, not skipping a beat.

"Done what?" asked Kristin's mother, walking into the conversation, from out of nowhere.

Kristin shot a look to her sister and friend and put up her index finger. "Do NOT tell her." And she meant it. But her sister cared not, as usual.

"Yoga. We want Kristin to try yoga," Sandy told her mother.

"Oh yes, that would be perfect!" Mom gushed, clasping her hands together and lifting her shoulders like a little girl who had just been given her first puppy.

Kristin sat back. There were the three women closest to her in her life, the three woman that meant the most to her, the three women that drove her the craziest, all going on and on and on about yoga. None of them had any real knowledge of yoga, and yet anyone walking into the conversation would think that they all practiced it daily. Kristin tuned out somewhere around

Hollywood bigwigs like Jennifer Aniston and Ellen DeGeneres doing yoga. Her eyes wandered again over to Joshua who had finally broken free of the dreaded basketball man. He flashed her a smile, pointed and mouthed, "You owe me," as he walked by her. She smiled and looked down at her feet, suddenly ashamed again about her lack of a good pedicure and appropriate party footwear. She must have allowed her brain to wander off on a shockingly deep story because before she knew it, her mother, sister and best friend had all planned to take her to this new yoga place as soon as it opened. She must have been either drunk or worn down, because she reluctantly agreed to it.

"Can't you all just leave me in my misery?" begged Kristin, smiling. She smiled because they loved her. She was grateful. Even though she didn't want to attend the stupid yoga class, she appreciated that they cared so much about her well-being.

"No we can't," said Melissa.

"Because we love you," Sandy responded.

And with that, her mother grabbed her face and planted a wet lipstick kiss on her cheek.

She supposed that having some people love her wasn't the worst thing in the world. But going to yoga? Really? How was that going to help her feel better? She knew that she wouldn't be able to do much of anything at the class. Or what if she got hurt in class? This would then make her feel worse about her condition. She made a silent agreement with herself that doing yoga was not going to change her. She was absolutely not going to give up eating meat, smoking, or drinking alcohol like she had heard some Hollywood elite discuss on TV talk shows. According to them, yoga and meditation had helped them evolve to understand how these things were not good for them or the world. She didn't get that. And, she liked who she was. She was a real person full of real problems. She had a good paying job (even though the people running the company were killing morale by the hour) and she had a home (even though she hadn't decorated it since she moved in five years ago). She had a car (although she could really use a better one that was more reliable) and she had family and friends who loved her (even when they drove her bat-shit-crazy). And even though she finally resigned to try the yoga thing, she knew that it wasn't going to last. The yoga place wasn't even open yet, after all. This gave her some time to potentially find a way out of it going at all. She smiled to herself, devilishly. Although she was happy to be loved, she really did wish that they would just leave her in her own misery.

Chapter 4

And the Hits Just Keep On Coming

"I am not what happened to me, I am what I choose to become."
~ C.G. Jung

The fluorescent lighting above her head began to feel as if it were burning her eyes. Kristin lay on her back in the doctor's office waiting for what seemed like an hour for someone to come in. She was in no rush since she had taken a half-day off from work to see this new doctor on the recommendation of a co-worker who had suffered from similar issues last year. Over the past three weeks her condition seemed to have worsened. Stress at work was at an all-time high and she often had to take four or six Advil during the day just to get through. Any minor movement seemed to aggravate her, so she tried not to move as much as possible. She could barely concentrate because she was in such constant pain. This caused her to make lots of errors at work lately, too. Even when she wasn't thinking about the pain and started to feel sort of "normal" — or whatever that meant — a pinching pain would stab her in her lower back and hip area and begin traveling down her leg. At times her leg would go sort of tingly and at other times it burned as if it were on fire. Her attitude, it had been pointed out to her by co-workers, had gotten even worse as of late. She tried to explain to them that it was because she was always dealing with this pain. They all replied with options for her. Even Brian seemed to be avoiding her on smoke breaks. Maybe that was in her head, but still, something obviously had to be done.

She shifted her head to look at the human body charts on the wall. One showed the human skeletal system. She looked at the bone near the top of the chest and felt for hers. *Clavicle*. She thought she had heard that name somewhere before. She checked out the ribcage and started to feel for hers. She wandered her fingers down her "sternum" to a rib and followed it down and around her body until she lost it under some muscle in her back. From there she guided her hand down the right side towards her "pelvis." Was this part of her problem? She wasn't sure. It felt kind of there and kind of not there.

The muscle chart was a little more confusing. The human body certainly had a lot of muscles. Although, on most days, Kristin didn't feel like she actually had any muscles. Back when she went to physical therapy she often felt as though her body was limited because she lacked certain muscles that maybe most other people had. "Can a person be born without certain muscles?" she had asked the therapists, but they only laughed at her. But she wondered why not? She had read about a little baby that was born with a heart on the outside of its chest. If an organ could grow on the outside of a body, then certainly it was probable that she could have fewer muscles than other people. This possibility would certainly explain her inability to do certain things with the ease that others seem to be able to do. Before the doctor arrived, she had convinced herself that this was her problem: she was a freak!

A knock on the door indicated someone was coming and although she wanted to sit right up, that wasn't happening today. The doctor entered the room and immediately told her not to bother sitting up. Kristin thought, *As if that was going to happen anyway.*

The doctor looked professional and well put together and Kristin guessed that she was probably in her mid forties. It was also comforting to be working with a woman. In her experience, men didn't always seem to "get" the intricacies of women and their parts, even doctors. Maybe this one had some new insights for her. She anxiously awaited the doctor's ideas based on the preliminary history and information she had provided her with.

"So, Kristin, I'm Dr. Bell. I have read your charts and your reports. I've checked out your X-rays and leg length tests. But I want to hear from you what you are experiencing and get to know you a little better. I feel that there are many aspects that contribute to our overall health as human beings, and sometimes tests and reports aren't going to tell me all that I need to know. So, can you just tell me about yourself, why you are here, and what are your experiences right now?"

These all seemed like reasonable questions. Kristin began with a brief history of key factors in her life. It was a short history, in fact, because she really hadn't done very much so far. She had graduated from high school, went to college, graduated, got a decent corporate job, and at some point developed these pains in her lower back and hip area. They seemed to have only worsened over the years. She never had any serious injuries, but when asked about her level of stress, she was quick to identify with a nine and a half out of ten, but couldn't cite many reasons why except for work and her physical issue. None of the other members of her family seemed to have these issues like her. She had to admit to smoking and drinking alcohol socially, but those were her only vices. Then when probed about her diet, she admitted that it could probably be better since she often didn't have the ability to cook due to her back. She also admitted to taking big doses of ibuprofen daily.

Kristin told the doctor that the pain seemed to come from somewhere around her right hip and lower back area. She explained that the pain used to be isolated near there, but had recently begun to travel down the back of her butt and hip causing her to have trouble walking, sitting, and doing just about anything at all. Since she had no traumas of which to speak of, she wondered if there was just something critically wrong with her body. She admitted to Dr. Bell that she must be broken or flawed in some way from birth, and wondered that perhaps it was all just catching up to her.

"You're thirty-four, right?" Dr. Bell asked. Kristin shook her head affirmatively. "Well, I think we can rule out birth issues. But since you are lying down I would like to try a few tests on you if you don't mind."

Kristin wasn't happy about the quick dismissal of her potential birth defect, but agreed and let the doctor run through a series of mobility tests where she moved her leg or body part and held it and asked Kristin to press this way or that way against her. Most times Kristin had a hard time pressing into anything, further fueling her argument that she was born with fewer muscles than other people. However, she did not share that theory with the good doctor. She felt that if the doctor was as good as she was supposed to be that she would soon discover this anyway.

The doctor poked around her hip and buttocks and had her stand up, asking her to perform a few minor movements, all of which hurt or were difficult for her to do. After about ten minutes of this type of evaluation Dr. Bell asked Kristin to take a seat.

"So, you say that you have a lot of stress in your life, right?" Dr. Bell asked.

Kristin nodded. "Yes, of course. I mean, who doesn't?"

"Well, you're right about that. Everyone does have stress. In fact, some sorts of stress are even good. But I want to know how you deal with your stress."

Uh-oh, here's where she recommends a psychiatrist, she thought. She didn't say anything about this out loud. Instead she offered that she relaxed on her couch, drank wine, used a heating pad and took ibuprofen. All of these things helped her to fall asleep and be in less pain overnight. During the day when the pain got worse she would continue the over-the-counter medicines to remedy the pain. That was her entire stress reduction regimen. Kristin smiled, thinking she nailed it.

"Okay, I think one thing is that you need a healthy outlet for your stress. Do you do anything creative? Did you used to participate in any sports before these physical issues began?" the doctor asked.

Kristin paused and shook her head. She could not help the onslaught of angry words that flew out of her mouth next. "Wait, I'm confused. There's something wrong with my hip or my back. I realize that stress is probably not helping, but what I need to know is what is wrong with me and how do I fix it? Do I take a certain medicine? Do you recommend an operation to fix something that is physically wrong with me? I mean, stress is always going to be there whether I paint or crochet or not, right? So, I mean, what is going on with me?"

It was obvious to Dr. Bell that Kristin was on the verge of crumbling into an emotional heap. Tact was needed most right now, and since she wasn't sure just how Kristin would react, she decided instead to try to explain to her the methodology of holistic medicine. Perhaps backtracking a little was best for her patient.

"Yes, you are correct in some of that. And we are going to address your body. But I believe in a holistic approach to wellness. Our body and our mind are intricately connected so what happens to one happens to the other, too. You have some issues with the muscles in your pelvic area. I think some of them are chronically locked up. Some are impinging on nerves and causing some of the tingling and the sensations that you are experiencing. Others are creating a weakness that may be shifting your pelvis into a different position, which is therefore pulling on other muscles causing even more strain in the area. You certainly have inflammation and this inflammation is why the ibuprofen gives you some relief. So while this all may sound like a lot, I want to stress to you that I do not think you need an operation. There doesn't seem to be anything wrong with your bones, in general, or with any torn musculature. But we have to work on your musculoskeletal system. And part of working on that is to work on the mental part of you that is connected there."

Kristin was at a loss for words. No other doctor had ever spoken to her about these things. Her options were taking medicine or getting shots. And the idea that her body and mind were connected and affecting each other was certainly a new concept for her. Her mouth must have been wide open. Dr. Bell realized this.

"I understand that is a lot of information. But if you trust me, I think that I can help you."

Kristin started to cry. She had no reason why, but before she knew it she was balling like a baby in the doctor's office. She still didn't really understand what was wrong with her, but she had a feeling that somehow this doctor may be able to help her in some way. Dr. Bell handed her some tissues and waited patiently for Kristin to collect herself.

"I'm sorry," Kristin apologized, wiping her nose.

"Please, do not be sorry. You are in pain. It is natural and it is good to feel what you are feeling and to let it out. You've been holding on to all of these feelings for a while."

This made Kristin cry even more. What exactly was it that she had been holding on to? What was this doctor doing to her? She felt like crawling into a big hole in the earth and being alone. She knew her mascara was probably running down her cheeks by now, too. And she still had to go out into public and drive home. *This is great. This is just freaking great*, thought Kristin, crying even more.

Dr. Bell excused herself to give Kristin some time alone, but let her know that she was right on the other side of the door. Kristin was grateful for this time to recollect herself. She was not comfortable crying in front of other people and showing that much emotion. She remembered when her father had passed away when she was very young and her mother had been crying just before the services and one of her aunts had come up to her mother and told her to get it together because people were arriving. She recalled that experience as if she were still a little girl standing there watching her aunt give her mother a tissue and help collect herself. It had made quite an impression on little Kristin. She always tended to recall that scene when someone cried in public and would think to herself, *get it together*. And just after that memory would come to her, she would also think about her favorite uncle, who would always find a way to make her laugh and make light of life or a particular situation. She thought about him because he was there that day when her aunt had told her mother to get it together. He was watching the situation and quickly came to her aid and escorted Kristin out of the room. He picked her up and carried her outside and showed her how to make Pinocchio noses out of the seedpods in the trees. They had stayed outside right up until the moment that her father's services had begun, and then they quietly slipped inside. Her uncle had taught her how to avoid bad feelings. She loved him for that.

After a few minutes, Dr. Bell returned. When she came back, she handed Kristin a small glass of water, which she gladly took and drank, even though she detested the useless tastelessness of water. Kristin was calming down and beginning to feel a little better. In fact, she even began to feel some relief in her hip, or was she imagining that?

"So," said Dr. Bell, "I would like to work with you on some of these issues if you can see me twice a week. I would also like to suggest something else to you, too."

Something within her told her that she could trust this doctor. "Sure, what is it?"

"I want you to think about starting yoga," said Dr. Bell.

And just like that, Kristin faded out. The good doctor almost had her, for one hot minute. And then, BAM: the yoga card is pulled! When would everyone leave her alone about that damn exercise?

* * *

The next day at work turned out to be a complete nightmare. Why not? *"The hits just keep on coming,"* she thought, referring to an old radio-programming slogan that her uncle used to say all the time. Her uncle had been the closest male influence in her life growing up and she always enjoyed spending time with him. Her mother would describe her uncle, her father's younger brother, as a real character. And because he would often make her mother uncomfortable with his stories, Kristin loved him even more. There was one time when her uncle started reminiscing about a double date that he and his wife and Kristin's mother and father had been on together. Something mischievous must have happened, because Kristin's mother began swatting at her uncle telling him to be quiet. And the more she swung at him, the more he laughed and tried to get the story out. Kristin didn't remember the details of this story, but she fondly remembered laughing until her belly hurt as her uncle sang, "Good Golly, Miss Molly" over and over as her mother beat at him to stop.

Kristin especially liked when her uncle would tell her a story and include something that her father would do or say. In a way, it gave her a window into her father's life. Since she never really knew her father, she found that very comforting. Her uncle had passed away just about three years ago, and since then she often found herself using some of his old sayings. Was it the memory of her uncle or the connection to her father that brought her the most comfort? Perhaps, she thought, it was a little of both.

Now on this particular day, her company had sent out an e-mail announcing impending major cutbacks. In fact, by the end of the week, one-third of the folks at her job would no longer be working there. The workload, however, would continue for the lucky two-thirds that would remain. Kristin changed her Facebook post to "And the hits just keep...on...coming..." It was random enough that if anyone from above her at work saw it they wouldn't know what she was really talking about. Yet her friends and family would probably get the gist. Within five minutes she had thirty-seven likes.

Kristin wondered if she would make the cut or not. As she looked around her group she realized that it could really be any one of them. She certainly was not the ideal worker bee. She had taken so much time off for medical reasons and even when she was at work she was rarely in a good mood, as they had all recently informed her. IT had also finally found the reason why Kristin's computer had been acting up when they did a virus scan. Apparently, something she downloaded created 237 viruses. And since she hadn't kept up with her regular maintenance, it continued to corrupt her files. Not that anyone had, in fact, taught her how to regularly maintain her computer system anyway. In the end, they had to bring her a new computer, but since they didn't know what she actually downloaded that caused the issue in the first place, there was nothing that they could do to reprimand her about it. Either way, it was another notch on her "bad-worker" belt.

On the flip side, the rest of her team was no better off than she was. Half of them came in late every day. One guy was continually insubordinate to Betty and basically a sexist pig. It was amazing he had not been fired yet for any of those reasons. Another woman on the team really was in over her head. This woman barely spoke English, let alone understood what she was supposed to be doing. But it seemed like the company was scared to talk to her about it. As she eyeballed her co-workers, Kristin caught Janice's glance. They locked eyes realizing that they were both most likely sizing up the possibilities of who would remain on Friday. Janice was probably the most likely candidate for staying at her location because she was probably the only person who actually did her job well and never even complained about it. For sure, Janice was safe.

Kristin's work telephone rang and she picked it up without looking, and sat down to avoid Janice's gaze.

"Hello, Kristin speaking."

She had failed to give her last name or department name. Again, bad employee! Hopefully it was not the boss man calling.

"Hey, sister. I just heard about your company's cuts. Don't worry. You will be fine."

It was Sandy. Of course Sandy knew about the cuts. Sandy knew everyone and everything about everything. Kristin let her talk for a few minutes before cutting her off.

"Listen, San, now is not the best time for me to be having personal phone calls," said Kristin. She really didn't care, but it was a good excuse to get her sister off the phone.

"Oh, of course. Well, listen, I just wanted to tell you that the new yoga place is open and we are all going this Thursday night to the 6 p.m. class. It's for beginners, so you'll be fine. Mom is even going. We'll go to dinner after. It'll be fun."

Kristin rolled her eyes.

"Stop rolling your eyes," said Sandy.

Kristin rolled them again, wondering how her sister actually knew that she was rolling her eyes.

"I mean it."

She rationalized Sandy was somehow watching her on a camera she had installed on a personal item of hers so that she could keep an eye on her all the time. While she searched for the hidden camera, Kristin changed the subject and said, "San, I wanted to ask you about that guy you introduced me to at Brenda's recital party last month? I think his name was Joshua."

"Yeah." Sandy waited.

"Is he still single? What's his deal?"

"Nope, he just started dating someone. A mutual friend set them up two weeks ago. You did say you weren't interested in someone with kids." Sandy took a deep, disapproving breath. Kristin was well aware that it was directed at her. And she didn't need a hidden camera to know that.

Besides, that was all very true. Kristin had said all of that about not wanting to date anyone with kids. But something about her interaction with Joshua kept coming back to her. She had even since had a dream about Joshua where the two of them were riding horses together in an open field around what appeared to be the late 1800s. Kristin had woken up in a sweat that night, completely confused since she had no affection for horses nor men with children. So why was she bringing him up now? Was it Melissa bringing attention to his magnificent jawline? Was it her imagination of his rectus abdominus muscles? Yes, she had thought of those six-packs when she read the name of them on Dr. Bell's muscle chart yesterday. But alas, it did not appear that Joshua had felt any connection with her since he had already moved on and was dating someone else. She wondered if it would have mattered if she had been more polite or asked about him sooner? Would he have been interested? Well, one thing was for sure, he still would have had kids. Either way, nothing was gonna happen between them now.

What *was* going to happen in the very immediate future, were cutbacks. By the end of the week she was going to either be out of a job or have a heavier workload. So, to go back and tally today's score:
Kristin 0, Work 1
Kristin 0, Hot Dad 1

"Of course," Kristin finally replied to Sandy, and then under her breath grumbled, "*And the hits just keep on coming...*"

Chapter 5

The Yoga Experiment

"In the beginner's mind there are many possibilities, in the expert's mind there are few." ~ Shunryu Suzuki

Kristin arrived early at the yoga studio and was sitting in her car sneaking a cigarette. She knew that her mother would be all over her if she saw her smoking at all, let alone before the yoga class, so she found a hidden spot near the back of the lot in which to conduct her "bad, dirty habit." The fact that she had shown up at all — let alone early — was a miracle. She still did not see the benefit of doing yoga when she was inflexible and had a serious injury. She again thought about the various famous people she'd seen on television discussing yoga and meditation. All of them had thin, yet muscular, bodies. Many of them talked about helping other people less fortunate by donating time and money to their particular causes. Kristin always thought this was a nice idea for those who had extra money. And then there was the whole vegetarian thing, which led to being vegan! Now people were not digesting anything from animals at all. When she thought about it she had a difficult time even trying to think of any food that did not in some way come from an animal...at least nothing that she tended to eat. Even pasta contained eggs. And as she puffed on her cigarette, she tried to remember just what pasta was made from. *Grain, right?* She was asking herself this question when she spotted her sister and mother pulling into the parking lot.

As anticipated, Sandy pulled up right at the front of the building. She watched as her mother and sister got out of the car smiling and walked happily inside. She took another drag of her cigarette and looked around for Melissa, who was still to arrive. She figured she could probably finish her cigarette and do her regular cleansing routine to eliminate the smell of the smoke enough to pass her mother's detection in time.

And bingo, just as she was spraying body spray on herself and washing her hands with perfumed disinfectant wash, Melissa pulled up next to her. Kristin winked at her, grabbed her purse, and got out of the car.

"Are you excited?" Melissa asked coyly.

Kristin flashed her *that* look and the two started walking towards the studio entrance.

"Just try to keep an open mind about it. I've heard good things about yoga, and what if this is the one thing that actually helps you?" Melissa said.

Kristin shrugged and kept looking ahead. She didn't even want to acknowledge that with any words. She was there and she was going to do it. And when she was sore the next day or worse, then they would all finally leave her alone, including Dr. Bell. Or at least she hoped that they would. Although knowing her mother and her sister they would come up with some other crazy idea that they heard about from Asia, like eating some fungus from the jungle.

Once inside, Kristin had to admit, the studio was quite beautiful. The mocha-colored walls and white trim with dim lighting gave off a beautiful appearance of being in a relaxing spa. There was a fountain near the front entryway with a glass jar of water with fresh orange and lemon slices inside it. There were some very small cups next to it that looked like shot glasses to Kristin, although these were not the type of shots that she was used to. There was a small counter where Sandy and her mother were standing filling out some paperwork and the woman standing behind the counter appeared to be an average person and not like the stick-figured models that she had seen touting yoga before. Was this place normal? For a moment she nearly smiled.

Looking around the studio she could see people of various ages and sizes and even a couple of men talking. Some of them were drinking the water, which made her giggle to herself with thoughts of "*don't drink the Kool-Aid!*" Kristin laughed to herself, wondering what kind of jokes her uncle would have made about this yoga scene. Back when Olivia Newton-John's single "Let's Get Physical" was popular, he had come in to their home with a headband and tights on, kicking his legs and singing the song. Even her mother had laughed that time. She imagined him pointing at the people who were all drinking the fresh citrus sprinkled water while trying to put his leg behind his head. He probably would have been able to do it too! But, much to her chagrin, she had to admit that the people standing there seemed like everyday folks similar to her and her family.

"Kristin, come fill out this student card," Sandy called from the front desk.

Kristin walked up and was greeted by the woman behind the counter, who smiled sincerely and held her hand out to shake Kristin's. Kristin extended her right hand expecting to retrieve it nearly right away, but the woman held her hand a little longer than a normal handshake. When Kristin went to pull it back she felt the lock on her hand and looked up. The woman was smiling at her. Kristin felt awkward and confused. She faked a smile, but the woman still held her hand. Then finally, she closed her eyes, took a deep breath, lifted Kristin's hand up and down, and then released it with another smile. Kristin looked at her family and friend to see if any of them also thought that was strange. They too all had the same goofy look on their faces. She wondered if they had drunk the water? Then the woman spoke.

"Hello, Kristin. I am Nayana. I'll be teaching your yoga class today and I wanted to welcome you to our studio. I think you will find that we are all an encouraging and welcoming community here. There are no judgments and no competitions at our studio. Everyone here is doing the best that they can at each moment. And if there is anything that you are unsure about or need, you just let me know."

Kristin looked at her goofy smiling family again, nodded her head at them all, and smiled weakly. How did the teacher even know her name?

"I filled out most of your card for you," said Sandy. "You just need to sign it and add anything else that you want."

That's how, thought Kristin. Leave it to Sandy to try to do everything for her. She gazed at the card and what she had written down. It was all valid stuff, although she wasn't sure why she had to go into such detail about her issues. *Christ, Sandy,* she thought. *Everyone doesn't have to know everything about me.* Sandy had even put down that Kristin suffered from stress-related mental exhaustion. *What the heck does that even mean?* she wondered. Kristin signed her name at the bottom of the card anyway, and slid it right back over to Nayana. She didn't need to see her issues in black and white.

"I already paid for us all," said Kristin's mother, smiling, then giving Kristin a big hug. "I just know that you are going to love yoga."

"Why? Because you do?" Kristin answered sarcastically, knowing that her mother had never done yoga before and thus had no previous knowledge of it, or what it could do for her.

"Well, I love anything that is good and helps people," she replied, smiling at her daughter. What else could a mother do?

Kristin rolled her eyes and turned away. There were some clothes on the other side of the registration area so she took a walk over. She was always in the mood for shopping, even if it was for "yoga" clothes. There was a really cute pair of stretchy pants with a wild trim that flowed down to a wide leg. It looked very Grecian, except that they were black. She picked them off the rack and looked at the price tag, which was quite shocking. The pants were $145! She looked again. *Is that in American money or Indian rupees?* Kristin thought to herself. She quickly put the pants back on the rack and checked some of the other tags just to make sure that it was not mismarked. No luck. They were all pricey. Even the capri style pants that had half the amount of material were $125. She shook her head thinking she would go to TJ Maxx later and find some designer clothes for a small fraction of the price of that one pair of pants. How could they get away with selling a pair of pants for that much money?

"Aren't they *DIVINE*?" Kristin's mother said, picking up the same pair of pants enthusiastically.

"Mom, if you buy those pants I will seriously kill you. They're $145!" Kristin scolded under her breath. She quickly looked around to make sure that nobody else heard her, but they were all busy discussing some retreat in Mexico that was coming up later in the year.

"Honey, you don't understand, these are made from bamboo," she replied to her daughter.

"I don't care if they're made from a baby's behind, you are not spending that kind of money on one pair of pants that you will wear like one time."

Kristin took the pants out of her mother's hands and hung them back on the rack. She grabbed her mother by the wrist and pulled her over to where Sandy and Melissa were standing near the front entry.

"Don't even look at those clothes; they are ridiculously overpriced," said Kristin to Sandy and Melissa.

"They're gorgeous," her mom told the girls, looking back over her shoulder longingly at the clothes.

"What are they, bamboo?" asked Sandy. "Because if they are then they are worth it."

Kristin flashed her sister a dirty look for agreeing with their mother. This would only validate her and award her permission to spend money that she didn't need to. Sandy always had a way of doing that. There was no reason to be spending that kind of money on clothing. Especially considering they might never be doing yoga again and when would they wear those crazy pants? She would never get away with wearing them to work. That was if she even had a job to wear those pants to! Kristin wanted to run to her car for another cigarette or go get some coffee. She even asked Melissa to take a walk with her, but she wouldn't budge. They seemed all hell bent on doing this yoga thing — this experiment.

"Everyone, how about we start heading in for class," Nayana said in one of the sweetest voices that Kristin had ever heard. She literally sounded like a Disney princess.

Nayana disappeared behind a curtain into a darker room and the rest of the folks started to follow her in. Then Sandy went in, followed closely by their mother, and then Melissa. For a moment Kristin looked at the door and thought that she could make a run for it. She realized it was probably better to just get it over with. But she was all alone in the front entryway. She looked at the clock and reminded herself that they were all going to dinner afterwards. This would all be over soon and she would have some wine and good food in her belly. She took a deep breath, and holding it, began to step into the yoga room.

"Kristin, I'm sorry, can you please leave your shoes out front," Nayana said to her, apologetically. "It's my fault. I didn't tell you about the shoes. You won't need them for class. And when you get back, I'll have a mat and a blanket set up for you."

Kristin nodded and walked back outside. Maybe this was a hint that she should run! She noticed all of the other shoes stacked and lined up outside the yoga room. She had not even noticed them prior to entering. Most of them were simple shoes that could be flipped off. Of course, Kristin had to sit down and untie her sneakers. She looked around for a "safe" place to put hers so that nobody would walk away with them. Then she realized she had no idea what that meant or if anyone even cared about her crummy Sketchers. She wondered if she was supposed to take her socks off too. There were no other socks sitting outside the yoga room, so she assumed it was okay to keep them on. It was clearly evident when she reentered the room that every other person was completely barefooted. She felt strange being the only one with socks on. But she still hadn't had a chance to get a pedicure and her feet were in even worse shape than they had been at the party several weeks ago. Besides, she hated her feet. Her second toe was bigger than all the others and it looked weird. Kristin kept her socks on and looked for the open yoga mat. It was near the front on the left side, wedged right in between Melissa and Sandy. She was thankful that at least her mother was on the right side of the room and not just next to her because she just had this feeling that her mother would talk to her throughout the entire class. She was, in fact, already talking to the one man in the room whom she had managed to sit right next to. That was no accident. She watched her mother giggle and flip her hair flirtatiously. Kristin rolled her eyes and plopped down on the mat, trying to avoid eye contact with her mother.

Ouch, she grimaced immediately. She already hurt just sitting on the floor.

Coming up to Kristin with a larger pillow, Nayana offered some advice, "Kristin, since you have some issues with your hip and back, I think you should sit up on this cushion. I'm going to offer you some other tools to help you be more comfortable as we go along, if that's ok. If you don't want to use them, you certainly don't have to. But you will see some other folks also using different things to assist them in postures too. Remember, it is about you being comfortable. Nobody looks the same in any pose."

"Well, if you want me to be comfortable, show me to the couch! Am I right?" Kristin said, heckling her loudly. In her head she heard the Ba-dum-dum-CHING stinger. In reality, it sounded like crickets in the yoga room.

Sandy shot her a "that's not funny" look but Melissa seemed to think it was funny and chuckled. So did Nayana, to Kristin's surprise. Kristin turned to her sister and stuck her tongue out at her, as if they were still five and seven years old and she had just won something from her.

"I hear ya! There are some days all I want to do is veg on the couch too. Well, give it a shot with the cushion and see if it can work for you. I also invite you to sit back against the wall if that helps," Nayana said, slowly walking away to the front of the room.

Kristin noticed a woman across the room take Nayana up on it and scooted herself back against the wall. The woman seemed to be much older than even her mother was. Yet Kristin thought to herself, *there's no way I'm going to lean against the wall like an old woman.* The class hadn't even begun, and Kristin was already judging herself and the others in the room.

There was soft music coming from somewhere. Once she realized it, the music seemed almost hypnotic in its relaxation effect. Kristin looked around and saw most of the people seated on cushions with their legs crossed. A few people, including the one guy, had foam bricks under their knees too. Folding her legs was easy, but her right hip certainly hurt. She wedged a brick under it and found it to be somewhat helpful. But the pain still shot down her back and leg. She took her right leg forward and shook it out. Then she moved it to the right, but Sandy flicked it off of her mat so she had to extend it forward again. This was not comfortable at all.

"Everyone, find your seat. It should be comfortable. And if you cannot seem to find a comfortable seat, I invite you to simply lie down," Nayana offered to the entire class.

Kristin thought, *Is that actually an option?* And then looked around to see that a couple of people had even taken Nayana up on lying down. Not the man or the oldest looking woman in the class, but two others did. So, Kristin thought she would join them and also carefully lie down on her back. That certainly felt a little better, but she had to keep her feet on the floor instead of extending them straight. Even when she slept at night she had a pillow between her knees to help alleviate the pain. She would never think of sleeping on her back flat. That was the worst position ever!

"So go ahead and close your eyes, relax, and take the biggest breath that you can in through your nose. Then, hold it for a moment, and then exhale it out through the mouth with a big sigh," Nayana guided the class.

Kristin took the breath in, but it wasn't very big. She could barely hold it but as soon as everyone started to sigh, which to her sounded a little orgasmic and hilarious, she began to giggle. Then, Nayana had the class do it again. Everyone else seemed at ease moaning in front of the group. But Kristin couldn't bring herself to do it. She also found that she sucked her breath back in on the exhalations instead of sighing like Nayana wanted her to. Something about it just didn't feel right.

Nayana continued, "That was great. Now, take a deep breath in through the nose, and then exhale through the nose. But, while you are doing these deep breaths, inflate the belly with the inhalations and then on the exhalations allow the belly to draw backwards towards the spine."

Huh? Kristin thought. *What you talkin' bout, Willis?* Another vision of her uncle arose and she laughed to herself.

"So for every inhalation the belly expands as if you are blowing air into a balloon, then for the slow exhalation the belly deflates and draws in as if you were squeezing the air out of the balloon," Nayana continued guiding them a few more rounds.

Kristin tried to do what Nayana was saying but it felt all-kinds-of wrong. The belly felt like it sucked in on the inhalations when she did it. She put her hands on her stomach to determine if that were the case, and yes, she was correct. Each time she took a deep breath in her chest inflated but her belly sucked backwards. She wondered if Nayana had been teaching yoga very long because she obviously had the breathing all wrong. She opened her eyes and peeked up to see what her sister and friends were doing. They all seemed to be fine with it. Maybe they just didn't notice it was incorrect. Maybe she was a yoga genius compared to all of the others!

Nayana approached Kristin and leaned down towards her. "Is it okay if I put my hand on your belly, softly?" she asked. Kristin nodded affirmatively, although she wasn't too keen on the idea. Nayana placed one hand on Kristin's stomach and with very little pressure asked her to inhale and push her hand upwards. Kristin tried to do this, but the breathing occurred just as it had before — the opposite of what Nayana wanted.

"I'm not sure you meant what you said. I think you want me to inhale and pull my belly in," Kristin corrected Nayana. Nayana smiled and responded kindly:

"I'm sure it may feel like that at first. I remember feeling the same way. But trust me, we aren't breathing to our full capacity if we aren't breathing the way I am guiding you to breathe. I don't want to bore you with the details just yet, but trust me. Try it again."

Kristin tried it a few more times and felt quite defeated. She just couldn't bring any opening to her stomach with the inhalations, or the exhalations, for that matter. Now that she was noticing, it certainly felt like she was sucking her belly back on both of the breaths and suddenly realized that this couldn't be right at all. Shouldn't at least one of them be outward? And then Nayana asked the question that she was dreading:

"Kristin, do you smoke?"

Kristin lifted her head and looked across the room. Yup, her mother was staring right at her, and her sister was looking down at her, quite literally, although she often felt looked down upon by her sister.

"Uh, is that important for some reason?" Kristin asked in a whisper. Perhaps her mother hadn't heard the conversation.

"Well, I often see with my students that smoke that it is even more challenging to start this breathing at first. But it's okay. If you smoke you can still learn the breathing. In fact, it will help you in many ways that you can't even imagine. Put your hands on your stomach and try to push them down into your belly when you inhale. The idea is to give your stomach muscles something to work against as you push up. So you can try to train them."

Kristin had no idea what stomach muscles had to do with breathing. Last time she checked the lungs were responsible for breathing. Nayana stood up and walked to the front of the room and spoke to the group.

"Remember, everyone, the diaphragm muscle is responsible for nearly 70% of our breathing capacity. Due to various stressors in our life, many of us have forgotten how to truly breath the way we did when we were babies. Now we rely more on our lungs than our diaphragm. So, we are never really fully oxygenating our bodies. The yoga breathing techniques are so important. In fact, I don't care if you never practice a yoga pose, as long as you practice the breathing and make it a regular practice. Then I'll be happy. I'll have done my job for you. And you will start to experience some of the truly life-changing affects of yoga just through the breath."

Kristin pondered all of that.

Was it true?
Where did Nayana get all of that information from?
And, what if she was never able to use her diaphragm?
What if that was her missing muscle?

Where the hell is the diaphragm anyway?!

Her mind was even more active than usual. Nayana continued.

"One more round and then I'd like you to take that *apana* or surrender breath again through the mouth with a sigh."

Soon everyone in the room was groaning like they were having an orgasm again. Kristin laughed out loud and Sandy swatted her disapprovingly with her hand. The swat made Kristin laugh even more, to which Sandy swatted her one more time. It was too late. Kristin was in the middle of a full-on giggle fit. And since giggling is contagious, soon Melissa was giggling, and then a few more people in the room chuckled too. None of this seemed to bother Nayana. In fact, nothing ever seemed to bother Nayana.

"I'm not sure what I missed, but it's good to have a good long belly-laugh. Nothing can be more healing than releasing through laughter!" she encouraged.

Is there nothing we can do wrong in this class? Kristin wondered.

Soon Nayana guided everyone to come up onto hands and knees and do a few movements with the spine. Of course, Nayana made it sound and look so simple and of course, Kristin couldn't perform these simple movements. This time, however, she noticed that her mother and sister were also having issues performing the spinal movements. She relaxed and felt a little less humiliated when Nayana came over to assist Sandy with it. In fact, she even smiled. That kind of made her entire day...week...month, even!

The next pose was called Downward Facing Dog. Nayana told the class to push into their hands and lift their hips up towards the sky. Then she rattled off about fifty other commands about feet, inner thighs, heels, shoulders, abdominal muscles and things she had never heard of before. Kristin's legs were shaking like crazy. The pose was really difficult to hold, so she came down onto her knees just as Nayana was offering that to the group. Several others came onto their knees with Kristin, and Nayana guided them into Child's Pose. That one felt all right. In fact, that pose actually felt good. There was a big stretch happening in her lower back and it seemed to relieve some of the pain in her hip too. She felt like she could stay in this Child's Pose forever, but alas, Nayana was moving on.

Nayana took her time guiding the class through a series of postures. Some of the poses were challenging, while others were more relaxing. There seemed to be some sort of scheme to the madness. It was hopeful to see other people struggle like she was. Kristin realized this may be perceived as selfish, but it made her feel good to not be the one having the most trouble in a class just for once. Even when she went to P.T. it seemed like the people who looked worse off than her were managing quite well. This assumption of hers really angered her.

Before she knew it, the entire class was lying on their backs in what Nayana called "Final Relaxation." Only it was not very relaxing. Nayana came over and offered a folded blanket under Kristin's knees, which seemed to relieve some of the stress for her. She was able to lie there without wiggling around a lot anyway.

"So, let go of all of your thoughts here. Maybe that's a challenge too. Maybe it seems like your head is like a snow globe that's just been shook up. And each one of the snowflakes floating around is an individual thought floating around in your head. But you know what? Eventually those thoughts will land and settle. And you can quiet the mind too. Let the mind settle like the snow and relax deeply here."

With that thought, Nayana slipped out of the room and closed the curtain behind her. The class was left in near darkness with soothing music playing. In peeking around, Kristin noticed that everyone seemed fully relaxed. She gave it a try but each time she closed her eyes more thoughts seemed to flood in.

Is there such a snow globe that is in perpetual movement? 'Cause if so that's my head, Kristin mused.

This final "relaxation" seemed to go on forever. In the span of time that they lay there on the floor Kristin had made a complete shopping list and "to do" list for the next day. Her body couldn't really relax and her mind was as far away from relaxed as one could be. But when Nayana came quietly back in and guided everyone up and into a seated pose, it appeared that most of the group was completely relaxed. And this perplexed Kristin. She just didn't get it.

"I want to leave you with one closing thought. A quote from Albert Einstein: '*Nothing changes until something moves*'. And that's why I love yoga so much. You know, someone else once said, '*If you always do what you've always done, then you'll always get what you've always got*.' Or something like that! Anyway, the point is, sometimes you just need to move or do something different in order to create the change you need. So with that I would like you all to take your hands into your heart in *Anjali* mudra. It's like prayer. We will all take a breath in and chant the mantra *OM* together. Inhale...Ommmmmmmmmmm..."

Kristin looked around the room again. The regular students were all chanting. Her mother was chanting, although she was quite sure that she had no idea what it meant. Sandy, Melissa and she were not chanting, but the other two seemed peaceful, unlike her. When the chant was over, Nayana said, "Namaste," and bowed. The rest of the class repeated the word and bowed as well. Kristin bowed, a little late, but didn't say the word. She had no idea what the word meant. She was also sitting upright again way before anyone else was. *What is with these awkwardly long holds around here*, she thought.

Everyone was pretty quiet while exiting the yoga room so Kristin went with it. The truth was she didn't feel too social at the moment. She wasn't quite sure what she was feeling. She didn't *hate* the class like she wanted to. She actually kind of liked the teacher too. It was kind of weird. She didn't exactly know what to say. So, quiet worked best.

Afterwards at dinner, Kristin found herself still a little quieter than normal. Not in her mind, because that was still raging on like usual, but something within her felt quieter. Melissa noticed.

"You OK?"

Kristin nodded and smiled, "Yup. Just tired, I guess."

"What did you think of the class?" Melissa asked.

"I don't know. I guess it was OK. I am sore. I don't think it helped. I had trouble doing most of it." That was all the truth too.

"I think I may try to go once a week. It really helped me to relax," Melissa said. "Do you want to try and go with me?"

"Yeah, let me think about it. I'll let you know next week. I have to get through tomorrow's work nightmare. If I still have a job and can afford yoga, then maybe."

"Oh that's right. The cuts..." Melissa stopped short of finishing her sentence, realizing that she most likely wouldn't want to talk about it.

Sandy brought herself into the conversation between Kristin and Melissa and dropped in her two cents. She comforted Kristin telling her that she had nothing to worry about because she was a trusted employee. She reminded her sister that her company couldn't fire her because of missed work due to illness or injury. Kristin did appreciate her sister saying these things, even though she didn't believe it herself. Even if she were the best employee the company had, it wouldn't stop them from cutting her job if they wanted to. At the end of the day, it was all about their bottom line. They had made this quite clear to the employees.

"How does your hip feel?" Melissa asked, changing the subject even though it wasn't a better thought.

"I feel it," said Kristin. "I don't think one class is going to fix what I have."

"Well, at least you tried it. I didn't think you would show up. I told Mom as much," Sandy admitted.

Kristin's mother nodded her head, throwing some spinach into her mouth and speaking while chewing, "Yes, you said that. And I told you, No, Kristin will be there. If she says she will, she will." She continued chewing. At least her mother stood up for her, sometimes.

"Well, if I do wind up going back to yoga next week, it will be as an experiment," Kristin laughed.

"Experiment?" Melissa questioned.

"Yes, the yoga experiment," said Kristin laughing louder.

Melissa put her hands in the prayer pose and started chanting *Om*. Sandy joined in. So did their mother, with mouth full of spinach. Kristin laughed and joined them too. This yoga thing was certainly going to be entertaining, if not anything else.

Chapter 6

When One Door Closes...

"When one door closes, another door opens; but we often look so long and so regretfully upon the closed door that we do not see the one which has opened for us." ~ Alexander Graham Bell

Kristin sat anxiously at her desk trying to pretend that this was a normal day like any other. The fact was that Betty and their boss, Tom, had been behind closed doors with some other suits for over an hour and everyone knew what was happening: they were going over who was being let go and who was staying. Why hadn't they figured this all out before the rest of the people came in to work that day, though? Wouldn't it have been better if they just called people at home and told them so that there wouldn't be all this buildup and anxiety at the workplace? Even though she had had her morning break already, Kristin had to go have another cigarette. Fortunately, she was not alone in that. The smokers' patio was full of faces that she normally didn't see there. She didn't even know that most of the people outside smoked! Nor would she have ever thought it. Within a moment of being outside Brian came over to her.

"What's up?" he said, as if he didn't already very well know.

"Waiting, just like everyone else, I guess."

"You have nothing to worry about. You're a good employee," Brian said. "It's the rest of us morons that need to worry!"

Kristin laughed. He was being nice, of course. He wasn't necessarily being truthful. "You don't have to say that. I know I am not one of the best employees. Now Janice, *SHE* is a good employee!"

"True," Brian agreed, taking a drag of his cigarette and then pulling out his lighter to help light up Kristin.

And just at that very moment, as if she knew that she was being talked about, Janice opened up the patio door. "Hey, everyone, they just let Betty go!" she told the group, astounded.

Nobody moved. Nobody spoke. Nobody smoked. There was a long pause as if the world stopped for a moment. Kristin could not believe what she was hearing. Betty was the right hand of Tom, the boss-man. How could they let *her* go? And who was going to do Betty's job now? It was surreal. *What the hell is happening around here*? she wondered.

Janice came over to Kristin. "Can I bum a cig?"

"But you don't..." Kristin stopped herself and opened her pack, handing one to Janice. Brian lit her up. The three of them took a long drag together, held the smoke, and then exhaled slowly, all in unison. It didn't matter if Janice had or had never smoked before, she deserved a cigarette at that moment. This news was shocking, to say the very least.

"I couldn't believe it," Janice said. "After like an hour and a half behind closed doors, Betty comes out crying and Tom walks her to her desk, hugs her, and she throws a few personal things in a storage box and walks out. That was it. No good-byes to anyone. Nothing. But she was upset. I don't think she had any inkling that was going to happen. Before this happened I thought that I had nothing to worry about. But now..." Janice paused, taking another long drag of the cigarette, and then exhaled without finishing the sentence. It didn't matter; they all knew where she was going with it.

And then they all took another long drag, paused, and exhaled together, in unison.

"Fuuuuuuuuuccccckkkkkk," Brian said slowly while exhaling smoke. Kristin nodded her head. Janice repeated Brian's long drawn-out expletive with her next exhale. Kristin had never heard Janice curse before, and yet there she was, cursing and smoking with the best of them. Or were they the worst? Only time would tell about that.

In no time, like men being led down death row, everyone started back to their office cubicles. With Betty gone, it would only be a matter of time before about a third of them would also be gone. Suddenly, the lonely stairway, dark hallway, and old, rusty file cabinets, seemed more important to Kristin. She noticed more things about her workplace on that long, quiet walk back to her desk. She never noticed that the paint in the hallway used to be bright blue because the newer gray paint covered most of it. But that day, she noticed some of the new coat peeling away to reveal it. She caught a glimpse of part of a yellow hula-hoop tucked behind one of the old file cabinets. She had never noticed it before. And there were many more "new" items that she realized on her way back to her desk that day. It was strange, she noticed, when she slowed down and took the time how she saw things that she'd never seen before. Today all the little things seemed to matter more than before. She found herself wanting to understand the story of how that hula-hoop had gotten there or why they had painted such a pretty blue wall dark gray. Alas, she would probably never know the meaning behind many of these things.

Before sitting back at her desk, Kristin found herself taking a deep breath. She thought about yoga last night and her teacher, Nayana; who, no matter what happened or what anyone said, seemed to have it all together. She didn't seem to worry much about anything. And even though she had just met her, she felt that to be the truth. And as she thought about that she wondered why she was reflecting so much about the truth in the last twelve hours. She had never thought about what was true or not so much in her life. She just sort of assumed everything was true. Suddenly, she was questioning a lot of things.

Tom exited his office and gazed her way. Kristin's heart began to race. She felt her body temperature rise and even a little perspiration accumulate under her arms. That all seemed to transpire within a second of seeing Tom walking towards her. But he paused for a moment at Janice's desk and motioned for her to follow him into his office. Kristin could not believe her eyes. Janice flashed Kristin a look and then followed Tom. There was no way in the universe that they would let Janice go. *No way*, Kristin thought. Now there was no point working. She just stayed standing up until Janice walked back out and back to her desk, wiping her brow line as she looked at Kristin. She was safe. *Maybe there is some sort of justice in the world of corporate America*, she thought. *Some sort of sick, twisted justice, but justice nonetheless.*

After lunch the rest of the afternoon went along in this manner. Someone would walk into Tom's office and either come out happily, nearly skipping back to their desk to get back to work, or, similar to Betty, they came out crying, quickly packed some things up and left, escorted by Tom. Kristin felt a little sorry for Tom now. She knew that none of these cuts were his idea, after all. The suits in his office were behind all this mayhem.

At 3:33, Tom came out and wiggled his finger to Kristin. It was her turn. She checked the clock again and thought maybe it was a good sign. Maybe 3:33 meant something good for her. She actually crossed her fingers while walking into his office.

In Tom's office sat two distinguished looking men in suits. If she weren't bad with guessing ages, she may have put them in their late fifties or early sixties. Both wore the same color gray jackets and dark blue ties and were balding in similar places. As she entered the room they both glanced at their watches.

"Ah, 3:33," said the one on the left to the other, "You owe me a beer."

This comment revealed to her that his age was probably a lot younger than she had initially guessed. The one on the right brushed his comment off as if it were the umpteenth time that he had heard this reference from the other guy. The first guy, who she now judged as the younger one, was smirking. The older one picked up a folder and began speaking:

"Kristin, it is?"

"Yes, that's me," Kristin said, semi-pleasantly.

"So, Kristin, tell us what you do here?"

The question was ludicrous. They were looking at her personnel file. It contained her job status and all information about her. All she could think of was what jackasses they were. Nonetheless, she went through a concise, but accurate assessment of her job and what she did for the company, including any special committees she had been on during her tenure. The two men perused her file together, pointing to this or that. She knew not what. Then, the one who held the file spoke up again:

"It says here that you have been missing some time out of work lately. Is everything all right?"

"Yes, yes, sir."

"Please call me Charlie," he interrupted her. It didn't sound right to do so, and she didn't feel like doing it, but she went with it, reluctantly.

"Sorry, Charlie, yes, I have missed some work the past year. I've had some issues with my hip and my back. I really can't pinpoint what it is. I've been to a lot of doctors and had tests, but nobody can seem to help me."

He nodded. "I have a bad back, myself, the thing goes out from time to time and I find myself unable to even lift my own body up. It used to be really bad. Sometimes I would be out for a couple of days, just lying on the couch like a deadbeat. Then someone suggested that I try yoga. It helps. I've been doing it twice a week for six months now and I actually feel better. Have you tried yoga?"

Hold.

The.

Phone.

Was she hearing this correctly, she wondered?

"Well, sir, uh, Charlie, it's funny you mention that because my last doctor recommended yoga and I just went last night, with my mother, who is sixty-four. She loved it. My sister went too. It was a family event. We are probably going to go every week together."

Kristin smiled brightly. She found it hard to stop talking up yoga and her experience as if it had been a completely good one and positive one. She felt that she had made a good, solid connection with the suit. She needed to work it.

"Good, good. You will love it. Just don't give up. It helps. You will feel better," he said encouragingly.

Kristin smiled. He smiled. There was an awkward pause again. She noticed Tom looking back and forth at she and the suit inquisitively. But Kristin felt relief. *This is good,* she told herself.

"Well, Kristin, we want to thank you for your employment with us. You have been a good employee. We see some remarks here in your file about working on sticking to deadlines, but who doesn't have some things to work on, really?" he questioned. "So, thank you, we are happy to have you as one of our employees and hope that you will want to stay on with us through the upcoming changes with the company."

And with that, he extended his arm to shake her hand. Kristin stood up and extended her hand to him. They shook, and she paused one moment longer just like Nayana had done in yoga. Well, not *just* like Nayana. Maybe hers was shorter than that, but in the same vein. The two of them locked eyes, smiled, and then parted. The second suit extended his hand to her and she also shook his. She looked at Tom. He didn't know what to do. He went to extend his hand, and then hug, but then in the end just reached for the door to let her out.

She walked past Janice, then turned and went back to her and gave her a big hug. She didn't know why. It was not like her to be touchy-feely. But there she was, taking long pauses in handshaking suits and now hugging a co-worker. Kristin nearly skipped back to her desk just like the others who stayed on. And at the end of the day when a third of the staff had been let go, the other two-thirds quietly turned off their computers and began walking out for the weekend. At least nobody was being asked to work overtime this weekend. She was betting that Tom was going to have a few drinks of his own, just like she and her coworkers.

Kristin walked towards her car and noticed Brian leaning against it. She had wondered how he had fared.

"I guess you're still here, too?" She smiled at him.

"Ah, well about that..." Brian paused.

Kristin hit him in the arm, "STOP IT!"

He nodded affirmatively. They had let him go. She didn't know what to say to him. So she hugged him. She hugged him long and deeply, like she should have at the holiday party when he had begun to show her some affection. When the embrace ended, Kristin held his hand a moment longer.

"What do you think you're going to do?" she asked him.

He shrugged his shoulders and kicked a rock near the car. "Take a vacation?" he said, unsure.

"I'm being serious. Are you gonna be OK?"

"Oh yeah. I'm fine. I have a mess of money put away. I'm not worried. I'm a computer geek. I can get a job anywhere."

"Oh," she said. "OK." His response made her feel a little better.

Brian paused again, kicked another rock, and then shook his head disapprovingly.

"No, that's not exactly right. Well, I mean, it is. I can get a computer job anywhere. But you know what? I don't want to. I'm sick of it, really. I don't like being in an office. I hate the fluorescent lighting. The whole thing is boring and exhausting. The entire process of being inside an office building and pretending every moment of the day that I am someone who I am not, well, it sucks. I want to be outside in nature. I want to do something good for the planet!" He was getting more excited as he spoke. "I want to really live, you know? Screw this corporate shit, I want to enjoy — no LOVE — I want to LOVE what I do!"

She had never heard him talk like this before. She had never really heard him talk much at all before, other than about work or smoking, really. She suddenly found him very attractive, sort of like the old basement wall color.

"Wow, Brian. That's a lot to digest. I mean, what do you think you want to do?"

He shrugged again. Kicked another rock, "I don't know, but not this. I'm done."

"OK. Well, I mean, I get it. I 'get' wanting to do something that matters and something that you love. But how will you survive? I mean, after the money you saved runs out? How will you live?"

Brian stood up and looked her square in the eyes. *Have his eyes always been this beautiful color green?* She pondered.

"I just know it'll work out. I can't explain it, Kristin, but I just know that if I'm doing what I love and I'm happy, that I will be OK. I'll survive. It's like what they say, *'when one door closes, another one opens'.*"

She had never heard that saying before. She didn't know what "they" he was referring to. She wondered if he had lost his mind. Yet, she wanted to support him. She was feeling confused and sad at the same time.

"Well, listen, if you need anything, you have my number," she offered.

"I know. I know. And you know, maybe we can have dinner soon and maybe just, you know, hang out, as friends..." he said, pausing at "friends" as if he didn't really want to agree to that agenda fully.

"Sure," Kristin began to say, when Brian interrupted her again.

"No, I don't mean that," he said, shaking his head again. "I'm done pretending and not speaking what I feel in my heart. You know that I like you, Kristin. I've always liked you. And it's okay if you don't feel the same way. You certainly don't have to. But, if there's a chance that you do or you might, then I want you to give it a chance. Here I am," Brian said opening up his arms wide and spinning around in a circle. "I'm just an unemployed guy who likes to play video games all weekend long, who has no healthy habits at all, but wants to start a new life doing something good for the planet and wants you in it in whatever way you are willing to be in it."

Brian smiled. He was truly happy with himself in that moment. She had never seen him look so open and carefree.

"Brian, I don't know what to say to all of that," Kristin started. "I mean, you know I care for you a lot. We are certainly friends. And I do want to get together and hang out. I mean, I don't know, maybe there is something more here. But…"

Brian stopped her by leaning in and planting a whopper of a kiss right on her lips. Although she was shocked, this had happened to her once before too. When she was in tenth grade she had double dated with Melissa and a friend of her then boyfriend. At the end of the night the guy leaned in and planted a huge tongue kiss on her and even though she hardly even knew the guy or what to do, she kissed him back. And the guy never seemed to notice that she was not into it at all. She was a good faker when she needed to be, just like in Tom's office a couple of hours prior. The kiss lingered for about forty seconds, although it felt like five minutes. When he was done, Brian gently pulled away and immediately stuck both of his hands into his pockets, looking at the ground, but smiling. Kristin touched her lips, wondering for a moment if she enjoyed it. She wasn't sure. She felt something, but this was Brian. He chuckled and looked up at her sweetly.

"So, you have my number," he said. "I'll leave it up to you. If you want to get together, you can call me or text me or email or IM or Facebook or whatever."

She nodded, and before she could say another thing, Brian turned and darted off in a sprint. Kristin opened her car door, sat down inside, and closed the door again. She did not start the engine right away. She didn't look at her phone. She just stared ahead towards her workplace building but not looking at anything in particular. A moment later Brian's Honda sped past her and down the road. He didn't look back or wave. But he was smiling.

This was truly the end of an era of her life. Although she had been spared her own job, Kristin felt like she had lost it. With the company making so many changes and all of the people who were let go today, it was challenging to think that come Monday she would still have the same job. Perhaps some of the job would be the same, but the reality was that lots of things were going to change. And Kristin didn't really like change very much. Her stomach started to feel even queasier than it had all day as the reality of the changes at work set in. And then she thought about the quote that Brian said: "When one door closes, another one opens." If that was true, there was no way of knowing if the new door was going to be better than the one that had closed. It had the potential of being a door that opened up to a horrific new place. Yet Brian seemed sure that it would be better.

How do some people have the capacity to believe in the positive in the midst of frightening or challenging times? she thought. Either they were blessed or she and people like her were cursed. Either way, doors were definitely closing. Only time would tell if new ones opened, and if they indeed led to better places.

Kristin took a deep breath and started her car. The deep breath felt good. She thought of yoga. Then she lit up a cigarette, opened the windows, and began driving home. It was Friday night, and the only doors that were opening this night were the ones to her townhouse that led to her couch. It was a Chinese take-out, wine and television kind of night.

Chapter 7

Take 2

"Our greatest weakness lies in giving up. The most certain way to succeed is always to try just one more time." ~ Thomas A. Edison

It was Thursday evening and Kristin sat in her car in the back of the parking lot at the yoga studio. Her mother and sister had already gone inside at least ten minutes ago. There was still five minutes before class started, but she was in no rush to get there early. Melissa wasn't coming tonight because she had to work late to finish up a project. So it would just be Kristin and her family. And after the week she was having at work, she just felt like staying in the car by herself a little longer.

She hadn't known what to expect on Monday morning when she returned to work, but the morning transpired rather normally considering that a lot of people were no longer in the company. Kristin arrived early to work and dove right into it. She wanted to show that she was grateful to have a job and she knew that she did not always show that. Janice was already in the office when she arrived a half an hour early and she honestly had no idea if that was a usual thing or if Janice had the same feelings as she did that morning. They exchanged pleasantries, but both got immediately back to work. Tom stayed in his office working all morning too. When she walked by his office to use the restroom she noticed that he had looked rather haggard, almost as if he had slept in the office all weekend. Again she felt bad for the guy. It sucked being on the receiving end of those meetings on Friday, but it certainly had to be tough for him being in the middle of the chopping block just watching it all happening around him. Then she had the thought that maybe his job had been on the line too. Or, perhaps it still was. It would definitely explain the aging he seemed to have done in the past three days.

Late afternoon on Monday, Tom called a meeting. He did it in a rather unusual way, unlike ever before. He emailed everyone to meet at 2:30 by his office and everyone gathered around in the hallway and around the cubicles that surrounded his area. Kristin leaned against a cubicle farther away with Janice while most of the other people stood with their hands folded across their chests in a defensive type stance right in front of Tom. Tom, on the other hand, looked more relaxed and casual than she had ever seen him before. Kristin noticed that he lacked a tie.

"Thanks for taking a few minutes away from your work, everyone, I truly appreciate it," Tom began. He took a deep breath and rubbed his eyes before continuing. "So, I know that Friday was a tough day for everyone. As I look around the office today, I realize that a lot of people that I considered friends are gone now. I know that as your boss I am often serious and don't always take the time to tell everyone how much I enjoy either talking with you about your children or grandchildren, or spending social time with you at the company outings, or even just asking how your weekend was. And I know that if I did that now it wouldn't seem very genuine to many of you. I've had a lot to think about the past week or so. When they told me of the cuts and the changes that were coming down the pike I tried very hard to be a company man and to stand behind it. But the truth is that I don't agree with the way that the company is going."

At this point, it seemed as if air had been let out of a balloon and the energy in the office changed. Everyone shifted positions and many people let their arms fall to their sides. Kristin and Janice both stood up and took a few steps closer to Tom. It felt like everyone for a moment was letting their guard down and actually coming together. And there was more to come.

"So, as of twelve noon today, I submitted my resignation," Tom said to a stunned crowd of co-workers. There were even a few gasps to be heard. Not from Kristin. Her mouth was open, but nothing had come out.

"I know this may come as a complete shock to those of you who felt like I was a real company man. I tried. But I simply cannot continue to work for the company any longer. I've decided to take a couple of months off with my wife and we are going to travel. I'm going to clear my head and decide what I want to do. I need to assess what is important to me and then decide from a more centered place, and not an emotional one."

The sincerity in Tom's voice was genuine. Nobody could deny that this man was indeed hurting and actually grieving something that he once loved and cared for. It sounded odd to think of a job as being that, but Kristin understood. Even though she didn't enjoy what she did, if she lost her job, she thought that she would probably grieve it as well.

"Jeez, Tom. If you were going to leave, why didn't you do it on Friday? Maybe someone who needed their job and the money could have kept theirs," said a man in the front. Kristin couldn't identify who had said it, but thought it sounded a lot like George from Accounting.

"I know. I know. I thought about that," Tom continued. "I don't want this to be perceived as me being ungrateful for having a job. I have honestly loved my job. I loved working here and I loved working with all of you. And you may not believe this, but I tried my best to save every single job that they wanted to cut. I went to bat for each and every person that got fired Friday, regardless of any personal feelings I may have had about them or even if I had given them a bad review before. Nobody deserves to lose a job like this. Nobody. That's why before I resigned, I made a recommendation that they hire someone from within to replace me. In fact, I gave them three names of recommendations out of all of you."

Everyone started looking around the group. They were all interested in knowing who it might be. But Tom wasn't saying. In fact, he didn't say much more. After that, he made some closing remarks, and then people started coming up to shake his hand. Tom smiled as each person came to say good-bye to him. Janice and Kristin waited until almost everyone else was gone before they approached him. Of course, Janice shook Tom's hand first.

"I want you both to know that you were two of the three people that I recommended to the company for my replacement," Tom told them.

"What? Me?" Kristin blurted out.

Janice looked at her and back to Tom.

"Thank you, Tom, for the opportunity. I promise you that if they choose me, I will not let you down," Janice said, shaking his hand furiously. When she stepped back to let Kristin in, instead of walking back to her desk like the others had, she waited and listened in.

"Tom, honestly, I know why you gave them Janice's name. She's an awesome employee. I'm not sure why you gave them mine, but thank you. And I honestly wish you the best with your future," Kristin said, smiling.

"Kristin, you don't give yourself enough credit. You are probably one of the most honest and reliable people in the company. And you are too, Janice. I know that if I want something done, I could give it to either of you and it would get done, even if that meant you coming in early or over the weekend. And that never went unnoticed. Again, I want to apologize if I didn't convey my sincere appreciation for the work that you did," Tom said with a smile. "I wish you both the best."

This was how the day went down.

As Kristin sat in the car waiting to go into yoga she repeated that scene over and over in her head. First, Brian sped off Friday feeling elated, as if he had just come out of the closet. Now, Tom appeared more human than he ever had, leaving the job. Kristin had been so worried about losing her job that she couldn't fathom the freedom that they had both displayed in leaving it. And she was starting to wonder if she was missing something — something bigger.

The rest of the week the workplace felt wrong. She could not put a finger on the reasons. Yes, many people were gone and yes, her boss and one of her best work buddies were a part of that departure. But everything in her cubicle was the same and her workload and nothing else had changed. For all purposes, most things were exactly the same as they had been. And yet, it all felt wrong and she just didn't understand why.

She shook her head, coming out of her daze and stepped out of the car to walk into the yoga studio. People were already heading into the yoga room when she arrived, so she quickly slipped off her sandals, grabbed a yoga mat and went inside.

Sandy and her mother sat near the front and waved to her as she came in. She smiled and waved back. She hadn't spoken much to her mother since last week, but Sandy knew about Brian and Tom and the rest of the week because she had called her to talk about it. Sandy had just told her to hang in because things would work out. What else could she say? Kristin took a place near the back of the room and sat down when Nayana began to talk.

"It is so great to see so many faces here tonight — some new faces, some returning faces, but all beautiful faces. And I want to talk a bit tonight about that — about the different masks that we wear. We all wear several different masks: the mother or daughter, the boss or co-worker, the scared little girl or the warrior princess..."

There were a few giggles when she said the warrior princess. Kristin smiled because it made her think of that 90's TV show *Xena* that Sandy used to like to watch. Nayana continued.

"So with all of these masks that we wear to show to the world, how do we know who we really are?" she posed as a question and waited. She nodded her head as people nodded and pondered. Someone finally said something:

"I think I am finally starting to know who I really am. And it's because of yoga. I think that before I just was whoever anyone needed me to be. I don't think I had a sense of who or what I was. Now, because I am centered and grounded and happier and healthier, I see that all the things I was doing was an act. They were not the real me, or what I even wanted to be doing. I tended to do things for external approvals. And I was an unhappy person then too. Now, when I am really being myself and honoring who I truly am, I find deep contentment and peace. I'm a happier person. And by changing my energy, I have noticed that people around me also appear to be happier. I guess, in the end, it's all about love," said a middle-aged woman in the room.

She started crying after she said what she said and Nayana came over and gave her a big hug.

"That is so awesome, Nicole. I couldn't have said it better myself." Nayana went back to the front of the room and offered that everyone lie on their back for a breathing meditation. Kristin was more than happy to do that and soon Nayana was guiding them to feel and honor their breath and reminding the class to honor their true self as they practiced.

"If something doesn't feel right for you, please come out of the pose. I can help you find something that works for you," Nayana offered. "If you focus and concentrate on your breath and what you feel in the body, you will not be wrong. But if you listen to your mind and your ego, you will never know if it is true or not. So don't do a pose for me or because the person next to you is doing it. Don't push yourself to the point that you can't breath or are holding your breath. Always focus on the deep breaths and concentrate on being in the moment, and then you will know what is real and true for you."

Kristin liked that. There was no competition when each person was allowed to be him- or herself and work at his or her own level. And she needed that, due to her physical issues. She listened to what Nayana said with more awareness this night than she had the first. She realized that she had a wall, a resistance, built up going into the first class. But in the wake of the week that she had from work, she was beginning to feel that there was more to life than what she had been allowing herself to believe. Brian was out there finding his path, Tom was traveling the world, and Janice, well, Janice was happier than a pig in shit. But that was also who Janice was. She was the ultimate worker-bee, always happy to produce for the hive.

But who was Kristin? And what masks was she wearing? She started to wonder if everything that she had done or was doing was for the enjoyment of her sister or approval of her mother or to be the perfect worker for her boss, or whatever else. She should have been focusing on her breathing, but her mind was focused on that whole other story. She clearly didn't know the answer to that question. That both fascinated and frightened her.

"Let's all release that final deep breath with a surrender breath. So inhale through the nose, and exhale through the mouth with a big sigh," Nayana guided the class. Then everyone groaned like they were orgasming. Just like at last week's class, Kristin giggled like a little kid. She didn't see that changing anytime soon either. She was happy that her sister was not sitting next to her to swat at her. She giggled again because that was her being herself. And the woman in the room that shared her story was right, that made her happy.

When Nayana had the class come into the downward facing dog pose again, Kristin lifted her hips with greater ease than last week. It was still quite challenging, but instead of dropping out of it in a second, she was able to hold it for a few moments without shaking so terribly. When she came down and "honored her body" and went into child's pose, she smiled. She smiled because she was being true to herself and it was an approved thing to do. She kind of dug that about yoga! And she found herself smiling quite a bit throughout the class; particularly when she came out of poses instead of staying in them. Each time, Nayana gave the class permission to listen to what they should be doing for their body and each time Kristin took the modification and came out of the pose or went into an easier variation of the posture. She noticed that some people stayed and some even did other things that looked harder than the pose Nayana was instructing. Nayana even made mention that it was okay to reach beyond the options that she was instructing because perhaps your truth was to do so. Really, "nobody can be wrong in yoga" was what Kristin got out of these classes. This was a mantra that she could get behind!

Towards the end of class Nayana came over to Kristin and offered a bit of advice to her:

"Kristin, I'd like you to try this pose lying on your back. It's called supine pigeon and I really think that it may help alleviate some of the problems you're experiencing with your hip and back. I think you may have sciatica. I'm not sure if anyone has ever said that to you before, but it is a nerve that's being pinched and the pain can radiate down the back of your leg."

"Yes. I'm starting to get that and some tingling and numbness too," Kristin whispered back to Nayana, as to not disturb the others who were doing their thing.

"Yeah, that's definitely nerve related. We can try this and see if it helps. If so, you can do it daily at home."

Nayana guided Kristin onto her back and had her put her feet on the floor hip-width apart. Then she told her to cross her right foot over and place it on her left thigh, flexing the foot. The flexing part took a little while, as apparently Kristin did not understand what she meant by "flexing." When she finally got into position, Nayana asked her to pull her left thigh in towards her chest. But Kristin could barely lift her left foot off the floor, let alone hold the leg in. She looked around and noticed that most of the other people seemed to be performing this pose in various positions but without effort, and she started to immediately feel pangs of despair. But Nayana, astute as she was, realized what Kristin might have been thinking right away and said to the entire class, "Don't worry about what anyone else is doing. Do your practice for you and for no one else, remember? Close your eyes. Breathe deeply." And then to Kristin she continued, "I'm going to just put a little block under your foot here to lift it a little off the floor."

Nayana set her up in the supine pigeon. It was difficult, but not hurting, so she asked her to stay and breath deeply, which Kristin did. She asked herself if she was doing it for Nayana or for herself, but finally decided that she truly wanted to feel better and ultimately she was doing it to relieve the pain she was experiencing.

She also noticed that the right hip was a lot tighter and painful than the left hip. She was able to perform the other side with more ease when she crossed the legs over. This was quite interesting to her. She hadn't really put much thought to how her body felt other than the painful sensations that she experienced. She was only now seeing that each side felt different and that the stretch on the left side was even quite enjoyable. She had focused so much on the pain and negative situation, that she didn't even realize there could be an equally good or positive one as well. This realization was a monumental moment for her. Kristin had finally re-connected to her body and mind.

After class Nayana asked Kristin to stay just a few minutes more to talk about her issues and Kristin did not feel a need to run away. She stayed a little longer, and she even asked her sister and mother to wait outside so that she could actually have a conversation with her yoga teacher without her family stepping in for her, as they usually did, or maybe more appropriately, like she usually allowed them to do.

"So, I think I noticed something, that my right hip is a lot tighter than the left," Kristin told Nayana.

"Well, you said that whatever pain you are experiencing seems to be happening in your right hip and that's the side you tend to hold onto when it acts up, right?" Nayana said.

"Right. Oh, so it makes sense that that side would be tighter, I guess," Kristin said nodding about the connection. She started to feel a little stupid — like she should have known all of this already. Again Nayana seemed to be reading her thoughts.

"Hey, don't judge yourself, Kristin. You're just like most people I meet. Most people have forgotten how to connect to their bodies because they have either spent their entire life abusing it or ignoring it. You're going to have a series of what we call A-HA moments on the mat. Every time you get on your yoga mat will be a learning experience, trust me," Nayana continued. "So, see how that works. I would suggest you do it every day if it feels good to do so. I also think that we need to strengthen some other muscles for you, but we will get into that more. I really think you should try to come regularly. I believe yoga can help you find the balance you need if you give it a chance."

"Yes, I think I'm going to definitely start coming once a week. Last week was hard; I'm not going to lie. But tonight felt better, and I've had a really tough week too. Even though I was really stressed out, I found myself smiling a lot at what you were saying and what I was able to do and even not do."

Nayana smiled at Kristin and encouraged her to continue to listen to what her body was telling her because it was incredibly knowledgeable.

"I find the idea of wearing masks really interesting. I never thought about that before," Kristin told Nayana. "I found myself thinking a lot about what masks I wear while we were practicing. I was wondering if I am *ever* being myself."

"I have a feeling that you are in the process of awakening to your true self now. This awakening is going to have some very interesting reveals for you. One of my favorite quotes is from Thomas Paine. He says, 'The mind, once enlightened, cannot again become dark.'"

Kristin smiled at Nayana and thanked her for taking the time to talk and show her some things that might help her feel better. If anyone had told her last week that she would be thanking her yoga teacher for anything, she would have thought they were crazy. And yet, here she was. She had a yoga teacher. She was becoming enlightened! Did that mean that in the process she would find her true self? Now that she realized that who she was being was not necessarily that, she suddenly felt a need to find out the answer to that very question. And so, it appeared that this yoga experiment would continue...at least for now.

Chapter 8

The Sun Will Come Out Tomorrow

"Every situation in life is temporary. So, when life is good, make sure you enjoy and receive it fully. And when life is not so good, remember that it will not last forever and better days are on the way." ~ Jenni Young

It had been three months since the mass shake-up at work. Kristin had been attending yoga classes once or twice a week and was feeling stronger both physically and mentally. She hadn't realized that she even had any mental issues prior to yoga, but through the process of reconnecting to her body, she found that her mind was equally, if not more so, messed up. She was working on it. And this time she was not so reluctant.

Work did change. A new boss was hired from outside the company, completely disregarding Tom's recommendation to hire from within. As for Janice, she was promoted to a position that they are not calling the same as what Betty had done, but she is in Betty's old cubicle basically doing all of Betty's work, plus her own that she had before. The promotion included a slight pay increase and a bigger workload, but also a new title, which seemed to feed Janice's ego perfectly. As for Kristin, she was basically doing the same thing that she was doing before, but working for someone else whom she had less respect for than the previous leadership of her group. She was grateful to have a job, but it felt rather empty and seemed to be growing emptier by the day.

Lately she seemed more interested in getting out of work and going to yoga or meeting with friends than before too. Her hip was definitely feeling much better. Of course, she had days when she woke up in pain or the pain radiated more as the day progressed, but she was starting to notice that the pain corresponded to particularly stressful events in her life. She could almost identify exactly when it was going to start up just by the level of happiness or lack of in her day. On yoga nights, she usually had less pain. Was it because her mind knew she was going to yoga later and she would feel better? Who knew? In any event, she definitely felt happier on days when she knew that she had yoga in the evening. She was considering purchasing a monthly pass and start going more often. She found herself starting to get to know some of the people who also came regularly and striking up conversations with them before class. She was even drinking the damn water with them!

In addition to the yoga classes, the studio also hosted many interesting workshops on the weekends. So if Kristin did not have plans with Melissa or other friends, or family obligations, she found herself attending some of the yoga related events instead of lying home on the couch. The topics at yoga were interesting and engaging. They talked about concepts of spirituality and energy that she had never even thought about before. This weekend a woman was coming to do a lecture and workshop on Vedic Astrology. She had no idea what that meant, but she did read her horoscope everyday, so she had at least an inkling about astrology. And next weekend a bunch of people from the yoga studio were attending a chanting event at a local church. She wasn't sure about that event yet. Attendance there would definitely mean that she had drunk the Kool-Aid and was all in. And although there were only positive things coming from yoga, there was something within her that kept her holding back just a little.

In her thirty-four years of living, it had been her experience that when things were going good for a while, that something always happened to throw a wrench into the flow and cause problems. Kristin was waiting for that to happen — for that second shoe to drop, as her uncle would say. Although when he said it, for effect he would usually take his shoe off and actually drop it on the floor. So while she was attending and most likely going to be attending more, and found herself googling different yoga references during her break, and looking into online yoga classes for when she was home, she still didn't want to go all in. She felt like she had to hold back just in case. That was just being a realist, she argued.

Kristin's mother had stopped going to yoga regularly because she had a new boyfriend twenty years younger than she who was taking up a lot of her time and interest these days. That was okay with Kristin. While she loved her mother and knew that she meant well, sometimes she just needed some space to do her own things. Even Sandy's interest seemed to diminish after the first six weeks. Brenda's schedule got busier. In addition to her music lessons, she was now taking tap dancing and playing softball. Sandy also had the family involved in some community events; so on a usual night there was at least one planned activity to do. Melissa started going to yoga fairly consistent with Kristin. They would often even go to dinner after class. But then when Kristin started attending more classes than Melissa, they somehow created a new pattern of hugging and heading in separate directions after class. Now the thing that her sister, mother and best friend had dragged her practically kicking and screaming into doing, most of them were barely into. And there was Kristin jumping in — even if she was using a floating devise. It was an interesting turn of events, for sure.

Even more interesting was the fact that Nayana had encouraged her to stop smoking and even though she had not completely stopped, she was down to one cigarette a day. She would allow herself just one during her morning or afternoon break at work. The group that collected at the smokers' patio seemed less than half the size that it used to be. Granted, many of the people who smoked had been fired. But even above that, a lot more people just weren't smoking anymore. Cigarettes were an expensive habit and everyone seemed to be watching their pennies just a little bit more these days.

Of course she had always known that smoking wasn't good for a person. It just seemed in the past that the more someone got on her about the smoking, the more she wanted to smoke. Her rebellious nature didn't want to listen to anyone telling her what to do and she used all the reasons that people gave her to stop smoking as fuel to continue. What she was realizing through her yoga practice was that she was breathing much more fully and deeply since she cut back on smoking. She had been quite upset with Nayana for bringing up the smoking the first night that she went to yoga, but now she could actually see and feel the difference. She even started to question why she had been so horrible to her body for so long. But Nayana would often remind her that everything that happened to her in her life had brought her to where she was at that particular moment. And she was feeling pretty good now in that moment.

She had taken the last ibuprofen for her back a couple of months after Tom had left the company. By then she had been going to yoga twice a week, which is when she stopped feeling the need to medicate the pain. She noticed that getting up from her office chair was easier, and she rarely had to grab her lower back or hip and wince like she used to do on a daily basis. At first, she hadn't realized that she was even feeling better. But then people around her — people at work, friends and family, and also people at yoga all started to comment that she was looking better and didn't appear to be in as much pain. Nobody came right out and said that she was acting much nicer or that she had a better attitude, but she knew that was a part of it too. She was feeling better all over and it was an awesome thing. She even stopped seeing Dr. Bell because she didn't feel that she needed to anymore. She had yoga in her life now and that seemed to be working for her.

Although she was feeling better physically and felt a positive change occurring in her life, work remained challenging. Things at the office had changed, but yet were still not positive or offering her anything that made her feel like she was doing something worthwhile. Her co-worker, Pim, from Thailand would say, "Same, same, but different." That seemed to sum it up just right. Until she was able to pinpoint just what was not right she figured she would continue to show up every day and just do the best that she could and eventually things would line up.

She was definitely living a more present and positive life than she had just a mere few months before. Things were moving and changing and she was trying to ride the wave.

* * *

That night before heading to yoga, as Kristin was walking out to her car she paused to watch the sun set behind her office building. The sky illuminated in pinkish-orange colors like she had never seen before. There was just the right number of clouds in the sky to reflect the light from them. The office looked serene and since most of the other employees (except Janice) had left for the evening, there was a peace and calm all about the area. Kristin sat on the hood of her car and took deep breaths as she watched the sun slowly set behind the building. She smiled, knowing that the sun would come back out tomorrow, resulting in it being a good day.

Chapter 9

Well, There's That Other Shoe...

Ego says, "Once everything falls into place, I'll feel peace." Spirit says, "Find your peace, and then everything will fall into place." ~ Marianne Williamson

Kristin had torn her closet apart looking for the right shoe to her favorite pair of sandals. She just couldn't find it. She walked in and out, around her bedroom, looked under her bed and dresser, and everywhere that she could think of. She wracked her brain, wondering, *when was the last time I wore them?* But nothing was coming to her. She was preparing to go to a different yoga studio located in New York City with some friends she had met at her regular yoga class. Afterwards they were going out to dinner. The sandals she was looking for would be perfect for going from yoga to a nice meal, but alas, the one shoe was MIA.

Within six months, Kristin had become addicted to yoga. Well, that's what her sister, Sandy, teased her. But Kristin didn't mind because she thought if there were something to be addicted to, a healthy lifestyle was probably the thing to be. She now went to yoga at least five days a week, and on some weekends she would attend either a workshop or special event at either her local studio or at another one. She didn't realize how supportive the yoga community could be before she got involved. In addition to regular classes, there seemed to always be lectures, concerts, workshops, retreats, and even food events involving yoga. Last week she had attended a "Yoga & Wine" workshop at a winery where another local teacher conducted a yoga class and paired wine to certain poses. They didn't actually drink the wine until after the yoga practice, but Kristin thought it was one of the most fun events that she had attended probably ever in her life!

The truth was that there was a lot to learn and to understand about yoga. Beyond the physical poses, which were challenging enough, there was an entire philosophy. And understanding yoga philosophy was not so easy. Nayana had recommended a book called the *Yoga Sutras of Patanjali.* She said this was the yoga "Bible," and this book had all the methods of yoga put together. Kristin eagerly dove into the book and soon realized that while it had a lot to say, something seemed to be lost in translation to her. She was finding that she definitely needed a teacher to help guide her through the book and put things into modern-day perspective.

For example, the most well known part of the book was a section described as the "eight limbs of yoga." These branches are individual concepts that make up the whole tree of yoga. The first two branches are guidelines and ethical disciplines. Considering that she thought that practicing yoga meant doing poses, Kristin was quite surprised about this. She understood that most world religions are based on the same sort of principles of being a good and moral person, but everyone in the community kept saying that yoga was not a religion but a practice. She realized that the extent to which one can take each part of these principles could actually differ quite a bit from person to person. And for someone like her who was really just beginning to understand how her body and mind were connected and how her thoughts and actions were linked, going deep into her everyday actions and accumulated karma seemed a little too much. And yet, she wanted to learn more.

Nayana suggested that Kristin begin any self-discovery with inquiry on the first branch called *yamas*. These consist of five guidelines that are translated to roughly mean moral conduct. And the first of the five is called *ahimsa*, which translates to non-violence. Kristin sat down and took out a fresh journal. At the top of the page she wrote: "Ahimsa = Non-violence." And she began to write about what non-violence meant to her and how she was relating it in her life. She thought about all the times she wanted to hit her sister or yell at her mother, and if those things had been acceptable behavior, she would have really liked to have done them. She wondered how she would have felt had she actually went through with them. It was difficult to say. Right now as she wrote, she felt shame for wanting to hurt someone that she loved. She considered the times she had yelled at strangers while driving in her car because they were either going to slow in front of her, or driving up on her rear behind her. Was it okay to yell hurtful things at someone that she didn't know? Somehow she felt a little shame there too.

She began to discover the many ways that she hurt herself too. All the times that she said negative things about her body, the work that she did, her attitude or any other aspect of her life, this was creating harmful energy towards herself. Truthfully, she hadn't realized that on her own. Nayana had to sort of guide her through this understanding. But now that she knew, the evidence was glaring at her with disdain. Again, she felt more shame for her previous behavior.

The more she journaled about *ahimsa*, the more difficult she realized that it was to really live a nonviolent life. And yet, she wanted to. She paused and sighed because this was only one tiny aspect of the branches of yoga.

For sure, yoga philosophy was no joke! When she was being honest, she had discovered that she was not entirely living in unison with all five of the *yamas* and all five of the *niyamas*, which are other disciplines. And these are just the first two branches! The yoga postures came on a branch after those. But Nayana explained to her that it was probably a good thing to keep practicing the postures and develop a connection to the body and mind through them while she worked out her issues within the first two branches. So under the guidance of her teacher, she decided not to give it all up. This made her very happy since the physical practice was doing so much to help her overall physical and mental health thus far, and to lose that would probably send her back to where she had been earlier in the year. She reminded herself that this was not a very good place.

Kristin was also quite intrigued with the origins of yoga. She knew that it had begun in India. She watched several online videos with renowned yoga teachers talking about yoga. Each one of them had a different thing to say about yoga and the history of the practice. This also confused her quite a bit. Both online and book resources seemed to have conflicting timelines for yoga due to the fact that it was a practice that had only apparently been passed down orally and not written down for a very long time. The one somewhat consistent timetable indicated that some evidence could be traced back to about 6,000 years, but other theories felt there was a most likely much older dating that just couldn't be proved yet. Even at that, to say that this practice was thousands of years old felt astounding to Kristin. Certainly, yoga way back then was much different from today, but to be a part of this vast lineage of realigning the body, mind and spirit to "Oneness" only fueled her fire to know and understand more about the practice. That is what drew her to a workshop in the city on this very weekend.

Nayana had announced in a class that she was attending a special workshop with a well-known yoga teacher. Kristin had never heard of this person, but certainly googled him after class that night and found that for certain, he was a yoga rock-star. With her body now feeling stronger than ever, she wondered what more she could do! So when Nayana offered to bring anyone along with her to the workshop, she readily agreed to go with her and some other folks from the studio. She was very much looking forward to the entire day of immersing herself into the yoga practice and surrounding herself with the larger yoga community. The only question was, where the heck was that shoe?

Kristin had a few hours before she had to leave to meet her friends. She grabbed an apple and plopped down on a chair in her living room. As she bit into the apple and enjoyed the crisp, cool juices, she tried harder to think about her missing sandal. A voice in her head asked her why that sandal was important anyway; why not just wear another one? She nodded to herself, admitting that she shouldn't be as attached to that particular shoe since she did, indeed, have other shoes that would work just as well. Once she aligned herself to that idea, she took a deep exhale and simply enjoyed the apple. It was in the midst of this when her phone rang. And without even looking at the number, she answered the call.

"Hello?"

"Hi! What's going on, stranger?" asked Melissa's friendly voice on the other end of the phone. It was good to hear from her. Instantly Kristin realized she did not know when she had spoken to her dear friend last. It seemed like they had both sort of taken off in different directions as of late, and with her newfound interest in all things yoga, Kristin seemed to have forgotten about one of her closest friends. Suddenly she was feeling a little guilty.

"Melissa! Hi! How are you?" she said, surprised.

"Good, good. I'm just wondering where you've been? I haven't seen nor heard a peep from you in weeks."

It was true. And somewhere deep in her abdomen she felt a sense of shame about that too. She decided to just be honest and not create some story about it, which in the past would have been very easy to do. But with her newfound interest in all things moral and just, she knew she had to simply acknowledge it.

"I know. I am so sorry. I'm a bad friend," Kristin admitted. "I've just been doing a lot of yoga and immersing myself in understanding more of it. I should have called. I feel like crap now. But how are you? What have you been up to?"

"Well, I'm glad that it's all good. I do want to get together with you though. I have some news of my own that I want to share. When are you around? Doing anything tonight?" Melissa asked her friend.

Kristin felt another twinge in her gut. She almost didn't want to admit to her friend what she had going on. But why lie.

"Argh, I'm sorry, again. I'm getting ready to meet some friends and my yoga teacher to go into the city for a workshop. We have plans to go to dinner after. What about tomorrow?" Kristin decided that an immediate alternative would be the best way to attend to her friend's request.

There was a pause at the other end of the phone — a very long pause.

In that pause Kristin's mind went to a million different places. She questioned if her friend was mad at her, if she had said the wrong thing, wondered if something big was wrong that she should have known about and been there for her friend, and on and on and on. It amazed her how quickly in the span of a little silence; her mind went to just about any negative possibility. She couldn't wait any longer.

"Melissa, is everything OK?"

Her friend responded immediately, "Yea, sure. You know what? It can wait. Tomorrow I have this other thing to do. So, I'll catch up with you next week. It's not important. I know you are busy."

Oh the guilt...the shame...and all she could think of was *"bad friend...bad friend."* But instead of reacting to her own stuff, she decided to step up for her friend.

"Stop it!" yelled Kristin. "You are one of my best friends. I always have time for you."

And the truth was that she did feel this way and always would. Her friends and family were of the utmost importance to her and no matter what she would ever have going on, she would drop it in a moment to be there for any of them if they needed her, even though the truth was that she hadn't actually acted that way as of late. Perhaps it was time to reevaluate this new "addiction" of hers.

"Yeah, yeah, I know. I just don't want to make you change any plans or anything. It's OK." Melissa didn't sound particularly upset, but she didn't sound particularly jovial either. After years of knowing her, Kristin couldn't tell what was going on with her friend or where she was with her feelings at the moment. And she was not coming right out with it either, which concerned her.

"What are you doing right now? I can come over."

The women agreed. Kristin grabbed another pair of sandals without a single thought, slipped them on, grabbed her bag and purse and headed out to see Melissa. In her mind she knew that she had plenty of time before she needed to meet her yoga friends, but she also knew that if Melissa needed her that she would be missing the workshop. *Because that's what friends do*, she thought.

* * *

Kristin arrived at Melissa's house in just about twelve minutes. The Saturday morning traffic was light and they did only live five miles from each other. This was another thing that made Kristin feel a little guilty on the way there. Why hadn't she just stopped by Melissa's house after yoga one night? It would have been an easy thing to do. And since they had started going to yoga together and Melissa had gone for several months before becoming less consistent, Kristin felt that she should have noticed her friend's absences sooner.

Kristin knocked on Melissa's door eagerly. There was a little bit of rumbling from inside and then she heard some giggling. This was rather intriguing since Melissa didn't have a roommate. It was obvious that someone else was inside the apartment with her. And it took a little while for her friend to finally answer the door. She had to really pull back from knocking again or using the spare key to her friend's house. When Melissa finally unlocked and opened the door she greeted her friend with a big smile and bear hug. Kristin was immediately relieved now that she was in the presence of her friend.

"I'm glad you came over," Melissa said. "Come in, I want you to meet someone."

Confused, but no longer concerned, Kristin entered her friend's home. To her astonishment, there stood a tall, handsome guy. He quickly stood up and extended his right hand to her.

"Hi, I'm Bob," said the unknown underwear-model-looking hunk in her friend's home.

Kristin shook his hand, mouth agape, and then looked at her friend, furling her brow, inquisitively. Melissa was just beaming from ear to ear. Kristin then noticed that her friend's shirt was also tucked half in and half out and her top, in addition, had the buttonholes mismatched. Kristin smiled. She looked at Melissa, then back at Bob, and back to Melissa again. Everyone was smiling in a goofy, "I'm in love" kind of way.

"What's going on here?" she finally asked, although she was already getting quite the picture of what indeed was going on.

Melissa's smile said it all, but when she whipped out her left hand, sporting a huge, shiny diamond on her ring finger, the story took on a whole new level. Kristin's eyes widened and she instantly grabbed her friend's hand to pull it closer to her so that she could see this rock closer up.

"Oh my god!" she squealed, as only a female best friend can squeal.

Melissa starting jumping up and down. "I know! I know! I'm getting married!"

Kristin started jumping up and down too. The complete love and joy that she felt in this moment took her back to the same time when she and Sandy were jumping, bouncing and laughing on their new mattresses. In that moment, she and Melissa were transported to the innocence of young girls, in love with life and expressing that love in the only way they knew how — complete abandon.

She looked over at Bob. He was smiling, but more reserved. He was a guy, after all. They show their affections differently. But it was more than obvious from the glow on his face how very happy he was too. And then it hit her that she had no idea who this guy was or anything about him. How had they met? What did he do for a living? Did he support her friend in her life? Did he have any deep, dark secrets she would need to look into? And suddenly her need to understand more trumped her enthusiasm.

The girls plopped down on the couch next to Bob, and Kristin immediately started grilling them both. This is what she pulled out of her friend, who was already very eager to share the story: Melissa had met Bob after a yoga class one night when she ran into the local organic market to get something to eat for dinner. Bob worked there and had helped her bring some bags to her car even though she didn't really need the help. After what seemed to be an immediate connection with each other, he asked for her number, they went out on a date and had been seeing each other ever since. Bob called it "love at first sight." Kristin had heard of these types of events, but had never quite had one herself. And although she had her reservations about how quickly the relationship was moving forward, she was happy for her friend and also quite relieved that this had all turned out to be good news and not any of the other potential things that her mind mulled over on the way to Melissa's house.

They spent an hour talking and discussing some of the upcoming wedding plans. Melissa asked Kristin to be her maid of honor, which both thrilled and terrified her. There seemed to be a lot of important responsibilities for the maid of honor, and she wanted to make sure that she could be there and do all of them for her friend. They were looking at an October wedding, so they had plenty of time to work things out. Both of them wanted a small, more intimate wedding with just some close friends and family.

Although they could have talked forever about the potential plans, she had to excuse herself to meet up with the yoga folks for the workshop. She no longer felt any pangs of guilt or shame nor worry for her friend. So she was open to move into the rest of her day. The actuality was that if she and and her friend had been together, then Melissa and Bob might have never had a chance to talk that day at the store. And they most likely wouldn't be talking about a wedding today. *Everything does happen for a reason*, she thought.

And with that, she waved good-bye to her friend and her fiancé, got in her car and headed out to meet her yoga friends for the rest of today's adventure.

Kristin smiled. Today was a good day.

* * *

Three hours later, amid a challenging yoga pose, Kristin was no longer smiling. She started to wonder what she had been thinking and how she had even gotten herself into the position that she was in — and she meant that quite literally.

With her legs stretched apart, and her front knee bent, Kristin somehow had wrapped her arms around her front legs to grasp them behind her back. The teacher had come up and sandwiched her back leg between his and was spinning her ribcage upward, while it felt like he pulled her torso backwards towards him. She knew that if he let go she would fall, or worse. Luckily he did not let go!

The sweat poured off her body like it had never before. Kristin had trouble breathing, especially while being held and forced into this awkward position. She felt self-conscious about the puddle of water that was building into a small lake down on her mat and felt like she was probably the only one who was practically slipping off her own body parts. She had never experienced sweat like this before — ever! Not even when she had visited the desert in Arizona when it was over one hundred degrees out. After several breaths in this position, gasping for breath and clinging on for dear life, most of the muscles in her body were shaking and she felt as though if she moved just a fraction of an inch in any direction that she might actually break.

This moment seemed to linger for a very long time. Her mind, suspended in fear, wondered what it was that she loved about yoga so much. All those positive feelings seemed to have existed a very long time ago.

When the teacher released her from his grip and the pose, Kristin forced herself to continue on with the group, even though she knew that she should have taken child's pose and rested. She caught a glimpse of Nayana, skin glistening, seeming peaceful and happy. Glancing about the room Kristin noticed many fit, young attendees, and felt out of her league. Many of these city yogis wore tiny little shorts with a bra-top. She now understood why. Her own expensive full-length yoga pants, which she was more than happy to now purchase, held the moisture everywhere, giving the feel that they were weighing her down even more. She was sopping wet, and at one point when she brought her right foot forward to the top of the mat from downward dog, her toe actually got caught on the other pant leg and she nearly fell over. Kristin caught herself and staved off embarrassment, then almost immediately felt something start to cramp in her back. Staying in the pose, she took a moment to assess the pain: was it real and important to come out of the pose or just a twinge that she could work through? She decided to do the latter, and another forty-five minutes later, in final relaxation, she exalted herself for making it through with everyone else. However, if she was being completely truthful with herself she should have stopped a long time ago and rested. Her body had given her many signs of this, but her mind just went to a need to push through and keep up with the others. Kristin felt that she had achieved some great status. Her ego was flying high. But physically she felt like crap.

As she lay there quietly on the floor with a hundred other people, she breathed in the smell of damp sweat, patchouli and feet. But this was the sweat of a hundred spiritual warriors and for a moment, Kristin imagined that they had all just been in a battle together and now that it was finally over, were reaping the rewards of rest. If this had been an actual battle, she knew that she would have been one of the bloody warriors that were just about to die, clinging to life but in excruciating pain. And Kristin wondered if any of her other friends from the studio felt the same way. She visualized Nayana, smiling peacefully, probably having slayed the dragon after saving the rest of them in this story.

Kristin was not smiling. She imagined her own death. Was she being overly dramatic? Or was something inside her dying? She must have fallen asleep because she awoke to the yoga teacher chanting. The other yogis chanted in unison. Nayana and some of her friends from her studio joined in. Kristin felt like a wet, dirty sponge that was heavy and smelly and ready to be tossed into the garbage. She had no desire to go out with the group for dinner. It didn't matter what freaking sandals she had worn. She just wanted to go home. And she wanted to cry.

When the class finally ended, Kristin stood up feeling some uneasiness in her body. She was most certainly weak and nearly fell over. One of her friends from the yoga studio at home, Neil, was close by and saw her take a step back and catch herself from falling down.

"Hey, you okay?" he asked her, reaching a hand out to take her arm.

She looked at Neil. He also looked like a wet sponge. His face, which was bright red in color, appeared as though it was about to pop and explode open. His disheveled hair and dripping body also revealed that he looked like he had been through a war too. Kristin didn't even need to ask him. She knew he felt similar to her.

"Yeah, I think. I don't know. Something feels off in my back." Kristin winced.

"Oh man. I hope you're okay. I was surprised you did that whole practice. I had to come out of the poses many times. My body just couldn't keep up."

Neil had been smart, she thought. Neil had listened to his body's wisdom.

"I think I just want to go home," she admitted to Neil. He was on board with that too. And after meeting with Nayana and the others, they politely excused themselves and made their way back home. She did not confide in Nayana or the others how she felt because they all seemed to be glowing from their experience. She did not want to rain on their parade. She and Neil quietly made their way home together; supporting each other after the difficult, bloody battle that they had experienced.

Neil made sure that she got home okay and made her promise to let Nayana know how she was feeling the next day. She said that she would, but honestly she just needed to rest. She would think about tomorrow then.

* * *

She got home and threw all her belongings down on the floor near the door. She immediately plopped on the couch and awoke the next morning, in her same wet, gross yoga clothes. She felt horrible and completely wiped out. She lay there for a while considering her next move because she had to reach inside herself very deeply to find the energy for it. Finally, reaching her arms back over her head and pointing her toes forward she took one big stretch. This took most of her strength but she knew she had to get up. So she slowly bent her knees in towards her chest and then swung her legs to the side and off the couch, pushing herself up...

...and then she heard and felt a pop in her lower back and fell down on her knees like a sack of potatoes.

The pain coming from her lower back took her breath away — the breath she had been working so long and hard on increasing. Nayana had taught her how her pattern of holding her breath was creating more tension and unease in her body, so she needed to breathe deeper and fuller and sometimes right into the discomfort that she was experiencing in her body. This had worked well for Kristin up to this point. But right then, in the midst of this agonizing pain, all she could do was revert to her previous pattern, and hold her breath.

While Kristin was on the floor in pain and holding her breath, she noticed something under her couch. And even though she was in intense pain, she reached under and pulled out what was suddenly quite obvious to her. It was the missing sandal that she had been looking for the previous day; the one that would go so perfectly from the yoga workshop to dinner in the city — the one that it turns out, she didn't need after all.

And there it was: the other shoe. And it had, indeed, dropped, just like Kristin had anticipated it eventually would.

Chapter 10

A New Perspective

"We cannot become what we want by remaining what we are."
~ Max Depree

Kristin lay on a white gurney in the hospital hallway. The white fluorescent lights were blinding, forcing her to close her eyes. It felt all too familiar. She tried to take deep yogic breaths, but every time she did, it seemed that a pain shot out from her back more fiercely. Nayana had said that yoga breathing could help with pain management. She had heard and read about that more than once, and yet, this was not her current experience. She didn't want to give up on some of the new things that she had learned that were helping her feel better and healthier. But here she was, in the hospital with a yoga-related injury and now the breathing, one of the simplest things, didn't appear to be helping either. Of course, she wasn't giving it much time or attention. She would take a breath, feel something, and then hold it again instead of exhaling all the way through. Her old negative thought patterns flushed into her brain stronger than ever, as if a floodgate had held them back all these months, waiting for the right time to be released. This swell of emotions threatened her progress thus far, but she was unable to think about it thoroughly due to the pain she was experiencing.

Kristin had called Sandy before she called the ambulance. That may have not helped her mental state too much either. Sandy had a tendency to be pushy. She could barely get out the situation when Sandy started her line of rapid-fire inquiry. She forced Kristin to hang up and call an ambulance, something she was trying to avoid by having her sister come and pick her up. Alas, that did not work out.

How embarrassing to have the ambulance come to your home and cart you away on a gurney, she thought, worried about what this would look like.

Upon the ambulance arriving, several of her neighbors had rushed to her side. At first Kristin felt honored and happy to know that they cared about her well-being. Then she noticed that Rose, the single woman that lived on her right side, was curling her hair around her finger while she talked to the cute EMT. Flirtation with a hot EMT at the site of her agonizing pain was the last thing that she wanted to witness. It made her think about her mother and how she reacted around cute men. Kristin started to immediately despise Rose. Mrs. Gunther from a building down had been walking with her children towards the playground when the ambulance rolled in. She seemed quite concerned for Kristin and had stayed by her side assisting with anything that Kristin could not do or answer. Mrs. Gunther's children, however, were acting like raging lunatics. The four-year-old ran around the house as if it were the jungle gym. Mrs. Gunther seemed to feel that this was okay and let the brat continue. When he knocked over one of her candles, she said nothing. She simply picked it back up and let the kid continue to run around. The older child, who could have been around nine years old, was quite busy taking photos with her cell phone, as if she had stumbled across the scene of a murder. She tried to get Mrs. Gunther's attention twice to discuss these things, but the barrage of questions coming at her during the painful interludes she was experiencing forced her to let it go. Not that she was doing well with the letting go, however. With those kids and her other "helpful" neighbors, there seemed to be too much to let go of.

And now that she was in the hospital, the humiliation continued.

The first nurse wanted a sample of her urine, but she couldn't stand up to use the restroom. So, she was nice enough to call in a young male nurse to assist Kristin in using the bedpan. Curling up and dying would have been easier. It took her nearly five minutes to relax enough to actually pee. Now she had been wheeled into the hallway since all the regular beds were needed for other more severe traumas. Her situation was deemed manageable and she was asked to wait until the doctor could come see her. This left her with a lot of time in which to let her mind wander. That was never a good thing for her because her mental activity always seemed to bring her down a very dark and unhappy road.

For the past several months she was living on a high. Kristin was sure that she had cured her back through yoga. She was feeling strong and wonderful. And now, here she was, right back where she began, or worse. What if she had injured herself even more than before? She started to cry. At first, Kristin felt embarrassed to be crying by herself in the hallway, but after she considered the urination in the bedpan with the cute male nurse, she somehow felt like she could just let it out. And so, Kristin wailed, blubbered and shrieked like she never had before.

A passing nurse stopped and handed her a box of tissues. She said nothing to Kristin, but simply patted her on the shoulder and walked away. It was actually comforting to know that someone had seen and cared and yet wasn't going to sit and make her talk about it. Sometimes talking about things just seemed to make them worse for Kristin. Especially when people made too much out of their emotions.

Enter Sandy. She arrived in the middle of Kristin's emotional outburst, and since Kristin was not one to usually have a crying fit, this startled her sister to witness.

"Oh my god, what happened?" Sandy said, rushing up to Kristin's side.

Sandy kept throwing questions at her, but it was all that Kristin could do to try to calm herself down. It took her a little time to stop the crying. In the meantime, Sandy took her sister's hand and held it tightly.

After several minutes, Kristin's emotions started to subside and after she blew her nose three or four times — each of which hurt her back terribly — she felt like she was able to talk. She finally took as deep a breath as she could and told her sister what had happened the day before and how she woke up on the couch, stretched, felt the pop and crumpled to the floor. She even told her about the stupid shoe analogy, as if that was important.

Sandy squeezed her sister's hand. Seeing her sister so upset, Sandy found the need to be a little more reserved than usual. She assured her that she would be okay, although she had no idea if this was true. Kristin's previous tendency was to be overly dramatic and negative. She could easily get stuck on something if she were not encouraged to see things in a more positive way. Sandy realized that today's reaction to being in the hospital was not Kristin's normal negativity, however. There certainly was something bigger going on. And she feared that her sister had pushed herself too hard in order to keep up with the others in class, when she should have heeded her teacher's guidance and listened to her body. Sandy zipped her lip about that because she had an idea that her sister had already gained that perspective. And, maybe right now wasn't the time to gloat about being right. Besides, who was she these days to be judgmental?

Sandy had wanted to continue taking yoga with Kristin, but she couldn't. She told Kristin it was because of her daughter Brenda's schedule. But the truth of it was that she couldn't afford to go. She knew that Kristin would want to pay for her to attend, but she couldn't let her baby sister know that she was having financial difficulties. She had to keep up all the appearances, after all. Sandy was expected to be the successful one in the family and she didn't want to worry anyone that she and Sam were having any troubles.

A nurse came and told Kristin that they were taking her for some x-rays of her lumbar spine to see what was going on. First they moved her into a semi-private area out of the main hallway of the ER and told her that a doctor would be with her shortly. The ER staff was winding down from that hectic incident that had occurred earlier when Kristin arrived. She apologized for making her wait in the hallway and assured her that she would be well taken care of. Kristin smiled weakly. None of that made her feel better. Sandy tried to keep her mind off the waiting with stories about Brenda's accolades and accomplishments. Kristin loved her niece, and she loved her sister, but she just wanted her to be quiet and let her rest just a little. She was finally feeling somewhat comfortable having not moved for a while. Kristin felt like she might be able to take a quick nap, but Sandy kept chatting on and on. That was her way of dealing with things: keep talking around it.

The doctor arrived for a quick, yet brief meeting. After asking Kristin to repeat what happened and asking her to perform a few things — none of which she was able to successfully do — he reported that he thought she may have injured one of her lumbar discs, but couldn't be sure without some films. Once he saw the extent, he could determine if she needed any procedures or if she could take medicine and rest. He told her not to worry, and squeezed her hand like her sister had done in the hallway. Kristin wondered if there was some kind of compassion training book that they had read about squeezing the hand.

* * *

Two hours after the tests were done, Kristin and Sandy still sat waiting. The nurse had given Kristin something to take for the pain, prescribed by the doctor, who she was still waiting to see again with the results. She was told it would be any moment about forty minutes ago.

With the edge off Kristin's pain, Sandy called the yoga studio and talked to Nayana about what was going on with Kristin. Nayana felt terrible and asked to speak to Kristin, which Sandy thought would be a good idea, since it was obvious that her sister's old habits had resurfaced.

Nayana asked Kristin to honestly let her know what had happened. She reluctantly admitted that she had known that she should have come out of the poses and rested much earlier, but had not listened to that wisdom because she wanted to show off and keep up with everyone else. Kristin was embarrassed to tell Nayana last night how she had felt because she knew what she was going to say. She knew this because it was the same thing that she had been telling herself over and over too. She knew that she could have prevented all of this from happening had she only been honest with herself.

As usual, Nayana asked Kristin not to judge herself too harshly and then assured Kristin that this injury would be a very good teacher to her if she allowed it to. Now that she was out of the acute pain, she asked Kristin to try some of the breathing exercises to help relax her even more. She understood that in the moment it would have been challenging for Kristin to go to the breath, but she told her that in time and with practice, that this too would become a more natural and better way of dealing with challenges; whether they were physical, emotional or mental, in the future. Kristin agreed to do some breathing and promised to keep in touch with Nayana upon her release from the hospital. She felt better already just having told the truth to her teacher. Then again, she had taken some medicine too.

Sandy went to make a phone call home and check in on Brenda and Sam, which gave Kristin time to do some breathing. She took a few deep breaths and realized that she could take them without experiencing any pain or worse symptoms. This empowered her to do some more. She began by focusing on her inhalation and exhalation and the sensations around her nose, just like Nayana would often guide them through in class. Out of nowhere she visualized a beautiful field. The wind was softly blowing gently against her skin and the sun radiating soft heat on her head and face. In the middle of the field sat a giant willow tree. It looked unusually out of place, but Kristin visualized herself climbing the tree and lying back against one of its massive branches. She let her right leg fall off the branch and dangle towards the earth, swaying gently back and forth. She felt completely relaxed and at peace. She stayed in this beautiful moment for as long as she could, centered in her breath and in this alternate reality.

After an indeterminate amount of time, she felt someone gently rocking her arm. She slowly blinked her eyes open and adjusted to the light.

"Where did you go?" Sandy asked her sister. She had tried to talk to her, and then resorted to rocking her for a minute or so. She could tell her sister was not asleep, but she was most certainly in a trance or something.

Kristin smiled and continued blinking her eyes until her vision focused. The handsome doctor was there too. They were both looking at her.

"How are you feeling?" he asked Kristin.

"Good," she said, smiling. "I was in a willow tree relaxing."

He chuckled and looked at Sandy, "Its probably the pain medicine kicking in. Unless, she usually has these type of visions," he teased.

Sandy shrugged her shoulders. The truth was she had no idea what had just occurred. But at least her sister was not in pain.

The doctor continued. "Kristin, so, we took a look at your x-rays, and it appears that you have a slight herniation of your L4 vertebrae. It's a fairly common type of injury and nothing to be extremely worried about. You do *not* need surgery. However, I am going to prescribe a dosage of anti-inflammatory drugs to take and give you something that says you are to stay out of work for the next two weeks. I want to see you then. But until I do, just rest. No exercise yet. You can ice it as well. Icing will help with the inflammation. Okay?"

Kristin smiled. She said nothing. She was still in her happy place.

The doctor looked at Sandy, "I'll write it all down for her, it will be in the paperwork."

Sandy felt obligated to step in on her sister's behalf, especially since her sister did not seem to be mentally present.

"You know, she has had back issues before. Do you think that this issue was something she had and just got worse after the class she took yesterday? Is this something she may always have?" Sandy asked. Kristin drifted back off to her willow tree in the field without a care in the world.

"Well, it's hard to know for sure. Kristin did present with pretty extreme pain when she came in. When there is inflammation in a joint, there are lots of things that could be happening. Did she have tests before that showed anything relating to this injury?"

That was a good question. Sandy wasn't sure. She knew that she had seen several doctors about the issue and Kristin said that they had determined nothing was physically wrong with her. Had they done that through testing of her body or other type tests? Sandy was unclear. She realized that she had let her sisterly inquiries lack, probably due to the fact that at that time Kristin was always complaining about something, and sometimes she was just tired of hearing it. She felt awful about that.

Sandy would have to inquire about all of this when Kristin was lucid. But she told the doctor about the pain that radiated down Kristin's leg sometimes and how it had gotten pretty bad just before she started yoga. However, it seemed to have gone away completely over the last six months with her regular practice.

"Well, what you are describing sounds nerve related. Again, I can't say for sure if it is related to this or not. Let's see how she feels in two weeks and we can reassess. And if you can bring in any additional tests or doctor reports, that would also be helpful. Right now, she just needs to rest and let her body start to repair itself. Does that sound good?"

He smiled at Sandy. She knew that he was probably worn out from the patient load that had come in before, but this was her sister and she had to be sure of things. She shook his hand and thanked him for his time. Kristin was still off in La-La Land, which was probably best. The nurse said it was okay for her to stay a little while longer until she was more coherent to leave. Sandy took it as a time to also close her eyes and rest. After all, Kristin wasn't the only one who was going through a challenging situation at the moment. But that was something for another time.

* * *

For Kristin the next two weeks were, well, humbling. She had gone from having to grab her lower back to brace it when she moved, to being able to effortlessly move about, and now further backwards, to having to mindfully think about even beginning a movement. It was certainly challenging work being that careful. She realized that most people who do not experience pain like this do not realize the effort and energy it can take to move about or to perform even the most simple of things. Kristin was having a real education in awareness and mindfulness.

After a few days, she reached out to Nayana, who came by to see her with a bouquet of flowers. Nayana offered to perform some Reiki energy healing on her. Kristin happily agreed since the only requirement was that she lie down and be open to receiving it. She got comfortable and Nayana put her hands on various parts of her body. She often felt great heat coming out of her teacher's hands and sometimes felt what she could only describe as vibrations. She saw a beautiful green light envelope them both while she received this healing energy and she once again drifted off to a happy place as she had in the ER, although this time there were no pain medicines involved in getting her there. Sandy was convinced that Kristin had been under the influence of the drugs in the ER, but this validated her own feelings that there had been more to it than that.

When the healing was finished, Nayana sat down on the floor next to the couch and talked with Kristin.

"So, tell me what you're thinking?"

Kristin took a deep breath. Truth was, she had been thinking about a lot of things lately.

"There's a lot going on in my mind," she admitted. "I'm not sure where to start."

Nayana assured Kristin that she could say anything she wanted or nothing at all. It was "all good," and she would sit with her for as long as she liked. Kristin smiled and nodded her head. Nayana must have noticed that she was biting her lip.

"You know, when you bite your lip I can tell that you are trying not to say something," Nayana told her.

"How do you know that?"

"Ancient Chinese secret," Nayana joked, in reference to an old laundry detergent commercial. They both had a good chuckle recalling the cornball advertisement from their childhoods. Then Nayana revealed, "After twenty years of reading bodies, you pick up a few things here or there."

Kristin nodded, still laughing. She did like Nayana. She was the real deal. She didn't pretend to be perfect, but she was genuine.

"You know what has been on my mind?" Kristin finally revealed. "My life."

Nayana nodded her head knowingly.

"I feel like I've just been going through the motions. I was really an unhappy person for a long time. I don't even know when that started or why. I don't think I was an unhappy kid. I guess I can ask my sister. She may have a different story to tell! But I guess I just was so unhappy for so long for some reason, that it became a way of being. When my back got worse, it was *'poor me.'* When relationships failed, it was because they were jerks and men sucked. When work got challenging and the company seemed to care less about its employees, I just bit down tighter on the negativity. It was such a part of who I was for so long, and now…" Kristin trailed off, as if she were embarrassed to continue.

"And now?" questioned Nayana.

"Well, I don't want to be a Negative-Nellie anymore. I mean, I don't think I ever *wanted* to be. I mean, who *wants* to be angry or feel victimized all the time?"

"You'd be surprised," Nayana interrupted. This gave rise to much shared laughter, even though it somewhat hurt Kristin to laugh that hard.

"I know, I know… Some part of me needed that for some reason, right?" Kristin waited for her teacher to say something poignant, but she did not. She just looked at her and smiled. Kristin continued.

"Here's the thing: I never wanted to work in an office. I never wanted to be a department head or whatever else is up the line. Yet, when I get looked over for a promotion, I do get upset about it. Anyway, I just don't know how I ended up where I am, doing something I hate. I feel like I actually despise myself some days. And then I started doing yoga and feeling better. My body got stronger, I felt more confident, I was feeling more positive, and then — BAM — I'm down for the count and I'm looking at my life and how I got here and I'm just at the point where I'm feeling like I don't want to do this anymore. I want a different life. I just don't know what it is yet."

And there it was — the whole ugly truth of it. She was unhappy and she didn't even know what the hell she wanted. She must have sounded so stupid to Nayana. Deep in the pit of her stomach she felt this disappointment in herself.

"I understand where you are. Do you think I was always a yoga teacher or knew that I wanted to be a yoga teacher?"

Kristin had never actually thought about Nayana's past before. She just seemed to have everything together all the time and she imagined that was just the type of person that Nayana was. Unlike most of the women that she knew, Nayana seemed to be so well balanced. For a moment Kristin wondered if she even wanted to know any deep dark secrets from Nayana's past, lest it ruin her idealized perception of who she was. But that thought process was unrealistic and unfair to Nayana. Each woman seemed to be in a world of her own for a couple of minutes, as Nayana gazed outward as if towards an image of a distant past, or maybe not so distant. She finally gazed down and let out a big sigh before sharing some of her story. Kristin was on the edge of her seat. Not really, she was lying on the couch. But whenever her uncle would share a story and she would lean in physically and listen with every ounce of her being, her uncle would make that joke and fall forward onto the floor from leaning too far in.

"When I was eight years old, my father left us. One day I woke up and he was just gone. My mother was crying at the kitchen table. We were barely making ends meet with my father there. They never fought and he was a good dad to me and my brother and sister, so I just couldn't understand it. I pleaded with my mother to tell me why he had left but she was so overtaken with grief that she couldn't talk to me. That was the first time she ever hit me. I remember running outside screaming. The neighbors came over and talked to my mother and the next thing

I know, my brother, sister and I were taken away from her. Then, two days later she killed herself."

Kristin gasped. She didn't know how to respond, but her first instinct was to sit up, which she tried to do too quickly. Nayana stopped her and had her sit back down.

"Oh, it's okay. You know, this was a long time ago. I've done a lot of work during my life dealing with it. I know it's not my fault my mother killed herself. The fact is, she was sick. She had been diagnosed with an inoperable tumor. And my father, well, he just couldn't handle it. I'm not sure why he left. I've never spoken to him. I don't even know where he is. I tried to find him a long time ago, but then I gave up. He just went off the grid. So, my sister, brother and I were split up. You know, they both went to one home that wanted two children and I went to another. It was not easy at all. I was not a good kid." Nayana paused and laughed at a memory that she chose not to share before she continued.

"So, anyway, I got into a lot of trouble. I drank a lot. I dabbled with drugs. And this one day, I was really high — like, *really* high. I was walking around in the city probably up to no good, when this guy stopped me and asked me what I was doing. He had on these weird saffron-colored robes and smelled like strange spices and he talked funny. I probably gave him some bullshit answer. He knew I was high as a kite, but he didn't judge me. He smiled, he chuckled at me, and he showed me love. He took me home to his wife and two children and they fed me. I'm not even sure why I followed him. I just sort of knew he was a good guy. My adopted parents were so used to me not coming home at night, they didn't even worry about me anymore. They knew that I would come home when I needed something. I'm sure they were doing the best that they could, but really, I was basically a kid living alone on the streets until then.

"So, here I am in this strange Indian family's home, eating weird food and you know, I felt so at home. In fact, I felt more at home than I ever had. And I just knew that I didn't want to leave. I started crying and the man who found me in the street said to me, '*My child, do not cry. You are a child of God. You are love.*' And I ran to him and wrapped my arms around him and cried myself to sleep. He was my guru, my teacher. I stayed and lived with him and his family and he taught me yoga through his tradition."

Nayana paused and smiled. There was a tear in her eye, but it was one built from pure happiness.

"Wow," Kristin exhaled. This story seemed like something made for movies.

Nayana smiled and nodded. Kristin realized that her own story was not that bad compared to Nayana. It gave a new perspective to her way of thinking.

"Kristin, don't feel sorry for me or about my story. Here is what happened: I found myself. I found a family that loved and cared for me and gave me the opportunity to change my life around. I learned how to stop feeling sorry for myself and start living a grateful life; because that is what life is. It is gratitude and it is love and it is amazing. My guru taught me how to love and that included loving myself. He gave me everything. I am who I am because of his grace."

Nayana wiped a tear from her eye and laughed. "I still get so emotional when I think about him."

"What happened to him?" Kristin found herself so enthralled in the story of her teacher that she wanted to know even more.

"He passed away about two years ago. It was very sweet the way he went. He told us all he loved us like he always did, went to bed, and never woke up. He had a smile on his face when we found him in bed the next morning."

"That's how I want to go," Kristin said.

"That's how we *all* want to go!" added Nayana.

Nayana spent a little more time with Kristin, talking and helping her make lunch. Then she had to go to the studio to teach her classes. Kristin sat quietly for a long time after she left, pondering. She thought a lot about her family and how much they loved her and how much they were always there for her no matter what. Kristin remembered how ungrateful she often sounded when they attempted to be there for her, too. She suddenly wanted to see her family very badly. Kristin thought she would call her mother later. For now, she sat still in quiet contemplation.

There were many things to consider in her life. Kristin wanted happiness. She no longer wanted to feel or be ungrateful. She wanted to heal her body, but she wanted to learn how to also treat it with kindness. Kristin wanted to be a better person. She wanted love. She wanted to stop being an asshole.

That last one hit hard. Kristin realized the truth it had. She had often acted like a jerk. And she had absolutely no reason to. *Asshole*, she thought again, but not with judgment, but rather, with recognition.

Nayana's story had really hit home. Kristin knew now what she had to do. She had to start being a better person, first and foremost. She realized that maybe her problem wasn't her body or her job or her relationships. After some contemplation, she realized that her problem was herself.

Chapter 11

The Long and Winding Road

"There are only two mistakes one can make along the road to truth; not going all the way, and not starting." ~ Buddha

Kristin had gone back to work on Monday. It was now Wednesday and she was working really hard on being positive. Not much of her work had gotten completed while she was out with her injury. It was mostly all sitting at her desk, waiting for her upon return, complete with all the new work orders and reports. With the new perspective on life that Kristin was holding on to, she got up every morning, said a gratitude prayer, headed in to work and did what she could before returning home for the evening, grateful to have employment that provided for her. She had two weeks of physical therapy under her belt and was surprised at how much of it was similar to yoga, yet her doctor was reluctant to let her return to her yoga practice until she completed a round of P.T. and received the go-ahead from the therapists.

In the meantime, Kristin practiced her breathing and meditation techniques and was finding that they were most helpful in achieving an attitude of gratitude every day. But it was not easy. The challenges to her old self remained, and it was really all up to her to decide how to react to any given situation. This was the basis of her problems, as she had determined: her own self. Thus, the challenge this provided. There were moments when this was an easier task than others. Today seemed to just be one, long challenging moment.

It began when her old co-worker, Brian, contacted her about being a reference for his new job. Her boss somehow found out that Kristin had taken a personal call from a previous employee and let her know that this was not allowed. Apparently while Kristin was out he had gone on a rampage into everyone's computer and phone logs and evaluated how much time was wasted on social media and personal calls each day. And although Kristin was not privileged to the number, according to him, it was appalling. Now nobody was allowed to have any direct phone calls or use their work computer for anything personal. There were firewalls and limits to what they could access on the Internet, and this was now starting to interfere with her work since there were times that she legitimately needed the use of the web for obtaining certain data. But he didn't seem to care about this fact. And although he could not do anything about the time off Kristin had for her injury, it was apparent through his interactions with her, that he was not pleased at the work she had missed and was holding her at fault for everything that had not gotten done in her absence.

Kristin realized that there was nothing legally wrong that she had done or that he could do about it. She didn't let it bother her for the most part, or at least not on Monday and some of Tuesday. But today, she was kind of over his behavior and this job in general. Gratitude was still there, but at another level, so was the understanding that perhaps the time had come to move on.

Kristin started daydreaming about the perfect job and what it might look like. She wandered off to another land where she worked four days a week and had ample money to pay her bills and live comfortably. She caught herself several times in this dream and tried tirelessly to bring herself back to the gratitude that she had for her job and her current life. But the hopeful thoughts of a better job where she was appreciated and felt as though she were helping the world in a bigger way was always on her mind.

Two weeks after her injury, her back was beginning to feel better, but the endless hours at her desk now seemed to discount any work that she did at P.T. or at home. Each time she stood up to take a stretch break her boss peeked out of his office to see where she was going or what she was doing. She would smile and wave, stretch and sit back down. He was a real Gestapo, this guy. Work felt more like prison, and yet, she was there struggling to be grateful about it.

That evening when she went home she decided to stop and say hello to Nayana and her friends at the yoga studio. Although she did not have the official okay to practice yoga yet, she had been doing her own things at home and wanted to just check in with everyone and say hello. The fact was she missed their positivity and camaraderie.

When she walked in, Neil ran over and planted a big kiss on her cheek. He was a sweet guy. Nayana and a few others came over to say hello and to hear the prognosis. They were hoping she was attending class, but she quickly caught them up to speed about that.

"I'm basically doing yoga anyway. They just don't understand what yoga is."

They all agreed and some shared their own similar stories about physical therapy. It seemed the medical world was more open to the healing practices of yoga, but not entirely ready to give it all the credibility it deserved. Anyone who had been injured and went through therapy shared how he or she had done it in conjunction with some home-based yoga practice. They all unanimously agreed that this had a positive affect on regaining strength of body and mind and that it helped the overall healing process quicker.

When it was time for them to start their yoga class, Kristin asked if she could just sit in the check-in area and relax before going home, and Nayana offered that she come in and lie down on a mat in the yoga room. She said she could just lie there and listen, breathe and just be in the energy of the sacred space. Kristin agreed. That sounded just perfect and Nayana helped set her up in a way that she would feel comfortable during the class.

The theme of Nayana's class that evening was one of the yogic philosophies called *Santosha* or contentment. She wondered if Nayana had chosen that just for her. She realized that it always seemed like Nayana had chosen things just for her, although she knew that everyone probably needed to hear the lessons just as much as she did. Still, she couldn't help but smile thinking that it was meant just for her own benefit.

According to Nayana, to work with *Santosha* means to "begin to stop complaining about the things that annoy us and gently accept the things that fall short of our desires." She went on, "It helps to recognize that anything we are struggling against in non-acceptance causes us to suffer. Most of the time, the question 'why,' as in why is this or that happening, is not helpful and actually locks us into an internal place of struggle. If we do not want to experience so much anguish, then we can approach all experiences life delivers as opportunities for our growth and understanding."

Wow, this was really hitting home at the moment. Kristin breathed deeply as Nayana continued reading from her book *True Yoga* by Jennie Lee about the idea of *Santosha*. She talked about accepting things that are not under our control. She dove into karma. And she effortlessly led the class in a practice where they could look to find peace and contentment in every pose and in every sequence. Nayana offered that when they felt struggle or heard the ego pipe up in defense, or realized that they wanted to get out of the posture, that it was ever so important to watch our response to these negative things. And she offered that these responses are probably the same as how we react to things beyond our control that happen in our everyday lives.

Kristin was well aware of her response: victim. She quickly devolved into the negativity that someone or something else was at fault for what was happening to her. It was difficult to continue to think that she was the one causing her own suffering at any time or moment because she chose to react to something in a certain way. When layered with the idea of karma, it was even more challenging to think that any particular situation was occurring because of things she had directly either done in the past or in a past life. It really forced her to take responsibility for every minor detail of her life.

This yoga tradition is hard! she thought for the umpteenth time.

When the class completed, Kristin thanked everyone for graciously allowing her to join them. Everyone was more than happy to do so. Nayana reminded everyone about a workshop on creating new habits that they were hosting that weekend, and Kristin immediately signed up, knowing that it would help her immensely in dealing with this newfound responsibility of attending to her life like an adult.

Kristin left the studio feeling much calmer and more prepared to continue the week at work and physical therapy. She maintained a fairly positive outlook throughout the rest of the week and was happy to hear from her physical therapist that she could resume gentle yoga on Monday. Things were starting to look a little better on a physical level. Now if only she could win the lottery and not have to work. Argh, there it was again! She reminded herself to be grateful. Yes, this mindfulness was not easy!

* * *

The weekend course on how to create new habits was amazing. Kristin learned that it took twenty-eight days to form a new habit. And if she wanted to be successful in creating it that she had to work at it every day. This made perfect sense to her. Mindfulness, as always, was the key. Once the instructor guided everyone to determine what the new habit that they wanted to create was going to be, she gave them little tips on how to create daily reminders. Kristin downloaded an app that chimes every hour. When she heard the chime, she was supposed to say her intention. She set it on low so that her boss wouldn't hear it at work, but it was loud enough to catch her attention even when she was doing something else. This worked and really kept her on track. She noticed during work that there were times when she found herself in the middle of a particularly big challenge, and would hear the chime. Each time she would take a deep breath, mentally repeat her intention, and immediately the energy of the situation would shift. It was like magic! In fact, the more she did it, the more she noticed how quickly her attention would shift.

The basis of her personal intention was to be positive. Her mantra, she decided, with the help of the instructor, was:
"I am love.
"The Universe protects me always.
"Positive energy surrounds me."

It was longer than some of the other examples, but it seemed to be what she needed. Her mantra packed a lot of power and she definitely needed all that she could get.

A couple of weeks into the use of the mantra, Kristin shared it with Sandy, and told her how it was helping her. She actually shared it with her mother first. And her mother loved it so much she created her own mantra:
"I am love.
"I attract love.
"Love surrounds me."

No big surprises, there.

Kristin thought, *now if we can just get Mom to commit to love once she finds it!*

When Kristin shared this information from the class with Sandy, she was astounded to hear how badly her sister needed to hear it. Sandy opened up and confided about the financial issues that she and Sam had been facing, forcing them to file for bankruptcy. Kristin was totally blown away by this news since her sister had not shared any of this information with her previously. Had Sandy not said anything, Kristin was sure that she would have never found out. Sandy was that good at keeping up appearances. She decided not to be overly concerned for her sister since it seemed that a new financial advisor was helping them get back on track. As she listened to Sandy talk, Kristin realized something. Being so involved in her own selfish issues in the past and so wrought with negativity, her sister had been dealing with these issues alone. Of course there was Sam. But, she meant that Sandy had no sisterly or female support network to count on. Kristin felt bad about this. It was another reminder how important family is and how she wanted to develop kinder and more supportive relationships with them.

Sandy assured her that once they eliminated the debt they had accrued that they would be back on track. The new financial advisor had a plan for them and she said that she was going to follow it and live more within their means. Kristin wanted to think positively about her sister's situation and their future. She figured that was the best use of her energy.

Kristin shared her mantra with Sandy and suggested that together they come up with a mantra for her and Sam to use. Sandy seemed interested, but she believed that Sam would most likely not want to do it. Of course, they both understood that you cannot make someone else do anything, and even though it would probably be best if they both worked on it together, that at least for Sandy she could work on creating the energy that she wanted. They considered that maybe if Sam saw her making progress, then he might also join in on the daily mantras.

As a mantra for Sandy, the girls came up with:
"*I am love.*
"*The Universe always provides for me.*
"*Abundance surrounds me.*"

This would be Sandy's positive affirmation and daily mantra. Kristin showed her how to download the app that chimes and asked her to commit to twenty-eight days of doing this ritually. Sandy agreed and she and Kristin pinkie-swore that they would both see their mantras through daily until they created the new positive habits that they wanted in their lives.

Kristin also shared her mantra and this information with Melissa. Although still basking in the light of her love with Bob,

Melissa was finding certain things that seemed out of her control to be building up and causing issues surrounding the wedding planning. She shared with Kristin that a series of setbacks seemed to have occurred all at once. And while Melissa still wanted to get married to Bob, she was less than enthused that it was going to happen at this point. So now, instead of being excited about her big day, she started to fall into daily despair wondering what else was going to go wrong. Kristin could completely understand this way of being, but now understood how detrimental it could be. Listening to Melissa talk was so interesting to her. Her friend sounded a lot like how she used to be! She wondered if that were also a pattern for Melissa, one that she had failed to see before, because of her own victimology!

"It's like, if one bad thing happens, then two more are coming, ya know?" she asked Kristin. She did know. The old Kristin would have agreed and gone one step further to work Melissa up. She now realized how this had been their pattern together in the past. But the new Kristin offered a mantra and a new way in thinking to create a new pattern for them.

"Maybe if we change our thought process, we can change the way things seem to occur. I'm not saying that challenges will not arise, but just maybe we will see that challenges are not really as bad as we sometimes think they are," said Kristin, paraphrasing her instructor. "In fact, it's really up to us to be the changes that we want, right?"

Melissa agreed that it was worth a shot. And Bob even agreed to use the mantra daily too. He wanted dearly to marry Melissa and he wanted her to be happy. He realized that a wedding is a celebration and together they needed to move into a better thought process regarding it if they were going to get it all done.

Together they came up with the mantra:
    "*I am love.*
    "*The Universe is love.*

"Together we are love."

Just watching them say it together changed the mood in the room. Bob kissed Melissa sweetly and then stood up abruptly, shouting, "I've got it!" Kristin jumped up too. She didn't know why, but something shifted. Bob offered to run away with Mellissa to Vegas and just get married.

"All we need is each other and the church of Elvis!" he said.

The three of them broke into sidesplitting laughter. There was something incredibly healing about those full belly laughs. While Kristin was wiping her eyes, she realized that the laughing had taken a turn towards the serious. Bob and Melissa were asking each other if they could do it. Could they really run away and get married? Was it really that easy?

And just like that, they were all going to Vegas the following weekend for a wedding!

"Just not the drive-up one," Melissa teased her fiancé.

"I don't care what happens, as long as we are together. Screw all this planning and worrying about venues and priests, and blah, blah, blah. All we need is us, baby!"

He really was the sweetest guy. And he was right. It only takes two to get married. Well, three if you count the person performing the ceremony!

* * *

The following weekend Elvis married Melissa and Bob, witnessed by Kristin and Bob's friend Mark. The four had a fabulous Vegas weekend. Hey, what happens there stays there, after all. They were all on a natural high from love. And it seemed like it would never end. The chimes went off during the ceremony and they all said Melissa and Bob's magical mantra together. It was an uplifting experience that made Kristin want to run and get married too. Fortunately, she had the wherewithal not to go and do that. Mark was married, after all. This left Elvis and a bunch of other strangers, all also waiting to get married, to which she could get hitched to. No, she was going to just ride their love high for as long as she could. Kristin figured that all this love and positivity was going to last her a long time getting through the daily grind at work. Or, at least, perhaps, it would suffice until she found the right thing to do with her life.

* * *

But the universe had other plans. That following Monday morning Kristin was fired from her job. Her new boss read a diatribe of things from her personal file that he had been amassing. Most of them were not valid, and Kristin realized that she could have very well taken it up with human resources and fought for her job. And yet, she noticed that she just did not want to. She thought of something Nayana would say, "When we don't have the ability or aren't doing what we are supposed to, the universe will often step up and make the difficult decisions for us."

She sat in the parking lot watching the sun go down behind the building as she had many times before. The difference was, this would be the last time that she would watch the sun go down there. Her old self would have been worried to death. She recalled her initial reaction to Brian's firing at this very spot. But she was changing. Kristin realized that things were going to be a little challenging. She was not sure what she was going to do or how she was going to pay her bills. Her sister had just filed for bankruptcy and her mother was busy paying for her boyfriend's next hobby: base-jumping...whatever that was. She would have to take care of herself this time. And she knew that she would...somehow.

As the sun went down she took deep breaths and opened her palms to face the sky.

> "*I am love.*
> "*The Universe protects me always.*
> "*Positive energy surrounds me.*"

Kristin repeated her mantra many times. Some fluttering in her stomach mixed with strangely happy feelings of freedom, and then it was back again to some pangs of fear. Kristin had only been saying her mantra for seventeen days, after all. *Rome wasn't built in a day*, she reminded herself. It takes twenty-eight days to create a new habit. If that was true, then the next eleven days were going to be one long and winding road to traverse. And yet somehow, in the deep recesses of her being, Kristin knew that everything would be okay.

This new positive outlook was a very new feeling for her. She liked it.

Chapter 12

What Do I Want to Be When I Grow Up?

"It is better to live your own destiny imperfectly than to live an imitation of somebody else's life with perfection"
~ Krishna, Bhagavad Gita

It had been several days since she had been let go from her job. Kristin still could not attend many regular yoga classes due to her recovery and now she probably shouldn't spend the extra money to take them anyway. She had decided to take a week off from pursuing any new jobs or going anywhere specific and assess her life deeper. This seemed like a very smart plan, at first. Now, three days in, she was starting to panic. The truth was that she had no idea what she wanted to do, should do, or even could do with her life. She was limited physically and while she knew that she was on to learning something about her true self and what she was meant to be and be doing, she was far from understanding that. And yet, the universe had seen fit to release her from her job before she had it all figured out.

Ain't that something, she thought.

It was Thursday afternoon and Kristin decided to take a drive. She didn't have a destination in mind. She just thought she would get in her car and start driving and see where she wound up. Funny, she instinctually started driving to work. That route was hard-wired into her brain for so long that she had trouble undoing it. When Kristin realized where she was headed, she knew that she had to veer off into another direction of uncharted waters. At some point she made an abrupt left instead of the right that would have taken her to the previous work building. Just after the turn she found herself trying to figure out what was up ahead. Just where was it that she was going? Her mind was trying to stay one step ahead of her trusting in the universe. But further thought brought Kristin to understand that this question of "where am I headed" had a much larger meaning than the destination she was driving to that day.

Kristin really wanted to trust the universe. Each time she found herself trying to think of what was up ahead, she would make another abrupt turn in a different direction. For twenty minutes she basically drove in a circle. She didn't realize how challenging it was going to be to not think about where she was going and to simply trust. As Kristin drove around she realized that in the past, she had thought thoroughly through and calculated her next plans for every major decision in her life. Letting go of her mind and trusting the universe sounded good in theory, but proved difficult with all of her previous conditioning.

Finally Kristin pulled into a park that was located just about ten minutes from her home. She parked her car, got out, walked over to the nearest swing-set and sat down. This had a very familiar feeling and was welcoming and inviting to her. She held on to the old chains, smiling, and began to push herself slowly back and forth. A twinge in her back reminded her to not push herself too hard, so she just sort of swung lightly and tried not to go high or fast and really let go, like her spirit wanted to, so badly. The little girl in her wanted to play, but her healing adult body wasn't ready to have the complete abandon Kristin so desperately needed. It seemed to be yet another challenge for her to navigate through.

Looking around the park Kristin noticed several moms across the way. They seemed to be enjoying conversations while their children played close by. It was a beautiful day out. Kristin let herself ponder what it would be like to be one of those mothers, hanging out with friends in the park during a beautiful day and feeling completely at peace and ease that her role in life was to raise little ones. She used to feel bad for women who married young and had children because she thought of it as giving up on their own dreams to raise a family. Today her jealousy revealed to her that perhaps she had judged that situation incorrectly in the past. Maybe those women had it all figured out. Maybe there was just something wrong with *her*.

As she dwelled in another thought of her own inadequacies, one of the children fell and banged up his knees. He began to cry. No, he began to wail. And this rippling effect started all the other children crying too. She watched all three mothers stand, pick up their children, then bounce them on their hips to soothe them. The wailing of the children didn't seem to subside, so the moms gathered up their strollers and their belongings and started walking away. She watched until they were out of sight and the lingering sounds of the children's sobs could no longer be heard. In the newfound silence she stopped judging herself. She liked the peace and quiet. And there was nothing wrong with that. Not everyone was supposed to have children.

The sun was shining bright with a cool breeze blowing through the park. Kristin's jean jacket felt sufficient for the weather, but she wished she had packed a scarf for around her neck. She reached up and tugged the collar of the jacket up, then smiled, recalling many movies where the lead character had done the same thing to look cool. In the movies this effect worked. She, however, felt silly, for she certainly didn't feel cool. In fact, Kristin had never felt cool. She was never a part of that group of kids in school, either. As she thought about who she was, it was easy to cross "cool kid" off that list and move on. Kristin could also cross off "burnout," "brain," and "jock." As she ran through the characters from the movie *The Breakfast Club*, crossing their traits off one by one, she found herself no closer to figuring out just who she, Kristin Marie Pierce, was. She seemed to have no particular outstanding traits at all. She was the typical boring, girl-next door. The girl who always did just what everyone else did or what her adults thought she should do. How was Kristin ever going to figure out what lit her up inside and gave her life purpose?

Kristin looked toward the west and noticed a large group of trees. To the east the city loomed. North of her seemed to be an extremely upscale area of single-family homes. She had come from the south — the land of the middle class where townhouse and condominium complexes were built on top of town centers with large chain stores and restaurants within walking distance. It didn't even matter which state she was living in because today they all had these town center areas that all looked the same. Everyone can identify with them. These sprawling complexes of a slew of corporate conglomerates took all of the character from small towns and made them all look dull. There was no style, no culture, and no taste. In fact, it was all quite vanilla. Kristin had never thought about all of this before. She was always quite happy with the convenience of these complexes in the past. But now that she was digging deep to get in touch with what distinguished her from the masses and what would make her happy, Kristin realized that she thought there was an epidemic of mediocrity sweeping across the country. She wondered if anyone else felt the way she did now about all of this or was she just being judgmental? Kristin wanted to think that her yoga friends would get it. She laughed to herself thinking that Nayana most definitely got it. In fact, maybe there were a lot of people that had gotten it way before now, but she was just too busy withdrawing into herself inside the cubicle from hell to even notice. Weren't there a lot of people just like her? Kristin wondered if one day they would awaken too, just as she was attempting to. In any event, Kristin still had no idea what it was she was supposed to be moving towards in this life. She was still quite lost.

Kristin took a deep breath and as she exhaled, wondered if she should consider selling her townhouse. That would certainly eliminate quite a bit of debt. But where would she live? For a hot minute she considered moving in with her mother. She was the woman who had given birth to her, after all. She would never turn her away if she needed a place to stay. Kristin entertained the thought again: *Can I live with my mother?* And she imagined moving all of her belongings into her mother's house. She thought about moving most of her belongings into a storage facility because her mother's house was quite full already. Kristin thought about what it would be like to have dinner with her mother and then realized that dinner would also be with her mother's young boyfriend or the next boyfriend too. She thought about all the new-age interest that her mother fell into and out of weekly and knew quite well that she would either have to engage in them as well or listen to her mother tell her why she should be doing them. Kristin realized that her mother seemed to still be searching, trying to find herself, too. And she also realized that her mother actually did not realize this about herself. Could two women who don't know who they are live together as they searched it out? Maybe it would be good for them both. Or, perhaps she would stick a fork in her eye one night. Maybe living with her mom was not the answer she was looking for, albeit even a temporary one. Scratch that idea!

It certainly didn't make sense selling her townhouse if she had to turn around and rent an apartment. Then Kristin wondered if she could find a roommate. Considering taking someone in and living with her sounded reasonable. *Why not?* She had the room and she certainly could bring in someone that she knew to live with her. The thought of living with a stranger certainly didn't feel right. She wondered if she knew anyone looking for a room to rent. Not off the top of her head, she didn't. She could always put an email blast out to friends or post something on Facebook. Maybe one of her friends was going through the same sort of life crisis that she was. There was a sort of relief to think that bringing someone in could help her pay for the mortgage and some bills for the home. This would actually take stress off of her as she looked for another job.

Yuck! Another Job.

Immediately Kristin felt nauseated. Just the thought of that phrase, "another job," gave her a gut-wrenching, sickening feeling. She knew right away that she didn't want just another job! No, she was over the whole job thing. What Kristin wanted was to do something meaningful. She wanted to be excited about getting up in the morning and happy about what she did for a living. Kristin knew that most of the things that she'd gone to college and been trained for were no longer going to suffice. That certainly did limit her options, which was something that was also not helping her to figure things out. Or was it? Was it narrowing down the field and getting her closer to what she really should be doing?

Kristin struggled with the idea of doing something different that lit her up inside or settling for something that would be easier and provide her with more immediate means in which to live. Her mind started to stress about the fact that she may have to just settle for something. She didn't want to. But, perhaps she would have to. Or maybe she would have to just for a little while, and until she figured it all out. Again, this displeased her, but there was a different feeling inside her when she considered doing something temporary while she continued to work on herself. And yet, what was that temporary thing going to be?

Out of frustration, Kristin kicked the dirt under her foot and, in the process of doing so hit a rock. Her toe started to ache and she automatically unleashed some profanities out loud, then quickly looked around to make sure that nobody had heard her — especially not the mothers and their little children who were nearby earlier. She noticed that way on the other side of the park some folks were gathering, but certainly they were out of range of her outburst. Her foot throbbed, her mind ached, and her gut wrenched. Why had she come to the park today? And what the heck was she going to do?

She took a deep breath and remembered her mantra:
"*I am love.*
"*The universe protects me always.*
"*Positive energy surrounds me.*"

Kristin said her mantra three times out loud, then smiled and felt her body release tension and begin to relax. She felt better. But still, there was no resolution to her dilemma. Her experiment of trusting the universe had gotten her no closer to understanding the big questions of her life. But at least she had gotten some fresh air and it had afforded her the time to ponder a few avenues, even if they hadn't led her to the right path.

Kristin decided to get up and head back to her car. She began meandering through the grass in the park on no particular walkway. On the way, she saw some papers on the ground and figured it would be a good karmic thing to pick them up and deposit them in the trashcan in the parking lot. After picking several up and acquiring quite a stack, she flipped one of them over and read the flyer.

"Make Money Working from Home!" it read.

Her eyes widened. Could that be a coincidence that she found and picked up this flyer? Did she want to work from home? She had never thought about that option. How does that work, really — working from home, that is? Would she be motivated to actually take a shower and get dressed each day or would she become a messy, dirty lump that never left her home? Working from home had become a popular thing and she did know several people who were happy doing that. It sounded like a potential idea. But the more she thought about it as she drove out of the park, she knew that she needed to be around people. It had killed her to sit in her previous cubicle and not talk to anyone for hours. The smokers' patio had been the one thing that she had looked forward to all day so that she could, well, smoke, but also talk to her co-workers. Although Kristin doubted it was going to work for her, she did, however, tuck the flyer into her pocket. She thought she would see how she felt the next day and decide from there if she should call and at least get some information.

Leave no stone unturned, she thought to herself. Ironically the stone that she had kicked was so deep in the earth that it wouldn't budge, let alone turn over. Her foot still ached, reminding her of that rock and her life. If she was going to move that rock; which was now the metaphor for changing her life; she was going to have to put more effort into it and do something.

That evening Kristin decided to make a light salad for dinner and go to bed early. The fact was that she did not feel very hungry. Time seemed to stand still with her suspended in it, not moving forward or backwards. Everything felt stagnant. And she was feeling tired. Kristin said her mantra again and headed for bed. That night she slept quite deep, dreaming of sitting in a small craft, while being assaulted by huge ocean waves. Many times she felt like her boat would capsize, and yet, it never did. She often had to hold her breath as the sea lashed about and tossed her tiny boat. The intense storm hid any sight of land from her. Kristin didn't even seem to know where she had come from or where she was going. The dream was tiresome, trying, and endless. And when she awoke the next morning she felt as though she had actually been through that terrible ordeal. Her mind was no better off than when she went to bed the night before. And now, Kristin felt an ominous presence about her and anxiety began to set in as she worried about what might be coming.

It was really a challenge to kick that thought out of her mind. She was not able to do so, and now she was rolling into her first weekend without a thing to do, no job, and no prospects. After four days of taking off, she realized that this was not good for her. She needed some sort of purpose. She needed to do something with all of this free time!

* * *

Kristin awoke Saturday morning and headed right to yoga. She didn't much care that she hadn't been given the OK to attend classes yet. She just needed to clear her head and be there in that space, even if she wasn't able to do a lot of the postures or sequences. None of the folks she knew from the studio were in that weekend. In fact, even Nayana was apparently away. The studio felt weird and she felt out of place. Feeling somewhat abandoned by the one place that she thought she could count on, she considered leaving.

Kristin must have been so deep in thought that she did not even realize she was standing in the way of anyone else getting into the yoga room. A voice that seemed muffled or far off in the distance started to come into tune. She heard the words:

"Excuse me, can I get by? Hello?"

Kristin snapped to attention with the "hello." There was a sweet looking woman standing there with blond hair. She was smiling and waiting patiently for Kristin to move. Kristin didn't compute whether or not the tone of her voice was that of being annoyed or simply trying to get her attention.

"Oh, crap, I'm sorry," Kristin said, moving out of the woman's way.

She laughed, "It's okay, you certainly looked deep in thought."

That was an understatement. Kristin just smiled faintly at the woman and followed her into the yoga room. They both sat their mats down next to each other.

"Hi, I'm Barb," she said, extending her right hand to Kristin.

"Kristin," she said shaking Barb's hand.

"I'm new," Barb said, excited. "I'm a little nervous."

Kristin smiled, but didn't say anything in return. She was in her thoughts.

"I'm not sure what to expect," Barbara said again, smiling at Kristin, obviously attempting to get a conversation going.

Kristin sure didn't feel like having a conversation right now. She just wanted to relax and soak up the energy of the studio. It was already challenging to do so without her regular friends and teacher. Alas, ignoring Barb did not work.

"So, have you been coming here long?" Barb smiled, leaning over towards Kristin's mat further.

Kristin took a deep breath and sighed through her mouth loudly. Barb immediately got the message.

"Oh, I'm sorry to bother you," Barb said in response to Kristin's surrender breath and quickly moved back on her mat and slumped over in defeat.

Barb looked like she might even cry. She realized, when watching the new woman hurting, that she was doing it again: she was being an asshole. Kristin felt horrible and sat right up.

"No, I'm sorry. I'm…" she paused, "I'm having a rough time. I lost my job and I'm just kind of lost. And now Nayana isn't in tonight and I just really felt like I needed to see a friendly face. I didn't intend to act mean to you. I apologize. I'm being a jerk." Kristin extended her hand to Barb, "I'm Kristin. I love yoga and I just really need to be here tonight, as you can see. I am not in a very good mental place. I'm trying, but I just really need to be here and I'm being mean to you when you don't deserve it."

"Wow," Barb said, shaking Kristin's hand. "That's the most honest thing anyone has ever said to me. And I'm sorry you're going through a tough time. I don't like to see people in any kind of pain."

Kristin smiled. Barb was being a super nice person. Kristin thought she would share some more with her to make up for her rudeness.

"When I first started coming here, I actually didn't want to. My sister and my best friend made me come," she confessed. "I had a bad hip and back, in fact, I still have a bad back. I'm not even cleared to be doing yoga yet. I just need to be here tonight. I just need to breathe. This studio has come to mean a lot to me. The people here are great and I am sure you are going to love it."

"My friend Sally talks like you about yoga. She lives in Seattle. She loves it. She started doing yoga because of an injury and she swears it fixed her. It didn't fix you though?"

Now that was a very good question. And this gave Kristin pause as she took a deep breath and pondered her answer.

"I am a work in progress!" she said with a laugh and a smile.

The girls started to giggle when the teacher walked into the room. Kristin had never met this teacher before and realized there had been a few more changes to the studio since she had last been in, as some statues and pictures seemed to be moved around. She loved the place so very much she was just scared of any change that may affect it.

The teacher reached back and swirled her long brown hair up in a ball and tied it somehow on the top of her head. As she sat down, she tucked her long, flowing pants around her legs and then invited everyone to join her. Each person in the class began to sit down on their mat, but she asked them to come even closer up to the front of the room.

"It's okay. Leave your mats and just huddle up around me," she offered.

People seemed a little reluctant at first, moving slowly, but eventually with her prompting, more folks got up and came over. Kristin nodded to Barbara and they walked up together, sitting down near the yoga teacher.

"So, hello. First of all, my name is Annie. I just moved to town, but I've known Nayana for years. We took some of our yoga teacher trainings together. So, I wanted to get to know you all a little before we worked together because I feel it's important to know and understand where my students are: physically, mentally, and emotionally even, before we begin to practice together. I also want to share that I, myself, am recovering from an injury to my rotator cuff," Annie said massaging her left shoulder a little and moving it in a slight circle.

She continued, "So, my ego thought that I should be kicking up my practice a few months ago and I started attending these boot camp yoga classes with some people about fifteen years my junior. Anyway, long story short, I didn't do what I was taught or what I knew I should do to care for my body and, 'Voilà,' here I am!" Annie pointed to her bad arm and rolled her eyes.

The comment received a laugh from the students. Annie smiled and nodded her head knowingly. Certainly many of them had done the same thing that she had, but it was always good to know what type of group she was working with.

"Maybe some of you can relate to this: I wasn't listening to my body, I was listening to the teacher and my ego and trying to keep up with this class of hard bodies. I knew I should stop, but I kept pushing. I felt my body weakening and needing to rest, but I pushed through. I am not even sure how I did it. There were several times when my body was shaking so bad, I almost fell over. Then the next day this terrible pain radiated down my arm and I could hardly lift it over my head. It turned out that I tore one of my rotator muscles. So, I had a little surgery, and I have been coming back very slowly. There are many things that I cannot do — many things I shouldn't have been doing in the first place!

"So, today, as we practice, I want to talk about *Acceptance*, and I welcome any comments about that idea as you share with us what is going on with you today. Who would like to share first?"

Annie smiled and looked around the room. Kristin deduced from the unfamiliarity of the faces that this was a newer crowd to the studio. If that were the case, and remembering when she was a newbie, she didn't think that many people would feel comfortable opening up right away. Annie kept smiling waiting for someone to share, but it wasn't happening. It began to feel a little awkward. Kristin knew that she should probably share her story as well since it was so closely related, but for some reason she felt reluctant to do so. She didn't quite know why. Was she judging herself among what she projected that these people she did not know might be thinking?

"Well, okay then. If everyone just wants to practice we can do that too," Annie said smiling weakly. Kristin had to save her. She felt it was her duty to do so.

"I can share something," Kristin said in a small voice.

Annie beamed with hope. "Yes! What is your name?"

Kristin took a deep breath and pulled some courage out from deep within her and began sharing her own story of her back and hip and either injuring or reinjuring it in the workshop she had attended in the city. Once she began talking Kristin surprised herself with how much fell out of her mouth! She just kept talking about how defeated she felt and unclear what to do next. She even shared about her recent loss of work and all the free time that she had to create something for herself, but no direction in which to do it in. When she finally stopped talking, she realized she may have shared a little too much or talked a little too long. After all, this was cutting into practice time for everyone else. Kristin smiled weakly, and looked around the group. Someone behind her put their warm hand on her shoulder and gave her a little squeeze. Another person laid their hand on her lap and patted it. Kristin felt relieved, and validated. And she felt emotions begin to well up inside of her.

Annie took a deep breath herself. She invited the entire group to do that as well. They all took a deep breath. She invited them to do it again but longer and louder. So they all took that

157

big, deep orgasmic breath that Kristin thought was so funny just earlier this year. Today she practically belted it out as loud as she could and just about anywhere. At the end the group erupted into a fit of laughter. They probably all thought it sounded pretty orgasmic too. And you know why? Because it did! It really did feel that good.

"That was awesome. Thank you for sharing that with us, Kristin. I can relate. How many of you can also relate to a story like that?" Annie asked the group. A few more people raised their hands.

Barbara chimed in, "I'm new to yoga. This is my first class. Now I'm scared!" she said, laughing awkwardly. She wanted to make a joke of it, but it was true nonetheless.

"The best advice that I can give you, and I think that Kristin and the rest of us who have had an activity-related injury, would give you, is to listen to your body's wisdom. Accept your limitations. Accepting your limitations does not mean weakness, however. It relates to possessing real strength. It takes a lot of courage to admit when you have met your edge. It is very easy to power through something out of ego. But that is a detached way to practice. I strive to be truthful, and yet, I let myself get hurt by pretending to be something else. Be yourself. Be where you are. Meet yourself where that is on the mat and you will be fine. It doesn't mean that every teacher will meet you. It doesn't mean that every class will be appropriate. It means to just be you no matter what. Yoga is a healing practice. But when we practice from an inauthentic place, it is never going to turn out very well. Does that make sense?"

Barbara nodded her head. In fact, the whole room nodded in agreement. Someone yelled out "A-Ho!" and Annie replied, "A-Ho!" That was a new phrase for Kristin. She had no idea what that meant, but she loved that about this place. She was always learning something new. Kristin did not feel embarrassed to inquire and was pleased to learn that it was a Native American word similar to amen. This word, Annie told the group, is often used to agree with a member of the tribe after they share their story, as a symbol of unity. In learning that, the class all yelled in unison, "A-Ho!" and applauded. Annie was feeling quite happy and there was a great sense of camaraderie in the room again.

"Well, let's all get back on our mat and practice with the intention of being honest in every pose and movement. And accepting whatever arises. Okay?" Annie offered the group.

They smiled unanimously, some nodded and some said yes, then they all got back on their individual mats to practice. Kristin knew that she wouldn't be doing very much that night, but also felt that it was more than okay to do that. In fact, even if she just lay down on the mat and listened and breathed, that would have been okay too!

Annie, it turns out, was an amazing teacher. She had a calm and gentle energy, but she certainly challenged the class. In the end, Kristin was able to do more than she thought. But she also didn't push it. Annie came over to her several times to check in and offered some different modifications that were new to Kristin, which she gladly tried out. She also noted that Annie gave fair time to Barbara and many other students as well, so nobody felt singled out or neglected. It felt great to be back on her mat again and back in the studio, even if it was a limited capacity.

Afterwards, she invited Barb to go out for tea and they stayed for at least another hour and a half, talking and sharing more about themselves. Barb told her that she was single, but had a daughter who was nineteen and in college. Her husband had passed away several years ago due to a cardiovascular disease and she had spent a long time feeling sad and lonely. For some reason, this made Kristin think about her father, who had died when she was so young. She also had thoughts of her uncle, who was the other man in her life. He was gone now too. She tried not to focus on these thoughts that were arising, but instead to focus on Barb's story about how she gained weight and detached from a few of her closest friends because they were also friends of her husband's. At the end of the day, Barb shared; being with them reminded her more of how much she missed her husband. Barb said that finally she felt like she needed to move on and perhaps she was ready to fully let him go. She was tired of feeling sad and lonely and she realized on the anniversary of his death that he would not have wanted her to be living in this way mourning him. So, she got up one day and decided that after her regular visit to his gravesite that she was going to say a real good-bye to him and get on with her life.

"Just as I finished telling him that I would always love him, but that I needed to get on to living, a beautiful red cardinal landed on his tombstone," Barb said. "He sang a sweet little song to me, nodded his little bird head, and took off. I really felt like that was my husband coming to say good-bye to me too."

Barb wiped a tear from her eye and Kristin reached out and held Barb's hand.

Barb continued, "That night I went home and made a list of all of the things I ever wanted to do and made a plan to start working on that list. So, that is what brought me to yoga tonight."

Kristin was moved and impressed by Barb's story.

"I think I was definitely meant to meet you tonight, Barb." Kristin told her new friend. "I'm going to go home and I'm going to make that list too. I'm going to get on with living my life too."

Barb smiled, adding, "Life is too short."

"Life *IS* too short!" Kristin agreed.

That evening Kristin made the following Life List:

Kristin's Life List:

1. Travel the world (or just start somewhere)
2. Learn to play a musical instrument
3. Read all the classic novels
4. Skinny dip
5. Ride in a hot air balloon
6. Find God
7. Cultivate only positive, happy relationships
8. Have a loving partner to share my life with
9. Live debt free
10. Touch an Elephant
11. Learn more about yoga and other holistic healing modalities
12. Create art
13. Make something meaningful of my life
14. Live free of back pain

Kristin took another long look at her list. She wondered if she had gotten a little too heavy with some of the items or if she went too superficial with others. But she had to be honest with herself; these were the things that seemed interesting and important to her now or at some point in her youth. It was going to be easier to do some of the items than others. Of course, she did not have the funds to go traveling the world right now, nor would it be that easy to just make something meaningful out of her life. But at the very least, writing them down gave her some sense of direction. The list was going to be prominently displayed on her refrigerator, where she would get to see it every day. This way she could easily see if she moved any closer to living those things or not.

At some point while she performed light housework and chores that evening she went back over to her list and read it through again. Kristin was trying to notice a common theme to it. There were definite cultural overtones. She wanted a fulfilling life on all levels. It looked like she had a desire to be creative and also learn more too, and not just about yoga but also about life and the world. Kristin wondered if she should take another course at school for a career change and decided that perhaps she should look into some programs at the local community college or online. In the meantime, she figured the one thing that she could start immediately was getting to read some of the classic novels. Library cards, after all, did not cost anything. She made a plan with herself to go into the local library the next day, get her card, and start looking for that first book.

Kristin felt good about her first intention on her list. Of course, she had no idea how many classic novels that there were to read, but at the very least she would pick one up. Maybe reading would also jolt her mind onto something about her own life. Kristin slept soundly and peacefully that night. There were no dreams of being in a small boat on the stormy seas. She had course-corrected herself rather quickly tonight and got back on a healthier, more positive path. Kristin was acting like a real grown-up. And tomorrow she would once again tackle the lingering question: *What do I want to be when I grow up?*

Chapter 13

Great Expectations

"Twenty years from now you will be more disappointed by the things that you didn't do than by the ones you did do. So throw off the bowlines. Sail away from the safe harbor. Catch the trade winds in your sails. Explore. Dream. Discover." ~ Mark Twain

Kristin had a routine morning. She got up around 8 a.m., made a cup of tea and checked her email. Melissa had sent her joke about cats. Melissa liked to send pet jokes to her even though she knew that Kristin had no pets nor had any inkling of getting any pets anytime soon. But because Melissa had a cat, she liked to share these jokes with her often. Usually once or twice a week there was a lively cat meme or video or joke. Today the obligatory cat joke was waiting in her inbox.

Kristin smiled knowing that her friend was very happy. Melissa had it all: great new husband, good job, loving cat, and happy home. Now she had it all together. Kristin was happy for her. There was once a time in the very near past when she would have just felt sorry for her own life and not happy for her friend. But luckily she was past all of that, at least.

After her morning routine, next on her list today was the last visit to the physical therapist. It proved a good appointment and she was cleared to resume all normal activities, but reminded to take it easy with yoga and only do the gentler classes. Kristin did not confess that she had already gone back because it was irrelevant at this point. And she already knew what not to do because she had learned that the hard way. Kristin smiled as she walked into the library to get her first library card since grade school.

The library proved more active than she had thought it would be. Kristin didn't realize so many people actually still used it. There were people on computers, people reading and looking at books, people chatting in some rooms on the side, and there were many people around the desk waiting to be helped. People of all ages seemed to grace the library too. Once again her judgment had been incorrect. She thought that she might only find a bunch of senior citizens there that morning. But alas, there were people closer to her age than anything else. She wondered if everyone was unemployed like her or if they were independently wealthy? Kristin realized that she was judging again when she felt a tap on her shoulder.

Turning around she was pleased to see her new yoga teacher, Annie, standing there.

"I thought that was you," Annie said with a smile. "How are you feeling after last night's class?"

Kristin smiled and hugged Annie. "I feel great. In fact, I was cleared from physical therapy just now, although with the warning to take it easy in yoga."

The girls laughed and commiserated about their hard-learned lessons again briefly.

"Hey, I am about to teach a meditation here at the library, would you like to come? Or are you busy?" Annie invited Kristin.

Meditation at the library? What a fantastic idea, she thought. Of course, she graciously accepted Annie's invitation to head to the meditation with her. Here, she was just moments inside the bustling library and she was able to attend a free meditation with her new favorite yoga teacher! She was feeling the blessing of having decided to visit the library on that day. It was certainly interesting how one decision in life can lead to another. If she hadn't had tea with Barb, she wouldn't have learned about the life list. If she hadn't made a life list, she wouldn't have come to the library. And if she hadn't had come to the library, well, she wouldn't be about to engage in a free meditation class there!

She and Annie headed into one of the smaller rooms. A group of chairs was already arranged in a circle and another woman went up to greet Annie with a handshake. She appeared to work at the library. She and Annie spoke for several minutes while some other people started to come into the room and sit around the circle. Kristin helped herself to a chair as well and slid her purse underneath. In just a few more minutes the chairs were all full and the librarian began to introduce Annie.

"Thank you all for coming to our first meditation group session. This is a free event, hosted by the library and donated by my yoga teacher, Annie. She is new in town, but we have known each other for many years through my own travels of practicing yoga. I know that many of you are new to meditation, but you are in good hands. I want to thank you, Annie, for donating your time and being here with us today."

The librarian bowed to Annie with her hands at her heart in prayer. Annie reciprocated that motion to her and spoke.

"I am so very grateful for this opportunity to share some insights on yoga and meditation with the group. So, as you just heard, I am new to the area. I am teaching some classes down the street at the local yoga studio in town for my friend Nayana. And I had the pleasure to meet one of her students there last night, Kristin."

Annie motioned to Kristin, and Kristin put her hands also in the prayer position and bowed her head to Annie. Annie again reciprocated that movement. Kristin smiled.

"So, I think the best thing to do is to just get right into some of the practice and afterwards we can talk a little bit about your experience," Annie offered the group.

She guided them to sit up straight in their chairs with their feet flat on the floor. For some people this required them to scoot forward on the chair so that their back was not resting on the seatback. She mentioned if there was any discomfort to sit back, but to try to draw the belly inward to keep the spine straight and the connection with the feet on the earth. She even offered for anyone to remove their shoes if they felt called to. Three people did just that. Kristin decided to join them.

It was challenging to sit forward and not rest her back on the seatback, given her recent injury. So she slid back quietly and tried her best to sit up straight with her feet on the floor. But she was too small to reach, so her feet hung like a little child. She smiled and giggled inwardly at the thought of her six-year-old self in a room full of adults at the library, attempting to meditate. She decided to cross her legs underneath of her instead.

Annie guided everyone to notice their breath and to watch the flow of it through the nostrils. She told them not to change it, but just to become aware of it. If they felt like taking a deep breath, that was fine too, but they didn't have to do anything but notice it. Annie spent several minutes guiding the class through an awareness exercise of the breath and the body. She continued to guide them to focus on specific areas within them and Kristin was able to stay focused and follow Annie the entire time.

When Annie brought the group out of the meditation, Kristin realized that she hadn't heard very much of what Annie had been saying. She had no idea where she had gone off to in her mind. She couldn't remember any thoughts that she was having, and it seemed as though time just slipped away. She recalled Sandy mentioning that this had done this at the hospital too. Immediately Kristin judged herself as messing up the meditation and when the group began to ask questions she struggled with what to say, if anything, about it. As if she knew that Kristin had something to share, Annie asked her directly to do just that.

Kristin felt embarrassed. So she shared that first, which got a few laughs and affirmative head-nods from the group. Then she admitted that she had drifted off somewhere but couldn't remember anything. Kristin just felt peaceful. She apologized for not being able to stay with the meditation.

"Oh my gosh, what are you apologizing for? Most of us dream of doing what you were able to do! That's meditation — you were completely at peace in that moment. You still heard me on some level. Your highest self just took over and went where it needed to," Annie shared.

"I'm working on it," Kristin said. "But it isn't easy. I still look to see if what I am doing or feeling is right by seeing how other people act or react. Even though I know I shouldn't have to," Kristin shared.

More folks nodded and this got the attention of another woman in the group who also began to share. "I know how you feel. I always used to look to my family or friends or others for approval. I realized one day that I was the only one who knew what I truly wanted or needed and only I had the answers to my own questions."

"That's very true," Annie said approvingly of the woman's comment. "Kristin, you don't seem to give yourself enough credit for how well you are doing."

"That's an understatement," Kristin said, recalling that her old boss, Tom, had told her the same thing. Obviously this was a pattern of hers.

The group laughed and Annie entertained a few more questions before thanking the group and ending the session.

"And don't forget, we are doing this every week for the next five weeks. So spread the word to any friends who may be interested in joining us."

The group started to head out. A few people stopped to thank Annie personally and she saw her handing out her business cards to them. Kristin sat for a moment, then finally reached under her chair to get her purse and began to get up and start the rest of her library journey in a peaceful state of mind. Annie came over to her before she had a chance to walk out of the room.

"Thank you for sharing that, Kristin. It took me a really long time to be able to quiet my mind in meditation. What a gift."

Kristin smiled.

"I'm sorry, you know I realized as you were sharing that I never even asked you why you were here at the library today in the first place!" Annie said laughing. "I just pulled you right into the meditation."

Kristin laughed. "Well, first of all, I needed that meditation. Secondly, I decided to come in and get a library card. I have wanted to read some classic novels my whole life and with being out of work I figured I might as well get to it! Do you have any recommendations?"

Annie admitted that she had never much liked to read in school, but in most of her adult life she had been reading various different yoga text. She offered to share some of her favorite yoga books with Kristin and they exchanged emails so that she could provide her with a list. Kristin thanked Annie and told her that she would definitely be back to her meditation next week at the library and hoped she would see her at the studio. Without a job, she had to be careful of what funds to spend, so although the yoga studio had become a meaningful place to her, she definitely needed to be more careful with how she spent her money until she could figure out her game plan. Annie understood and wished her well, reminding her to trust that the universe had a bigger plan for her. After all, with needing to be a little thriftier with her money, the universe had planted some free meditation classes in her lap!

Kristin knew this already and was working on it. She left the room and was so deep in thought about how the universe should get to it with revealing to her its plans that she nearly walked into a man coming around the corner.

"Oh my, I am so..." she began to say. Immediately Kristin recognized the gentleman. It was Joshua, the cute, smart, single dad with the amazing jawline she had met at Sandy's house. She felt a little flush come over her face uncontrollably and tried to look away from him as to not draw attention to it.

"Hey, it's you!" said Joshua, smiling. "Don't you owe me a beer?"

More blood flowed up into Kristin's face and she could feel her body temperature rise about twenty degrees in a flash. She knew that he had to have noticed by now but she still played coy, looking towards the ground and around the library to avoid eye contact.

"Yes, yes, I suppose that I do," she said, trying to sound uninterested.

Kristin took a deep breath, exhaled, and then looked up to see his beautiful smiling face. She felt flushed again. He smiled. He had to have noticed. But, Joshua was still standing there and what was she to do? Kristin decided to just suck it up and stop worrying about revealing her feelings. Then she decided to deflect a bit by saying, "What are you doing here?"

"In the library?" he asked.

Kristin squinted her eyes and pursed her lips, "Ah, yeah..." she said, mocking him.

He laughed and hit his head with his hand. "Of course you meant the library. Well, my kids are with me this whole week and I saw that there were a few fun things happening at the library so we came by." Joshua pointed to the other side of the library to an area that seemed to be dedicated for children's reading. "They're over there now having a blast."

Kristin lifted up on her toes to see over to the other side of the library better. There was a swarm of kids sitting around in a circle. She recognized his son from the party, but didn't remember if she had met his daughter. Kristin tried to figure out which one might be a little-girl version of Joshua.

"I would have never thought the library would be such a fun place. But they love it," he offered, shrugging his shoulders.

"Did they get a free snack?" Kristin asked, smiling. She knew that with her niece, Brenda, that a free snack was always a good trick to keep her interested.

Joshua smiled and nodded his head. "Yup, chocolate chip cookies, I believe."

Kristin nodded and smiled too. "Yup, that would keep my interest too."

They both laughed and it looked like maybe his face had flushed a little this time too. Was she imagining that?

"So what brings you to this wild and crazy place?" Joshua asked Kristin.

"Ah, well, I came in to get my library card and check out some books. Then I ran into my yoga teacher and she was doing a free meditation lesson, so I just came out of that. Now I have to get said library card and then the big question of just what I want to read."

Kristin filled Joshua in on her interest in the classics, but complete openness as to where to start. He offered up Charles Dickens.

"As in *A Christmas Carol* Charles Dickens?" she asked him, indicating that she was not as enthused about the idea as he seemed to be.

"Yes, but he's written many other books," Joshua replied sarcastically.

Kristin waited for a response from him as to what other books he was recommending but he didn't seem to understand. She raised her eyebrow and rolled her right hand in a circle as if to say, *come on with it then*, and he finally recognized that she was waiting for more details and began to list some Dickens classics.

"Ah, yes. Well, there's *Oliver Twist*...*David Copperfield.* There's a lesser known work called *Nicholas Nickleby*..."

Kristin interrupted him. "There seems to be a lot of books about young boys," she said, trying to pretend that she may be as uninterested in boys as she was his book suggestion.

"Well, don't they say to write what you know about?" Joshua said dropping his gaze towards her, then smiling. He rubbed his hands together nervously, and then pushed them into his pockets. Kristin remembered her co-worker Brian had done that when he was nervously talking to her, knowing that he liked her.

Kristin suddenly realized that they were in a full-on flirting mode at this point. Something inside her swooned with exhilaration. She felt her body heat rise dramatically as her face flushed again. She wasn't sure what her next move should be. Thankfully, he reacted first.

"*Great Expectations!*" Joshua said loudly and completely out of flirtation mode. An angry "shushing" came from across the library and they both threw their hands over their mouths and ran behind the closest set of bookshelves. Kristin felt as if she were a teenager again, hiding from her mother in an effort not to get caught kissing a boy. She felt youthful joy at the moment. It felt good to be a little bad again.

Once behind the bookshelf they both put their hands in front of their mouths, attempting to stop the sounds of their happiness. Joshua leaned against the shelf and a handful of books fell out on the floor with a loud thump, inciting angrier shushing from the library. This now forced them to head outside of the library to let it all out. They both had a full belly laugh about the situation. Joshua wiped his eyes after a minute and tried to catch his breath. Kristin snorted — twice!

"Oh my God, I haven't cracked up like that in a long time!" he said.

Kristin kept trying to stop, but each time she looked at Joshua she'd lose it again. This only made him chuckle more. It took several minutes for them both to fully calm down. Everyone walking into the library seemed to smile at the apparent happiness too. And then they would smile brightly. Their joy seemed to be contagious.

Wiping her eyes, Kristin finally commented back, "Oh my God. Was it even that funny?" She didn't care if it was or not. It was funny to them.

Joshua looked down at his watch.

"Oh my God, your kids. Do you have to go?" Kristin asked him, worried. "I'm sorry, we shouldn't have left them inside."

He shook his head and let her know everything was okay. The kids were in good hands and he had plenty of time. Then he continued. "So, there are some very interesting women in *Great Expectations*..."

Kristin grabbed her stomach feeling another fit of laughter coming on. "Stop it!" she cried out. They both laughed again for a good full minute. "People are going to think we've lost our minds. Wait, I don't care! Let them think what they want."

"Yeah, I've always felt what other people think of me is none of my business," Joshua said.

"I like that." Kristin nodded approvingly.

Joshua pointed to a small bench beside the main walkway to the library and the two walked over and sat down. It was a beautiful day and the sun was shining and birds were singing. Why did she suddenly feel like Snow White just meeting Prince Charming? What was this connection that she felt to this man that she hardly knew? She somehow felt that she could be herself with him because he actually *got* who she was. Then Kristin remembered that he was dating someone else, and visualized that woman as the villain, the wicked stepmother, in the movie in her mind.

"So, I'm unemployed," Kristin blurted out, figuring it didn't matter what she said. She guessed she could be herself. She didn't have to impress him and, when she thought about it more, she wondered why in the past she had changed herself in order to impress another person. That didn't seem quite right now. Either way, she decided to just be herself. Maybe at the very least she would have another new good friend.

"Really? I'm sorry to hear that. Are you looking for a job now?" Joshua asked.

"Well, that's the million-dollar question. I mean, yes, I have to work. I have to start looking on Monday. But truthfully, I don't know what I want to do. I am really kind of perplexed and I'm at a bit of a crossroads. Do you have any wisdom to share about that?" she asked coyly.

They both smiled. Joshua interlaced his fingers and leaned forward onto his thighs. This gave Kristin a chance to check out part of his buttocks, which appeared equally as amazing as his face. She flushed again, but he was leaning forward and didn't see her. She thought about how lucky his girlfriend was.

"I could ask around for you if I knew what you were looking for. I have a lot of friends who have businesses," he offered. "And we are usually hiring at the bank too. If you are interested in coming in and filling out an application, I can always find something for you there."

"That's sweet!" Kristin thanked him. "I don't know what to say. I certainly do need to work. But I also want to do something good. I don't just want a job. I want to work somewhere that is nice and the people like each other and the company respects you. Maybe I want to do something that helps people in some way. I know I definitely don't want to do what I was doing before. I don't want a mindless job sitting in a cubicle not talking to anyone all day long." She shivered after thinking about her last job.

He nodded. "Yeah, I get that. I get that in a big way. I'm the bank manager. It's not glamorous work and I don't consider it exciting. But, every now and then when someone comes in and they are down and out, I can make decisions to help them out and to help them get back on their feet. And that makes me feel good. I like the rich clients well enough — the ones who need asset management or protection, ya know? But the little guy who is about to lose his farm if he doesn't get a loan, well, I can help that guy out. And he can feed his family and in the process feed others. So, even though I'm not saving the world, I do what I can to help out. My staff is all hand-picked by me and they are amazing people. I just love going in every day and knowing that I'm working with a group of people that are kind and good to each other. I can't say much about the owners of the bank. They hired me years ago, and because I guess I run it well, they pretty much leave me alone. I do have to navigate through new systems and changes from time to time that I do not always agree with. But we make it a good day every day by focusing on what we can do."

"Wow. That's actually amazing." Kristin was even more impressed. Good body, good heart. What else did this guy have?

She couldn't have been more attracted to him at this moment if she tried. In fact, the only thing that seemed to be the tiniest of drawbacks about him was the fact that he had kids. And suddenly that didn't seem to be as big of a deal as she had thought it would be. Of course, they weren't around at the moment, so that probably helped.

She thought that he had to feel what she was feeling in that moment. Anyone who walked anywhere near them smiled because it was so obvious what they were feeling. The energy between them was electric. And although it was not her norm to put herself out there she decided to do it anyway — girlfriend or not.

"So, how about I buy you that beer this weekend?" she asked, face flushing.

There was a slight pause and she felt his energy change.

"Oh, unless you're busy. It's okay." Suddenly she felt silly for asking him.

Joshua shook his head and sat back on the bench. He had to be honest with her and he didn't want to have to tell her about his girlfriend. He hadn't been this attracted to a girl in a very long time, including the girl he was currently dating. And even though she was going to be out of town this weekend, it just wouldn't be right to go on a date with someone else, no matter how attracted he was to another woman. He honestly shared all of this to Kristin. And there they sat, two grown adults, completely honest with and drawn to each other like moths to a flame. For the first time they both sat quietly, wondering how to handle the situation or what to say. There were not many options. They were both thinking of all of them too.

Joshua found himself thinking about his ex-wife for a moment, and how they had remained close friends since the divorce because they had always been honest with each other.

Honesty was very important to him. He liked his current girlfriend quite a bit because she had many of the same qualities that his ex had. He certainly wouldn't be dating her if she hadn't. But he also didn't feel the same chemical reaction with her as he did with Kristin — thinking back to the first time they had met he had felt the power there. Joshua was quite close to his mother, and even she had recently told him in relation to his current girlfriend, "She's very nice. But she's not the one either." When he kissed his mom she had finished up, "When it's the right one, you'll know it because you won't be able to stop smiling." When he was with Kristin, he was certainly always smiling.

Joshua stood up with a jolt. Kristin thought he was going to say goodbye, ending their time together. Her heart sank a little. But he said something else entirely.

"Forget it."

Confusion, followed by a fluttering in her heart, with excitement came flooding in!

"Let's go out this weekend. I want to see you again. I'll talk to my girlfriend and let her know. It isn't fair to anyone if I lie to myself. And it would be a big lie if we didn't see where this could take us," Joshua said, smiling.

Kristin stood up. She felt like kissing him. She smiled instead. She knew the kiss would eventually come. And she was learning to trust, after all.

They exchanged phone numbers, made a date and headed inside. Upon entry, the kids ran up to Joshua. His daughter, Gabriella, grabbed her father's legs yelling, "Daddy, can we come back tomorrow, that was so fun!" Kristin noticed that nobody in the library seemed concerned or bothered by her talking loudly. She rationalized that maybe kids get a pass on that there.

Kristin smiled. They exuded love for their father. He patted his son's head and picked up his daughter and threw her over his shoulders in one clean sweep. This wasn't their first rodeo together. Gabriella giggled and raised her hands over her head completely confident in her father.

"Who is that?" asked the boy, pointing to Kristin.

Joshua smiled at Kristin and answered his children, "This is my friend Kristin. Do you remember her? This is Brenda's aunt."

"No," said the little girl, shaking her head and reaching for her father's shoulders, then leaning down to hug his head awkwardly.

"She's prettier than Tina," said the little boy.

Ah, Tina must be the name of the current and soon-to-be-ex-girlfriend. Kristin kind of felt bad for Tina all of a sudden. Tina had no idea she was about to lose a very cool boyfriend. She decided to let it go. She didn't know Tina. She only knew what she felt and what Joshua shared. And it was now important that he share some time with his family. Kristin decided to give them that space. Plus, she had her own things to get done.

"I'll talk to you later," Kristin said. She smiled and waved goodbye to the kids and soon Joshua and his little ones were walking out of the library together. She thought what a cute little family they made together. They certainly didn't seem to be the same sticky, dirty kids that she used to think all children were. Was that true? Or were her perceptions changing?

Two and a half hours earlier, she had walked into the library to get a book. She still had to tackle that errand. But it didn't take long to get her library card and she already knew what book she wanted to get. Minutes later she walked out smiling, holding her copy of *Great Expectations*.

Chapter 14

Manifesting a Right Life

"You have to participate relentlessly in the manifestation of your own blessings." ~ Elizabeth Gilbert

Three and a half months after that day in the library, Kristin sat in front of her refrigerator reviewing her life list. She and Joshua had been dating continually since then. Together they had taken a hot air balloon ride, discussed three classic novels, including *Great Expectations*, cultivated a happy and positive relationship, and discussed taking a trip together. And every Sunday she spent at least a couple of hours painting. She didn't think that she was very good at it, but Joshua's kids seemed to think that she was. She would sometimes have her niece, Brenda, over with Joshua's kids and they would all create art together. She actually found herself enjoying this time with the kids and helping them learn different techniques. They were receptive, she was patient, and together they created good art too!

Joshua had gone to the owners of the bank to frankly discuss his relationship with Kristin and her job application with them. They trusted his judgment and offered her a job working there. She was happy with that choice because her co-workers were amazing people and Joshua had created an enthusiastic place in which to work. She still wasn't sure that she wanted to work at a bank the rest of her life, but at least the job could afford her the ability to continue to take yoga classes and other workshops and to grow and learn. In the end it was a compromise, but a very wise one. Joshua was well aware that Kristin would not be working at the bank forever. But he certainly enjoyed having her there in the meantime.

With their relationship being fairly new it was certainly too early to call him her life partner. The thought of that actually scared her a little bit. Kristin was stepping into new and uncharted territory for herself with this relationship. And although things were feeling right and going well, she still had some unresolved fears. Kristin was not clear where they came from and she didn't want to scare him off with her issues. She had talked it over with Sandy and Melissa. They had both agreed that Kristin would work it all out in due time.

Living debt-free was a little far off to check on the list too. Kristin considered what other items on the list that she might want to work on. Joshua was ready to go skinny-dipping any time. She argued that when they were meant to do that, they would. When she considered what was left, it was the big ones on the list. While Kristin continued to take her regular yoga classes, she realized that she really could dive into other holistic modalities more. After all, she wasn't sure what else was out there that could move her into a new direction. She thought about quizzing Nayana and Annie a bit about that the next time she saw them.

With regards to her body, Kristin was feeling pretty good. Although she sometimes felt a little something limiting her, it was a reminder to be mindful about her actions and movements all the time. There was no way around not being mindful. She had learned that this way of being had to be a daily intention. Kristin noticed that the more she practiced yoga correctly, with proper alignment and giving herself permission to come out of the postures as needed, and with emphasis on strengthening her core, the better she felt. So even if in a seventy-five-minute yoga class, she really only worked hard for part of it, that was good. She didn't have anything to prove to anyone. At the end of the day, Kristin just needed to feel good in her body, her mind and her soul.

So body was feeling good. And mind was feeling content too. Now what about that soul part? She wondered why she had written: "Find God" on her list. She didn't even know what that meant. Joshua teased her about that one often. He was brought up Catholic. He said God was always present but he did love that feeling at church when the sun came through the stained-glass windows. He said he always felt God's presence the most then. Feeling God's presence was not that easy for Kristin. She was Methodist, but her family only attended church for weddings or funerals. She hadn't even ever gone for the major holidays like the "good Catholics do," she teased Joshua.

She talked to Joshua about getting a monthly pass to her yoga studio again, because she knew that making a commitment to her yoga practice meant potentially less time for them together. He was for anything she wanted to do, always supporting her without judgment. He offered to go with her from time to time, but they both agreed that it was good for her to have yoga for herself just like he had running to himself. Running wasn't for her. Besides the constant compression not being good for her back, she also kind of despised the idea of it. She joked to him that she would run to the mailbox if it was raining, but that was about the end of it. He, on the other hand, was considering signing up for his first marathon. Nope! He could have his running and she would keep her yoga. They would meet on other nights. They agreed.

Kristin was also working through getting to know Joshua's children, without pushing herself too strongly into their lives. Truth be told, she did not want to be a mother to anyone. She liked the kids well enough, but that role was not something she was ready to step into. Luckily, their mother was a very important part of their lives and Joshua continued to have a good relationship with her. He even called his ex-wife one of his best friends. This foreign concept to Kristin was surely a beautiful thing to behold. For no matter what their personal differences were that ended their marriage, they came together for their children and for each other as needed. This fact did not threaten Kristin in any way. In fact, Kristin was happy to not be in between the drama that is often involved in broken marriages. This made the whole relationship flow even easier. The kids seemed to like her well enough, but she and Joshua also made sure that they had their time alone too. This was a new frontier for Kristin, so she was trying to trust that the universe was leading her down the right path. So far, she was following it.

One night Kristin went in to take a gentle yoga class with Nayana, and some of her yoga friends were there too. Her friends Neil and Barbara as well as her other yoga teacher Annie, and some other friends who she had met at the studio all seemed to

182

meet that same evening. *Some days you can just feel Divine energy calling you somewhere*, she thought. This was one of those evenings.

Nayana began class by reminding everyone about her exciting yoga retreat in Mexico that she was hosting soon. Situated right on the beach, the retreat would have regular daily yoga classes led by her, three vegetarian meals per day, meditations and group meetings, individual healing and massage sessions and free time too. For those interested in going to see some of the Mayan sites, there were also some excursion options. Kristin recalled hearing some of the group talking about this when she had first started doing yoga. She remembered how strange it all sounded to her then and how she had dismissed the idea entirely. Now, it was sounding a bit different to her.

A yoga retreat sounded overwhelmingly inviting, but she wondered if that was something she should be doing. The last thing Kristin wanted was to overstrain her body again by going gung-ho into something. She wondered if she should go with her yoga friends, whom were all discussing that they had just made their final payments. She recalled the last time that they had done something together by attending that yoga class in the city. That didn't turn out too well for her. But Kristin was a very different person today than she was then. She had learned a lot from that injury and continued to learn daily. Barbara leaned over and shared that she was also reluctant given her limited knowledge and practice of yoga. They both approached Nayana after class to discuss their interest but shared trepidation.

"Well, while I would love to have you both attend the retreat, I wouldn't want you to do anything you felt was wrong for you. I promise you, you can always come out of postures and only do what is right for you. There is never judgment about that. If you feel like you can't practice every day, then that is also your option. But it is there for you as a part of the experience. And you both know very well that you can also just come to class and lie down when you need to. It has to make sense to you.

Have either of you ever gone to Mexico before?" Nayana asked the women.

Neither of them had. Kristin's travels were so far limited to a five-day trip to the Arizona for a work-related training, a Florida road trip with her sister and some friends, the Las Vegas trip for Melissa's wedding, and some other places along the eastern coast of the USA that were within a day's driving distance of home. But other than that, she was certainly no world traveler. The thought of going out of the country without family or close friends scared her a little. And although Kristin knew that she would be going with people she did kind of know and considered friends, she still felt as though this was something that she would, for most purposes, be doing alone. Not that this was a bad thing, but it certainly was something Kristin needed to mull over.

Personally, Kristin was also concerned about the vegetarian meals, rooming with someone that she didn't know, and the basic uncertain fear that was there about just diving so fully into a twice-a-day yoga practice.

"I am interested," Kristin said. "But honestly, I am a little scared too."

Barbara nodded in agreement. This trip seemed to be way outside either of their comfort zones, and yet they both wanted to consider it. Kristin entertained the thought of inviting Melissa to the retreat so that she could have a person with her that she was comfortable with. She started to question if she was being herself when she was with her yoga friends. Then she went back to questioning who she was on a whole. She realized that this was all coming up for a reason. Maybe this retreat was exactly what she had been looking for. Somehow she felt that it was important, but she wanted to get someone else's view.

She took the information home with her to go over and read it multiple times before showing it to Joshua. He, of course, thought it was a wonderful idea, encouraging her to attend the retreat for sure. The week of the yoga retreat was the same time he would have his kids for the entire week again and he had decided to take them on a trip to his parents' house in South Carolina, anyway. They had talked about Kristin coming along on the trip but nothing had been concrete. Kristin was a little scared to meet his parents and go on a family vacation with him and the kids. She wasn't sure that she or the kids was ready for that. Honestly her heart said she was, but her head said something different.

They talked it through together and ultimately decided that it was up to Kristin and what she wanted to do, including going on neither trip. Either way, Joshua told her that whatever she decided to do would be what she was supposed to be doing. And although Kristin knew this to be true, she didn't know what the right thing was. Would she be missing out on an important bonding experience with Joshua and his children if she went on the yoga retreat? Would she be missing out on a chance to go deeper into herself if she went on the trip with Joshua? Would she be kicking herself real bad if she did neither? That was for sure. No, Kristin knew that she was going on one of those trips. She just needed to figure out which one felt right. Actually, they both felt right. So Kristin needed to figure out which one she was guided to do more.

Is going on a vacation supposed to be this difficult of a decision? she wondered. The truth was, she felt very grateful to have the opportunity to go on both of these trips.

She decided to call Melissa and see if she was interested in going to Mexico on the yoga retreat with her. Melissa hadn't been to yoga very often since she got married and had a new routine, but she still dropped in for a class every now and then. Kristin explained all of the details to her and Melissa was very intrigued with the idea of going on the trip. But as a woman who was now sharing bills and income with another person, she needed to talk to Bob about it first. Of course there were other necessary household things they needed to do and she wasn't sure if she would have the extra money to go either. But it wasn't out of the question. So she asked Kristin to give her a couple of days to look things over. That wasn't the problem. Kristin was more than obliged to let her friend have some time to discuss and look at finances. However, the trip was coming up soon and the final payments were due. They both needed to know in two days. That was the truth of it.

Kristin decided to call Nayana and talk to her more about the trip. Nayana was always available to talk or help her out with whatever she needed. She was a good teacher that way. Kristin sometimes wondered if she bothered her too much, but it always seemed to her that Nayana was more than happy to help people. And if she wasn't available, she wouldn't answer the phone, right? Kristin also appreciated that Nayana also always talked to her without judgment, even when it was apparent that Kristin was a little bonkers sometimes. So, she was also grateful for that.

"So, realistically, is this yoga retreat something that someone like me should do? I mean, I had that major injury because of yoga. I am doing pretty well, but I do practice mostly gentle types of yoga. I come two or three times a week now but I have to be super mindful when practicing. Honestly, it's not even the yoga. I am not a vegetarian, you know? I don't even understand what vegetarian food is! And who decides who I would be rooming with? I would have to room with someone I don't know I guess since everyone I know is already going or rooming with someone. I don't know. I guess, this is all just outside of my comfort zone, really. The truth is that I want to go and I want you to tell me why I should go. But I know you aren't going to do that, because you always say to trust my own path and do what is right for me. Anyway, I just wanted to say all that and get it out. So I guess what I am really saying is that you can count me in on the retreat. I am going."

Kristin got that all out without skipping a beat or taking a breath.

Nayana started laughing. "Ok. So, do you have any real questions for me?"

Kristin took a breath. "Not really. I guess I just need to hear from you that you don't have any concerns with me coming with you on the retreat given my last injury."

"Kristin do you remember the workshop you came to on creating new habits?"

Kristin affirmed that she had. She also realized that she had not been saying her mantra much lately. She admitted to Nayana that things had seemed to be going well with her and since they were, she kind of forgot about saying it every day.

"Ah, that's the thing. You have to do it every day. No matter what things are like in your life, you have to stay strong to these daily commitments of your practice and your mantra and whatever else you do. They will set the necessary groundwork for you for when you need it, like in times like this. If you don't, the energy sneaks back up on you. So, I'm curious, what was your mantra?"

Sharing, Kristin told her,
"I am love.
"The universe protects me always.
"Positive energy surrounds me."

"Do you believe that?" Nayana asked her.

"Yes, I do believe that," said Kristin. It was true. Even just saying it again made her feel better and released her fears. Of course the universe always protected her and she was surrounded by positivity. Her negative thoughts and fears were coming from somewhere else. Nayana reminded her that it was the ego.

"The thing is," Nayana, continued, "you don't need me to tell you anything that you don't already know. You learned a valuable lesson the day you got hurt. You learned what your ego was and you learned that when listening to it, you are surrounded by *maya* or illusion. So now you know what *not* to listen to. You are now very clear on what is untrue. So, in all the chatter of the fear and worry about the trip, wasn't that all ego speaking?"

Kristin had to agree. It was ego.

"I knew all along that I wanted to go on the retreat. But it was like something within me woke up and couldn't handle the idea of it or what I might actually come to terms with in doing it. I don't even understand what I'm talking about," she admitted.

"Well, I am glad to have you on the retreat with us. All you have to do is fill out the paperwork you took and hand it in with your payment. We have a meeting scheduled with the group next week where we will discuss more particulars. You just need to manage your personal affairs to get ready to go. Are you sure you feel good about coming?"

Kristin was sure. As soon as Kristin made that decision and told Nayana that she was going everything felt fine and all the physical sensations and mental anxiousness ceased.

"You know what I think scares me the most?" Kristin admitted to her yoga teacher. "What scares me most is that I am starting to get all the things that I ever really wanted — and more. They are just showing up in my life sort of effortlessly. And there is just this little part of me that is worried about it all going away."

This was a true and deep lesson to learn. Nayana knew it all to well herself. It was that of detachment.

"Someone great once said, 'attachment leads to suffering.' It's a tough one. We make connections with people, places and things. We enjoy how we feel with them and we cannot sometimes think of a life without them. But the reality is that everything is impermanent, and the more we cling to something, the more difficult our suffering when it finally does leave us."

"I like my attachments," Kristin said. "Does that make me a bad yogi?"

"That makes you a real person. It is the struggle, Kristin. We all go through it."

"What are you attached to?" Kristina asked Nayana. "I'm sorry if that is too personal for you to answer."

"No, no, its quite all right. I'm a real person like you. I came from very little. I got a lot in return. And somewhere in there I really like what I have. I love my life, my studio, the people I meet. I loved my guru and miss him every day. But he taught me that he is still with me. And I do feel him when I teach. So, I am therefore attached more to my teaching. I wonder some days if I did not teach, would I lose him forever. I know that not to be true, but I struggle with it nonetheless. Sometimes I think it is he that is teaching through me and not me speaking at all. But then I realize we are one. So it is both of us truly in the end who are teaching." Nayana paused. "Wow, that got deep real fast!"

The women laughed.

"All this yoga stuff is deep to me," Kristin said. "Does it get easier?"

"No." Nayana admitted. "Does that scare you more?"

"No, I think it makes me feel better, actually. Like we are all always learning and growing. Nobody has all the answers," she said.

"Or, we all have all the answers," Nayana offered. "But a part of us, that ego, doesn't want to listen or believe it."

"Like in the movie, *The Matrix*, when the guy said that they had created a first Matrix that was paradise, but we humans rejected it," Kristin said. "Sorry, I like movie references. It helps me understand things."

Nayana agreed and shared a few of her favorite movie references too, including a few that Kristin had not seen herself. She wrote them down so that she could remember to check them out. Kristin knew that Joshua would be interested in watching spiritual movies with her and now she had a good list of about five of them to get.

Kristin was feeling much better about their talk and her decision. But she did have one final question for Nayana.

"So, if ultimately we are supposed to let go of attachments, then what are all these manifestation ideas about? I mean, if I am ultimately not supposed to have things, why should I try to manifest them in the first place?"

Nayana was quick to offer some insights. "That's a good question. I see where that can be confusing. I think we can all be confused with that. But you know, ultimately the universe wants us to be happy. God wants us to be happy. We are in this human body because it is a blessing. We are meant to experience life and joy and all the things that the human experience can give us. But in the end, we are to realize what the truth is."

"And what is the truth?" Kristin wondered.

"The truth is that we are spiritual beings having a human experience, right? We are supposed to realize that we are beyond all the stuff, but at the same time, we are all the stuff too. We are all. We are 'One.' I AM. Amen. OM."

Mind-blowing, Kristin thought.

Kristin and Nayana talked a bit more about these philosophies. She was starting to understand more about manifesting a right life and a purposeful life. She understood that all things were temporary in this life and in the next. And she was trying really hard to get to that point of manifesting who she was truly meant to be. Things certainly felt as if they were going in the right direction. And at some point Kristin had to trust that she was being guided on the right path. But there was still that nagging thing on her life list: "Find God" that she was not 100% sure of. And somehow Kristin seemed to be feeling that it might be the missing link to everything.

Chapter 15

Comfort Zone? What Comfort Zone?

"A comfort zone is a beautiful place, but nothing ever grows there." ~ John Assaraf

There is no name of a color to describe the blue of the ocean on the southern tip of the Yucatan peninsula in Mexico. Kristin drank in the beauty of the sea. Up to her ankles in the pristine waters, she breathed in the warm salt air and felt the hot sun's energy radiating over her in the sort of healing that you can only get from being in nature. She had only just arrived at her yoga retreat a couple of hours ago, and she was already in love with being there. In fact, she wondered for a moment if she could just stay there in paradise forever without a care in the world. Well, *maybe*, she thought, *I'll fly Joshua here too.*

Kristin had flown down with a group of people from the yoga studio, but in the end Melissa was not able to attend the retreat with her. And although she was a little scared of being there without anyone who really knew her, she realized that since she had made connections with several of the people who were attending the retreat that she wouldn't be so alone in a strange land. Being there now and feeling the warm sun and watching the endless crystal blue ocean, she knew that she had made the right decision. Kristin couldn't have been happier about it.

The only schedule that the attendees were given was to arrive at the hotel that day and to meet in the yoga room that evening at 5 p.m. for a welcome class. They had all decided to arrive early and get a day of sun and beach in before any of the yoga-related activities started. Kristin was not used to traveling abroad so she did not know how long it might take her to acclimate to the new destination. However, she could hardly remember why she even gave that a thought now that she was there. She was more than happy to have the extra time on the beach with her yoga friends, relaxing and allowing herself some down time. The resort was beautiful and the people who worked there were very attentive and nice too. It seemed that wherever she went, she was greeted warmly and asked if she needed anything or wanted a fresh squeezed juice.

One of her biggest worries, the vegetarian meals, turned out to be pretty fantastic too. Fresh fish was available in addition to all the vegetarian items. The colorful and playful display of fruits was enough to fill her alone. She bit into a mango for the first time and had a sensory explosion! She never knew fruit could taste that juicy and alive. She ate a huge bowl of mixed fruits before even looking at the rice and other lunch specials. The meals were served buffet style, making it easy to see what she was putting on her plate — an important thing for a virgin vegetarian like Kristin. She was careful to put small amounts of each item on her plate so that she could taste and not feel too bad about throwing out anything that she didn't finish. But the truth was that she loved most of it and wound up not just finishing one plate, but also going back for another. She and her yogi friends joked that they were eating more as vegetarians than as meat eaters! But it all tasted so sweet and fresh that there was no way to pass it all up. It was with a nice, full belly that they put on their bathing suits and headed into the water.

Neil approached Kristin with some sun block and offered to put some on her back. At first she felt a little strange about having a man who she was not in some way romantically involved with slather lotion on her. But Neil proved to be very modest and appropriate with his touch and she soon offered to get his back too. In total there were twenty-one people who went from their local yoga studio and she understood that some others would be joining them at the location. Each time she passed an unknown face she wondered if they were part of their retreat group or if they were there at the resort for their own R & R. She thought that maybe another time she could bring Joshua and maybe even the kids back here for their own vacation. Only time would tell.

As if the view and the food weren't amazing enough, the bungalows that they used for their accommodations were tremendous. These individual double occupancy units sat directly on the beach. Sand carried right up to the entryway and into the room. The stone flooring seemed easy enough to sweep off and there was even a broom right by the front entrance in the event that she needed to do it herself before the cleaning staff had a chance to. The showers were open in the bathroom, and there were no doors on that either. The bungalow seemed to be set up perfectly for a romantic couple retreat or honeymoon even. The windows had palm tree shutters that you could close for privacy, but then there would be no airflow in the room. Since the bungalows sat directly on the beach, there seemed to be little electricity in the room except a small light in the bathroom and one above the bed, which also had mosquito netting around it. The small, quaint room had a perfect view. Kristin didn't even mind that there was no television or telephone. She figured she would be busy enough anyway.

She went to slip her flip-flops on to head to the beach and realized quickly that even those were not necessary. So, armed with only her beach towel, she walked out onto the sand and just a few steps to a beach chair where she promptly left her towel, and headed directly to the ocean to put her feet in. It was a few minutes after that when Neil caught up to her with the sunblock.

"How is your back feeling after the flight?" Neil asked Kristin.

Neil was a kind man with honest eyes. Kristin liked that about him. Joshua had met Neil a few times at the studio when he had either come in to meet her for dinner or attend a special event there. The two had become fast friends. In fact, sometimes she wondered if they hadn't been friends in another life. They seemed to get along that well. Then again, Joshua seemed to have many connections like that with people. He had a way of finding and building honest and deep relationships with just the right people. That was another thing that she loved about him. Kristin was still learning how to navigate around those people who seem to create too much drama. Now that her life was on a good track, she was able to see those folks more clearly from a further distance. But Joshua had much more experience with it than she had. According to his mother, he was born with that gift.

"I've been feeling good, thank you for asking," she responded. "How have you been?"

Neil had no complaints. He was a simple guy just looking to enjoy life. Soon Barbara and a few more folks who had flown down to Mexico together on another flight all came to the water and decided to jump in and float about with their travel clothes on. The gentle waves lifted and moved them about softly. They all laughed and spoke about things that they enjoyed spending time doing and things that they wanted to someday do or places that they wanted to see. Kristin was amazed to learn how many people had recently changed or lost jobs or gotten divorced or separated. It did seem that most of them were in the midst of a life change of some kind and had found yoga to be a helpful way to work through these changes. Everyone there was generous and often thought of the others in the group in the event that they were heading inside or somewhere else where someone could use something. It was a thoroughly enjoyable afternoon and the time seemed to fly quickly by when a staff member alerted them that they had an hour before the scheduled yoga class was to begin. And although they had all come down for a yoga retreat, they reluctantly headed out of the water to their bungalows in preparation for class.

When Kristin arrived back at her bungalow, she noticed another set of luggage and heard someone in the shower. She had forgotten that she would be rooming with someone that she did not know. Kristin wondered who it was, but felt strange just announcing that she was there in the room. Although, where was she going to hide? The woman was going to see her there any moment. She tried not to look into the area of the bathroom and gave the woman as much privacy as she could by keeping her head down and going through her luggage and reassessing what she had brought with her. In no time the shower was off and the woman emerged. She was familiar looking — like a yoga magazine cover model .

"Hi, I'm Jill!" she said, smiling and extending her hand.

Kristin shook Jill's hand, not able to miss the beading water that was dripping down her body and all over the floor near her things. Jill did not seem aware that she was drenching the floor. She did have a towel on, but had thrown it around her quickly and walked directly out of the shower from there. Kristin usually made sure to dry off before she even stepped out of the shower at home. Jill's drip-drying shower habit was a little unusual for her. She recalled an episode of the talk show *Ellen* where Sean "Diddy" Combs told the star-crazed audience that he liked to air dry after his showers. Although she couldn't personally get past the wet mess this would create, she was aware that others did the drip-dry thing. Of course, Diddy probably didn't care about making a mess since he probably had people to clean up for him. Kristin wondered if Jill was wealthy. She immediately wanted to nickname her "Little Miss Diddy."

"I'm from California, where are you from?" Jill asked Kristin.

"New Jersey," Kristin replied.

"Oh...fun..." Jill responded, pausing as if to think of the appropriate word to use.

Kristin took a deep breath and tried to shake off the feeling that she was having. She was sure Jill was a very nice girl and she didn't want to be judgmental about her in the first few minutes of meeting...although she was well aware that she already was doing that. The trip thus far had been tremendous. Kristin wasn't going to let her discomfort with her roommate affect her amazing trip. She was going to find a way to get along with Jill, even if she did things differently from her.

Within five minutes Jill was dressed, but her clothes were scattered about the room, encroaching on Kristin's area. Kristin pulled some of her things closer to her suitcase in an effort to give Jill more room, in case she felt she still needed it. But that was not the issue. Jill seemed to be unaware of social boundaries. She deducted that Jill was messy.

"So, I'm going to head into the shower. I hope I gave you some privacy for yours. I apologize if I startled you when I came in." Kristin gave that speech more for Jill to recognize what she wanted and not so much for what she was saying; although, it was true.

"Oh, no worries. We're both girls here. We have the same parts, right?" Jill said, smiling.

Jill pulled the mosquito netting back and plopped on one side of the bed, then stretched out across it and twisted from side to side, her blond hair whipping water droplets along the way. Kristin reluctantly headed into the bathroom. Why did she feel like she was in middle-school gym class all over again?

Then a few minutes into her shower it happened: Jill walked into the bathroom to brush her teeth. It was as if Kristin was not even there. She tried to play it off, but she was terribly uncomfortable. She told herself, *we have the same parts,* yet kept her back to Jill while she washed. Then Jill decided to talk to her, with a mouthful of toothpaste.

"Sho, ay you yo-a tea-ar?" Jill asked, continuing to brush.

Now, with the water running, Kristin could hardly hear her as it was. But with a mouthful of toothpaste it was even more challenging.

"I'm sorry?" she asked, keeping her back turned to Jill the entire time. She felt more comfortable showing Jill her ass than her front, for some reason. She somehow felt less vulnerable.

Jill spit her toothpaste out and without washing out the sink, twirled around and faced Kristin, "Are you a yoga teacher?"

Kristin was beginning to wash her hair. She thought she could give her a quick answer and she would leave her alone. "Oh, no, I'm not."

Jill sat down on the toilet seat, which, by the way, did not have a lid on it.

"I just finished my two-hundred hours. This is my graduation gift to myself. Are you going to enroll in a teacher training? It is so worth it. I've met so many amazing people through the process of my training. And now, here in Mexico, oh my God, I cannot wait to meet so many more fabulous yogis!"

Jill sure was perky.

"Well, I'm going to head out towards the yoga room and try to get a banana or some tea before class. Do you want me to grab you something?" she asked Kristin.

"Ah, no, I'm good. Thank you." Really, Kristin was just pleased that she would have the bathroom to herself for a moment. Kristin finished her shower in peace, got her towel and dried off while still inside the shower area, and then came out like a normal person to get changed.

The yoga clothes she had left on the bed were slightly dampened by Jill's hair. She threw the pants on but chose a different top. This was going to mess up her entire wardrobe selection for the week, but she had planned on wearing those pants the first night because they were her favorite pair. She tied her hair up in a ponytail, rinsed the sink, and brushed her teeth, and then rinsed the sink again just for good measure.

Before heading out, she pulled the mosquito netting back over the bed, thinking it would be dark by the time they returned, and in the event the bugs were out and about, this would keep them out of the bed for the evening. She took one last look around, grabbed her yoga mat and her small purse and headed to the yoga room.

She met a couple of friendly faces along the way. Everyone seemed excited to get on their yoga mats after the day of travel and frolicking in the sun.

Nayana was set up in the room and invited everyone to create a circle around her. Since the yoga room was circular, it created a beautiful look. Nayana had taken time to arrange an alter in the center of the room with a small statue of the elephant god, Ganesha, and some local flowers and seashells. She went around greeting each person and checking to to see how everyone was feeling after the first day. Everyone seemed pumped and excited and even though some folks had the usual aches, pains and issues, nobody was complaining about them at this time. Jill popped in just before class was about to start, and a few people had to make some room for her to squeeze her mat in. Kristin noticed that this threw the circle off just enough so that it was not perfect anymore. She wondered if this mattered to anyone else but her.

Nayana gave a lovely welcome speech and invited everyone to let go of everything including all the things they brought, physically, mentally, and emotionally. She invited everyone to bring in the energy of Lord Ganesha, who is known as the "Remover of Obstacles." And together they chanted to him 108 times, to invoke his energy and light. Kristin asked to release judgment. She hoped that the little elephant god understood what that was about.

"Om Gum Ganapatayei Namaha," they chanted in unison. Kristin swayed her body to the melodic chant, at once getting lost in it. She hardly realized that any time had passed when they held the last round, indicating that they were finished the 108 rounds. She felt that it would have gone on much longer. Kristin smiled, knowing that Ganesha had heard her prayers. She was already feeling lighter.

After chanting, Nayana led the group through a gentle class to stretch and open the body and release tensions. It was exactly the type of class that Kristin had been taking and it made her feel comfortable to know that she would be able to do the practice. After the yoga class was over, Nayana invited everyone to go around the room and share what they were letting go of. Kristin felt her heart start pounding. Immediately she worried about what she should say that would not be offensive about how she was feeling about her roommate. She was incredibly grateful to not be going first. She needed time to think.

Many people shared what they were letting go of. Some included the stresses of home or relationship or work-related issues that they were going through. Someone said that they were letting go of expectations. Another said fear. One of the men even joked he was letting go of watching television before he went to bed at night and everyone laughed with him. When Kristin's turn to share came up, she was surprised at what came out of her mouth.

"I want to learn to let go of anything that no longer serves me in being a better person."

Everyone smiled. A few people nodded in agreement. Kristin felt a lot better. It was not what she had anticipated saying. She found that quite interesting.

Jill said that she wanted to let go of needing to be perfect. Kristin wanted to tell her that she could let that one go right away, but she bit her tongue. That certainly wouldn't have served her intention. Nayana would probably argue that even thinking it was creating the negative energy. She tried to let that go too. She hoped Lord Ganesha heard her inner voice as well as her outer one.

Nayana made some closing remarks:

"Thank you, everyone, for sharing. I want to say that we have a special dinner waiting for us in the dining hall. After dinner you have open time to do whatever you want. We are meeting at 6 a.m. for mediation on the beach tomorrow morning. And; remember; do not drink the water from the tap here. Always drink bottled water — even when you are brushing your teeth. See you all in the dining hall." Nayana took her hands into prayer and nodded to the group, finishing, "Namaste."

Kristin failed to bow to Nayana with the rest because she was still processing the line about not using the water from the tap to brush her teeth, which she had done already. Now that she thought about it, there was a five-gallon water jug in the bathroom on the counter. She hadn't considered that it was for brushing teeth. She silently blamed Jill for throwing her off.

Kristin immediately felt sick to her stomach. The last thing she wanted on this trip was to get sick. As everyone began to clean up his or her yoga mats, she sat there, worrying. She started to vaguely recall a comment about the water upon checking in, but everyone was laughing and enjoying their welcome drink of fresh pineapple juice that she wasn't really paying attention like she should have. Yet, it was all coming back to her now.

Pulling herself out of the daydream, Kristin started to roll up her yoga mat and head out of the room. Most of her friends were ahead of her. The queasiness in her stomach deepened as she started to make a list of all the things that she suddenly felt were way beyond her comfort zone:

1. In a foreign country
2. Don't understand the language
3. Rooming with someone I don't know
4. Bathroom with no privacy
5. Weird vegetarian food
6. Yoga I cannot do
7. A roommate who is messy and inconsiderate

8. Water I cannot drink
9. So many bugs you need a netting around the bed at night
10. Nobody cares enough to wait for her

She was amassing quite an irrational list.

Kristin decided to go back to her bungalow and toss her yoga mat in before heading to the dining hall. Jill had already been there. She knew this because Jill had pulled the mosquito netting back and tossed her yoga mat across the bed.

Kristin wanted to cry...just a little.

She removed Jill's yoga mat and put it on her suitcase, pulled the mosquito netting back to cover the bed, and headed, reluctantly, to the dining hall. A part of her wanted to stay in the room and protect the area from Jill's impending invasion. But she was hungry, and for some reason she started to worry about when she would be able to eat again.

While walking to dinner she thought to herself, *Comfort zone? What comfort zone?*

Somehow she had a feeling that she was going to be letting go of more than she bargained for before the week was up.

She didn't eat much that night for dinner, and was relatively quiet among the group. The next morning, Jill was up at 5 a.m. going through all of her things with the light on, humming lightly. Kristin pulled her weary body out of bed and barely made it to the bathroom for her first of many rounds of what they refer to in Mexico as "Montezuma's Revenge."

Chapter 16

Letting Go

"When I let go of what I am, I become what I might be."
~ Lao Tzu

Jill informed Kristin that she had missed a fabulous morning meditation on the beach, followed by a yoga class and breakfast to die for. She herself had spent the morning curled up in a ball moving from the bed to the bathroom and back again. Jill told her that she would let her have some privacy, but if she needed anything to just call her. Kristin didn't have the strength to let her know that there was not only no phone in the room, but that she had not purchased an international plan for her cell phone. She had told herself she was going "off the grid" for the week and she was now regretting that decision, as she was feeling quite alone and frightened.

Just after breakfast, Nayana stopped in to check on her and brought her some coconut water to replenish her electrolytes, if she could get it down. Kristin broke down crying during Nayana's visit, explaining and practically pleading to her that she wanted to go home. Nayana understood, but pointed out that she was in no shape to leave or fly. She also felt that the sickness would soon pass, leaving Kristin feeling much better. She urged her to journal about anything that was coming up for her on any level: physical, mental, energetic and emotional, and to breathe through the discomfort in her body, wherever she was feeling it.

"Think of this as a real purging — a true letting go," Nayana offered.

Kristin was not open to the new age, hippie stuff during this time of agonizing pains in her stomach and frequent trips to the bathroom. She was tired, weak, and felt a complete mess. There was a part of her that wanted to believe that this was all energetic and a cleansing, but another part of her, the part that was conditioned to survive and often moving from a fear-based place, felt like she needed to be smart and find help. Maybe, she thought, she should see a doctor in the event that this was more than an energetic cleanse.

"Remember, yesterday you asked for the assistance to release anything holding you back from being a better person." Nayana continued, "So sometimes those are heavy energies to move through. I completely believe that this is what is happening to you right now. And I know it may not be of any comfort to hear at the present moment, but if you can in some way come to peace or understand what it is that you are releasing on this deep cellular level, then that will go a long way to moving through this painlessly and quickly."

Did she just say painlessly? Kristin was definitely certain of one thing that Nayana was correct about: that was not of any comfort to hear.

Nonetheless, she did trust her yoga teacher, and she did understand that she had a long way to go in being a better person. She either couldn't find a pen or forgot to bring one with her and asked Nayana to loan her something to write with. Nayana soon returned with a pen from the gift shop that read: "Letting it Go in Mexico" which had a funny cartoon picture of a woman throwing her top off. Nayana thought the humor was appropriate. Kristin smiled, trying to go with the flow, but she just wasn't there yet. She kind of wanted to stick that pen in Nayana's hand, disregarding her teachings on *ahimsa* for good old revenge…albeit not a very fair type. Her higher self took the pen and smiled, holding her lower self back from making any attack.

Once Nayana left, Kristin pulled the one chair in the room up to the open window so that she could look out at the ocean. She saw her yoga friends frolicking in the surf. There was beautiful, tan, blond Jill, her roommate, cavorting around like a pro. And there was Neil and Barbara and her other friends all laughing and enjoying Jill's company. The pains intensified in her abdomen the more she watched everyone in envy. At first, she was merely angry. But soon she began to cry. The tears came out gently in the beginning, but it did not take long for her to be in full gut-wrenching hysteria. This was no small feat since her stomach was already churning from the tainted water she had brushed her teeth with yesterday. Kristin hurled herself back on the bed and into a tight ball. She closed her fists, and squeezed every muscle in her body and let out a blood-curdling scream. She didn't even care that the rest of the resort may have heard her either. She belted it out. Somewhere in her mind she imagined droves of people rushing to her rescue, but alas, no one came. She managed to go to the window. They were all still in the ocean, having a good time. Kristin's cries intensified when she realized just how alone she was. And she thought to herself, *I could die here right now and nobody would know*. She continued to cry and wail until she somehow she fell asleep.

She woke up a couple of hours later. She went to the bathroom with somewhat less pain and cramping than before. But it was immediately clear that she was not out of the woods yet.

Kristin walked back over to the open window, holding her stomach. Her friends were now lying on the beach laughing and burying Neil up to his neck, then making a sand mermaid body for him. Nayana was there too. It appeared that everyone from their retreat was collected there together enjoying some down time, except for her. This saddened her. Kristin had spent a lot of money for this retreat, after all, and she was getting nothing in return but a horrible reaction to bacteria!

She was angry and upset, but didn't want to just waste her time away. So with a sigh Kristin reluctantly opened her journal. Tossing the pen with the topless woman over towards Jill's side of the room, Kristin rummaged through her things until she found a pen of her own. It read: "Marriott New York City." And she thought, *that's better*.

At the top of the page Kristin wrote the date and the location, then underneath penned, "Yoga Retreat — ?" Since she was wondering just how much yoga she would be getting out of this retreat it seemed only appropriate to end the title with the question mark.

Kristin wrote effortlessly about her amazing first day, the ease of travel to the destination, the instant camaraderie with the yogi friends she had made, the amazing food and the beautiful scenery. She talked about the blissful day in the surf and the sun and how she felt comfortable and fully alive. Her journaling went to discussions of Joshua and what he was coming to mean to her, how yoga had changed her for the better, and how losing her job was the best thing that could have happened to her. She wrote about how her life had changed and how she welcomed this change and craved to understand more and be an all-around better person. Kristin also discussed her fears of coming on the trip and how they were all starting to actually come true. In her journal, Kristin began to write about all the things that had gone wrong starting with Jill arriving to wreak havoc on her little zen sanctuary and up to the moment where she was left out of all the events and by herself sick in her room with nothing to eat, nothing to watch to take her mind off of how she felt, nothing to read, and nothing to do. Tears dripped slowly down her cheek and onto the page as she wrote. Not the hysterical tears from her deluge before, but quiet and sad tears of loneliness and abandonment. And then, suddenly, somehow the journal turned down a totally unexpected road.

I miss my father. He would call me "Princess" and carry me on one shoulder all around. When he came home from work I would light up with love. I loved my mom, but there was a special bond with Daddy and me. I loved him so deeply and purely and I felt him love me the same. I felt safe and secure with him around. He was the first man in my life and the only one who mattered...when he died, a part of me died too. I wasn't told what had happened to him. When Mom and Sandy got to go up to the body during the funeral, I had to stay and sit with my uncle. Even though my uncle tried to make light of the situation, I knew that my dad was never coming back. My mother never discussed Dad again after that day. My sister barely brought him up either. My uncle was the only person who gave me any glimpse into the man that he really was. And through his eyes, I knew that my father was an amazing man and that I was truly missing someone special in my life. All I have left of him now are some pictures that showcase his smile and his happiness. He was taken too soon from his family. I never got a chance to say good-bye. I never got a chance to even really know him. He never got a chance to see me grow up or become what I am to become. He never got to meet Joshua...

Kristin's emotions took over and she found herself unable to write anymore. She hadn't thought of her father in some time and certainly never in this way. Kristin felt this tremendous void within her that she had carried since that day. She realized that her previous relationships had been challenging because she made them that way. There had been men — some good men — that loved her or wanted to love her. But Kristin had always kept them at a distance and never truly let them in. Until she met Joshua, she never had even wanted a serious relationship. Just like her mother, she had a little fun and then kept a distance. Now in this moment Kristin realized that she had a fear that these men might leave her at some point. And so she never allowed the relationship to get that deep. As soon as she felt any significant emotion, she would withdrawal before she had time to be hurt again. And yet, somehow, her heart had softened enough to let Joshua in. What had changed? The only thing different was that she had been practicing yoga and had begun to change her mind and her habits because of it. Somehow this practice had begun to open her heart.

She never remembered crying so deeply from within like she did that day. There seemed to be no stopping it. The floodgates were now wide open and she had been holding back those dammed-up emotions since her father had died.

* * *

Later on that afternoon Kristin wrote some more in her journal about how she felt about her father, her mother and the entire situation. She wrote about how she learned to stifle her feelings. And she started to recall and journal about the first time that she started to feel the pain in her lower back and hip area. She had noticed it first at work.

She had spent the week trying to move rapidly through her work so that she would be able to leave early on Friday afternoon to go away to Martha's Vineyard with a guy that she was dating from work. Jeff worked in Marketing and every time that she saw him she had a physical reaction where her stomach fluttered. They had gone out for drinks one night after work with a group of friends. Brian had been there that night too, but he had left early. Kristin hadn't noticed that he was trying to talk to her because she was too smitten with Jeff and her attention was completely on him. That night drinks turned into dinner, and dinner turned into a make-out session in her car. She tried to keep their relationship quiet at work to downplay it. After all, if people knew about it then it might feel more serious. And back then Kristin had serious commitment issues.

One night after drinks, dinner, and their usual hook-up, Jeff asked Kristin if she wanted to go away for a weekend together. She had told him that it might be too soon for them to do something like that. She was already feeling scared that they were getting too close. He asked her several times over the course of the next few weeks until she finally broke down and said yes. But in doing so, Kristin made Jeff promise to keep it just between them and to not take it as a step in advancing their relationship.

The real truth of the matter was that she liked Jeff and Jeff also liked her. The fact that her stomach fluttered when she saw him proved that she had feelings for him. But her words and behavior were coming out of fear. If she didn't have a real relationship, then what could she lose? So Kristin kept Jeff at arm's length, even though she really felt differently, yet wasn't consciously aware of it. Her subconscious patterns took over, as usual.

In the two weeks leading up to their trip, Jeff became more distant. When she made an excuse to come by his office to see him, he would give her a disapproving headshake. When she called him after work, he always had something else to do and couldn't talk or did not answer. And even though he was acting like she had asked him to, the more he pulled away emotionally, the more she felt drawn to him. The less available he was, the more she wanted him. They hadn't discussed the trip for weeks, but Friday morning Kristin packed a bag and went to work with the intention of leaving early and going away with him. It turned out a little differently than planned.

Jeff hadn't come in that morning. He was not returning her calls. Kristin finished her work by noon, expecting him to show up. He never came into work that day until just before 5. She saw him walk in and head to his office as most of the other employees were heading home for the day. Her stomach fluttered seeing him and she smiled, thinking, *what is my problem?*

When the coast was clear, she headed to his office, ready for their weekend together. Jeff seemed to be waiting for her. She walked in and, out of habit, closed the door behind her.

"Are you ready to go?" Kristin asked Jeff, smiling.

He looked at her and took a deep breath. "About that..." he began, and then went on to tell her that they would not be going away together, and that he was no longer interested in seeing her since she was not interested in pursuing a deeper relationship. Kristin sat there listening to Jeff explain how he felt, but she could not bring herself to share her feelings. Instead she felt the need to keep them to herself. She nodded politely, and told Jeff that she understood how he felt and hoped that they could remain friends. He smiled, but did not comment. Instead he told her that he had been offered a job at another company and was there to collect his personal things and would be leaving. Kristin never saw or spoke to Jeff after that day. She never told him that she did have feelings for him. Instead, she focused on the fact that he had pulled away and left her. In the end, he was doing what she had always thought men do and why she always kept her distance — he was leaving her.

She was angry. She was disappointed. She began to feel abandoned too. And as she walked back to her desk, keeping all of these feelings to herself, Kristin tightened up her abdomen to hold them in. And with every step that she took towards her desk, she could feel her body tensing up more, until eventually a painful sensation lodged in her lower back and right hip. She found it difficult to get out of her car that night when she got home, and immediately began her ongoing remedy of wine and couch sitting.

Kristin's writing stopped abruptly there. She could see so clearly now what had remained clouded for so long. These feeling of abandonment triggered the emotions she had spent a lifetime hiding inside her about her own father's death. In her attempt to erase both those old feelings and the new ones sparked with Jeff's recoiling from her, Kristin had created a life of ill health, distrust and sadness. And now, here she was, changing and healing her life and plunging into her first serious romantic relationship with a more open heart. Her back was definitely feeling better these days since she had begun to move into her body, trust, and let go. But this had all been happening behind the scenes and completely unconsciously. Now, in the midst of this "purging," as Nayana called it, she realized that the dots she was connecting were allowing her to finally make peace with what had happened in the past.

Nayana had talked in classes about shifts. She had talked about connections with the body and mind and how we hold on to emotions and traumas in our tissues. It all sounded interesting. But finally she was beginning to understand what it was all about. It was not easy. But it sure was enlightening.

Now, how was she going to proceed from here? What would be her next step? She decided to let go of those questions because, honestly, she was still reeling from her recent realizations.

That night around dinner, Kristin felt good enough to make her way down to the dining hall. Everyone was glad to see her and welcomed her to the tables. She drank some coconut water and had some broth, but that was about all she could handle. She decided not to share with the others about her cathartic release because she knew it was still working itself out. Instead, she chose to listen to the activities of the day and what she had missed. Learning what tomorrow brought, she assured everyone that she hoped to join them at some point, but wanted to spend a little more time resting and recuperating first. The fact was that she still needed to be pretty close to the bathroom. And as she thought about the open bathroom that she shared with her roommate she realized that for Jill the last twenty-four hours were probably no fun having her as a roommate. Kristin decided to talk to Jill about it that night before bed.

"Jill, I want to apologize to you," Kristin began.

"Oh, you have nothing to apologize about. It's not your fault you got sick." Jill smiled as she tossed her day's clothes on the floor and changed into her nightie.

Kristin took a deep breath. "No, I need to apologize because I haven't been fair to you. I wasn't very nice to you when you arrived and I should have been nicer. The fact is that I was scared of a lot of things coming here — some things that I wasn't even aware of. Now that I'm here they are coming up. And I am realizing that I need to let go of a lot of things still. I'm just sorry for you, as my roommate, that some of what I am letting go of is coming out of my other end!"

Jill and Kristin both burst into laughter!

"Well, it certainly wasn't what I thought I signed up for," Jill mused, then continued. "But on a serious note, I'm glad you're getting some clarification for yourself. These yoga retreats always turn out to be so transformative one way or another!"

Jill was, in actuality, a kind person. Sure, she was messy, but why had she chosen to focus on that? Kristin was now glad to have a person like her as a roommate.

"That Lord Ganesha is a powerful dude, isn't he?" Kristin asked Jill.

"Yup, you can say that again."

Kristin and Jill talked a little more about the elephant god before heading to bed that night. Kristin's stomach was feeling better and the coconut water and broth appeared to be staying in. Kristin was feeling more hopeful about the rest of the week. In fact, she was feeling lighter than she had in a very long time. As she tossed her clothes on the chair, got changed and went to bed, Kristin left the mosquito netting open around her side of the bed.

Then, Kristin drifted off thinking to herself, *How's that for letting go?*

Chapter 17

Renewal

"Every now and then, go away, have a little relaxation. For when you come back to your work, your judgment will be surer; since to remain constantly at work will cause you to lose power of judgment." ~ Leonardo Da Vinci

Kristin awoke the next morning with many bug bites, but feeling a lot better. She missed the morning meditation because she still was not feeling 100%, but made it to breakfast and also to morning yoga, where she spent most of the time on her back breathing. But all was okay.

After breakfast Nayana said that she was taking a few of the folks into the local town to look around and asked Kristin if she wanted to join them. But Kristin felt that she should still stay close to the hotel for the remainder of this day, and just rest and relax. After all, her first full day there had been a doozy and she just felt like she needed to integrate everything. A few others decided to stay at the resort, but it looked like they also had the same things in mind, and took to finding a quiet space by him- or herself. Kristin pulled her beach chair up under the palms right near her bungalow so that she had some shade. The hypnotic flow of the sea calmed and relaxed her body and mind. She thought about her father. Had he known about yoga? Would he have joined their family the first time that they had gone? Would she have ever even gone to yoga if her father was still alive? Would she have had a reason to be pulled there? Would she be sitting there at that moment in paradise?

As Kristin traveled into those thoughts, the hair on her arms stood up and a chill ran through her. The heat and humidity of Mexico wasn't causing that sensation that was for sure. She pushed her feet around in the sand and gazed around the ground. Kristin wondered if her father was in fact there with her, as she noticed a small crab meandering across the sand close to her chair. She watched it move here and there. It seemed to have no particular place to be. Kristin smiled. She thought that she would call the crab "Padre," which is Spanish for father. When she first called it out loud, she swore the crab stopped and turned to look towards her. Kristin said the name again but it did not move. She waited for some time, but it seemed to have just fallen asleep or something.

As Kristin lay back into the chair, the crab began to walk quickly towards her. Kristin shrieked and pulled her feet up onto the chair. The crab ran under her chair and suddenly she couldn't see it. She feared it was too close and may bite her, so she jumped off the chair to see where it had gone. But alas, she couldn't find the little critter. Checking under the chair, around the side of her bungalow, and back into the sand, she chose to believe that it had gone deep into the sand somewhere. As Kristin stood there she took a big stretch and then someone from the hotel approached her.

"Would you like me to bring you some lunch? I understand that you are still not feeling well today."

Kristin thanked the woman, but told her that she would help herself very soon. The woman smiled and bowed to her and walked away. Kristin returned the gesture. Then turned to face the sea.

Taking a deep breath, Kristin reached her arms behind her back and clasped them together, stretching her chest and shoulders. She bent to the left and to the right, holding each side for a couple of deep breaths. She felt so open today. The daily hesitancy in her hip seemed to be gone at the moment. It felt strange to not be in pain. Strange, but good, that is!

And while Kristin still had the thought in her mind, she decided to get her journal and write a little more about how she was feeling today — in her body and her mind. It was interesting to her that after a day of purging, quite literally, she felt so much better and lighter. Kristin did not have all of her energy back yet, but she did not feel heavy or inflamed. Her heart felt light too. She began to think about the amazing guy she had waiting for her back home and how through some interesting circumstances they had come together. She smiled as she thought about Joshua. Kristin knew that her father and her uncle would both approve of him. She smiled at the thought of them meeting and imagined the friendship that they would have. As she envisioned this day that would never happen in the real world, the hair on her arms and neck stood up again and a chill ran down her body.

Kristin closed her journal. It felt like the appropriate time to go get something to eat, so she went into her room and put on a cover-up and some flip flops, and headed down to the dining area where another beautiful display of food was waiting. The good news was that now she was ready to eat it.

The hall was emptier than usual this afternoon. Kristin wondered just how much she should eat, given she was still recovering from yesterday's illness. Looking at the food, she wanted to eat it all. She knew there should be a compromise. As she was determining where to start, the woman who came by her beach chair walked out with a drink for her.

"Take this. It's coconut water and some special home medicine to make you feel good." And with that, the woman bowed her head at Kristin and walked back towards the kitchen.

Taking a closer look, Kristin could see some things floating inside the drink. She didn't know what they were and wondered if they were alive or just bits of something. Normally she did not enjoy pulp. But she decided to give it a shot. Before she took a sip, she placed a petite portion of a hardy-looking rice dish from the buffet and a sliver of fresh grilled fish.

Kristin looked around the dining hall and noticed only a few people, but none of them looked familiar. As she scanned again Kristin noticed one woman with a lovely teal blue top waving her over, asking Kristin to join her for lunch.

As Kristin approached her table, the woman said, "Please, I am dying for some good company! I'm Jean. I don't think we've officially met."

Kristin smiled and extended her hand, "No, I don't believe so. I'm Kristin. It's very nice to meet you. And thank you for inviting me to lunch. I've been enjoying my rest and meditation time today, but I was starting to feel like I needed to talk to someone!" she admitted enthusiastically.

"I know what you mean," Jean said, chewing on a piece of pineapple. "I love the going within part, but sometimes you just need some social time too. After all, this is also vacation!"

Jean was from Minneapolis, so the Mexican climate was a big change for her. She said she had done a yoga retreat last year in Costa Rica and the year before that also in Mexico, but on the western coast.

"Once I felt this warm humid air I said to myself, 'Jean, this is what you've been missin' baby!'" Jean laughed and chomped on another piece of fruit. "And I'll tell you another thing, these cute little Mexican men are not that bad to look at either!"

Jean was a hoot! The two women spent the entire lunch laughing and talking with food in their mouths like nobody cared. At one point, Jean wiped her hands on her yoga pants instead of the napkin that was still sitting neatly folded on the side of her plate. She didn't care. Kristin didn't care. It felt good to cut loose a little and not give a crap about what people's impressions of her were. Kristin was thinking about how badly she needed a person like Jean in her life. Suddenly, Kristin had a thought that came to her unexpectedly.

Confiding in Jean, Kristin admitted, "You know what I miss a little?"

Jean was on full alert. She stopped chewing to hear the answer as if it might actually make a difference.

"Smoking," Kristin admitted. "I just want one cigarette."

Jean snorted a little when she laughed. The girls laughed even more.

"I smoked when I was young," Jean said. "Everyone smoked then. One day I just stopped. I didn't want it anymore."

Kristin knew what she meant. She had done the same thing. And yet, suddenly, she felt like she really wanted a cigarette. Kristin shared that she didn't understand why that was coming up. She wondered in the back of her mind if her father had smoked. She couldn't remember.

"Uh-oh, you're getting too clean!" Jean cried out. "You are cleansing and eating all this healthy food in this healthy place and your shadow self is peeking up going, *Don't forget about me!*"

"Shadow self? What is that?" That was a new term for Kristin, but something about it really sounded interesting.

"Oh, that's the side of you that you try to hide because you feel like for some reason it is wrong. You feel ashamed or like it isn't PC, so you stop allowing for it. But the problem is, it's still a part of you. You can't just pretend something away, ya' know?"

Kristin didn't. But she was learning.

"Shadow self," Kristin repeated. "I think my shadow may be larger than the rest of me."

Jean snorted again and they laughed louder. There was nobody else in the dining hall at this point, so the women felt fully free to be whoever they needed to be. Kristin really enjoyed Jean. She felt like she could be completely honest and not judged by her no matter what she said. Somehow, it felt like she'd known Jean for a very long time, like Jean was one of her very closest friends.

"So if I'm a smoker, but I stopped smoking one day like you just because, but now I want to smoke, you're saying that is part of my shadow self — the part that I am denying. But since I quit, I really didn't want to smoke until now. So does that mean that I really wanted to smoke then, but I just denied it? Or what about us all being light beings and positive, love energy? If that is what we truly are, why would a part of me want to smoke?"

Kristin thought too much. Jean let her know about that right away.

"You're overthinkin'. Stop." Jean wiped her hand again on her yoga pants, then picked up another piece of fruit right away and threw it in her mouth. She spoke with a mouthful of pineapple. "I just can't get enough of this stuff. I swear, it's like we don't have real fruit in Minnesota!" Jean cackled and snorted another time.

Soon both women found themselves laughing hysterically, unable to stop. It reminded her of the time she and Joshua had to remove themselves from the library. She felt a similar connection to Jean, although not a romantic one, but as if she had known her somehow forever. If anyone else had been in the dining hall, they might have thought that the two women were drunk. Well, they sort of were drunk on life! Jean toppled over and fell off her chair onto the floor. Kristin thought she felt herself pee just a little. She admitted this to Jean mid-laugh and the women hurled themselves around uncontrollably for several more minutes, until the fit began to wind down, ever so slowly. Finally Jean picked herself back up into the chair and took that unused napkin and used it to wipe the happy tears from her eyes. Kristin used the palms of her hands. She noticed several members of the resort staff giggling, as they watched. She waved at them and they waved and smiled back.

"Shoot, Jean. You are a ton of fun," Kristin said, feeling full of love and happiness.

"Hey, baby, you only live once. You gotta find a way to have fun. Otherwise, life is one really long shit storm." That was the most serious Jean had sounded during their entire lunch. But Jean was right; life could sometimes be a real mess. But other times, life could be really awesome. They agreed that life is what you make of it. Jean offered one more bit of Minnesota wisdom:

"You may not always be able to stop that storm from coming, but you can certainly get out of the way."

Indeed, Kristin agreed.

Jean smiled at Kristin and thanked her for joining her for lunch and having a great laugh with her. Then she excused herself, telling Kristin that she was off for an afternoon siesta. Kristin waved good-bye to Jean, telling her that she would look for her later at yoga. Jean replied, "Sure, if I'm up!"

When Jean left the table Kristin realized that she had not yet drunk the special concoction that was made for her. She looked at it again. Some of the floaters had settled to the bottom of it and she wondered if she should stir them back up, or drink it without the sediment so that she got less of the pulp. She went with the latter and took a tiny sip. It didn't taste too bad. There was some spice in it, that was for sure, and something minty too. But it surely wasn't something that she would have ordered for the pure enjoyment of it. She swallowed about half of the glass and decided that she just couldn't finish it off at that point. She started to get up and leave the glass when the woman who had given it to her came around the corner and out of the kitchen. Seeing Kristin about to leave, she ran up to her.

"No, you must finish," she said pointing to the glass.

"Oh," Kristin said looking for an excuse. "I'm so full," she said rubbing her belly.

"No, you finish." She was adamant.

Kristin took a deep breath and picked up the cup. She swallowed a little more and then set it down. The woman shook her head at her. Apparently she was not leaving until the mixture was finished. Kristin looked at the sediment sludge on the bottom of the glass. She just knew that it was going to be gross going down, just like most medicine. She looked at the woman and shrugged her shoulders, pleading with her to let her go. She shook her head again at Kristin and told her to finish it. Even her own mother had never forced her to finish something that was supposedly good for her. Kristin wondered what Jean would have done about this situation. She figured that Jean would have just swigged it because life is too short to be sick. So, in honor of her new friend she picked it up and drank the rest. And after she set the glass on the table, Kristin shook her body uncontrollably, stuck out her tongue with disgust, and nearly gagged. Yup, it was disgusting, just like she knew it would be.

As she gagged and coughed a little, the woman laughed and picked up the cup.

"Good, now you no sick. Go siesta," she said, shooing Kristin away like a bug, giggling.

Kristin shook her head again and goose bumps ran down her arms and neck.

* * *

Waking from a midday nap became one of her newfound joys of life. Kristin felt completely renewed after the amazing lunch, the disgusting health drink, and a beautiful day of fresh salt air and pure pranic energy from the sun. Jill had returned from town with a cute little hat for Kristin as a gift and the two of them sat on their beach chairs discussing the sweet little town that some of them had explored. Jill told Kristin if she was looking for gifts that going into town she would find great prices and good deals. Kristin thanked her but told her she wasn't into buying lots of gifts. She was on a little budget for the trip.

Initially she had been worried about spending the money to go to Mexico, but in talking to Joshua she realized that she had to seize the day, and that if it was the right thing to do, the money would be there. Of course, she didn't want to miss out on any brilliant opportunities, so she thought that if everyone was going somewhere tomorrow that she would join the group.

"In fact, I think Nayana is going to arrange a trip to the Mayan pyramids tomorrow. Almost everyone wants to go."

This intrigued Kristin. Other than in Egypt, she didn't know that there were pyramids anywhere else in the world.

"Oh, sweetie, there are pyramids everywhere!" Jill beamed. "South America, Central America, China — some people say that they found some under the ice in Antarctica. Pyramids are ancient energy conductors. There is so much we still don't know about how they worked," Jill schooled her.

"I thought that pyramids were tombs?" Kristin inquired.

"Well, I think that is part of it. But there are lots of people talking about other ideas these days. It's all over the place in books and television shows and of course all over the web. What we learned in school is only part of the information."

"I'm not sure I learned much in school," Kristin told her roommate. "I can't think of one thing that I retained."

"That's because they didn't teach us about the interesting stuff. I still want to know why I had to memorize multiplication tables."

Kristin concurred.

"There is so much to learn about the world," Kristin said. "I feel like a student again. I have learned so much through yoga and I continue to learn so much every day. I wonder why these useful things aren't being taught?"

Jill offered her thoughts, "Maybe it's our job to teach them to other people."

Kristin smiled. She liked the idea of teaching something valuable to kids that they could use to make their lives easier or happier. She considered keeping the shadow side off of that curriculum though. That might be difficult to discuss. She herself still didn't fully understand it.

Jill shared her favorite quote, from Socrates, "'The only true wisdom is in knowing that you know nothing.' Now, that somehow I remembered!"

They laughed. Not the kind of laugh she had done with Jean during lunch, but a laugh nonetheless. Kristin hoped she would see her new friend in yoga that evening. Kristin didn't know if she could practice next to her, however. If Jean snorted in class, then it was all over for both of them for sure. And yet somehow, she didn't think that Nayana would mind.

* * *

The yoga room was pretty packed that night. Jean was there, but she sat across the room and seemed to be a much quieter version than the Jean that Kristin had had lunch with earlier that day. Another group was joining theirs and Nayana and the other retreat hostess co-led a beautiful Sun & Moon class. Each of them brought in one of the energies and they practiced slow, mindful meditative movements of both sun salutations and moon salutations.

They ended the class in a long yoga *nidra*, which meant "yogic sleep." While one of the women guided the yoga nidra, the other went around and did some energy work on people. By the time the class was over, Kristin did not want to get up. She felt so at peace and so completely renewed.

The entire day had been heavenly from nearly start to finish. With yesterday's purging and releasing, today's day of rest and renewal was exactly what she needed to get herself on a new trajectory. The only question was, what would that new direction be?

Chapter 18

Pyramid Power

"If you want to find the secrets of the universe, think in terms of energy, frequency and vibration." ~ Nikola Tesla

The next morning after breakfast, the group boarded a tour bus for the Mayan ruins of Chichen Itza. Kristin felt like she was on an adventure of a lifetime. Her yoga buddies surrounded her with compassion, insisting that she carefully select what to eat and stay near them in case she felt dizzy or needed to go back to the bus, which also luckily had a bathroom on it. She let everyone know that they needn't worry much about her now, as she felt that her purging was most likely over. But it sure was nice to know that the bathroom was there, especially with several hours of riding into the jungle before them. Yet Kristin was feeling truly renewed and ready to conquer the pyramid and its distinguished area that day. She awoke with a fury of energy and was determined to put her best intentions forward to create a day like no other that she had ever had in her life. And she was well on her way.

The ride through the more remote areas of Mexico shed light on how the people really lived. Most of the smaller shacks had large pieces of aluminum resting against each other for the sides. Kristin noticed elder women sitting in the shade near clotheslines while small children ran around barefooted waving to the buses as they drove by. The women just watched them drive by, unreactive, and she wondered if they were happy people. Kristin pondered if the nice people who worked at the hotel lived here or in this area. And while at first the situation seemed depressing, she couldn't help but notice the smiling faces on the children. They seemed to be happy, despite their seemingly dire circumstances.

Although the sights were sobering, someone on the bus began to sing some various yoga chants and it did not take long for others to join in. Some of the tunes Kristin was familiar with like, "*Om Namah Shivaya*" and "*Hare Krishna.*" But some of the chants were so long and so unusual, she wondered how Nayana and some of the others could even remember them. She thought, *I wonder if I'll ever know those chants by heart too?*

The lively chanting juxtaposed strikingly against the impoverished areas that they were traveling among. This shined great light on the gratitude that Kristin felt for having the means to travel here on vacation. She hadn't traveled abroad much, but now that she was there in Mexico having life-changing experiences, her heart heaved with immense joy and happiness to be given the opportunity. She decided to send a silent prayer out to the people of Mexico, and to wish for them the same happiness that she felt in her life. Maybe they already did feel happy. Perhaps it was her judgments thinking that they were not. *But saying a little prayer doesn't hurt anyone*, she thought.

The several-hour bus trip to the pyramids felt like no time at all once they arrived. The parking lot of the site hid the massiveness of what lay ahead of them. One by one they gathered their personal items and stepped out of the bus and stretched like good little yogis.

Nayana gathered them all around to say a few words before entering into the site.

"Before we enter, I want to say that it is my honor and privilege to be taking you to such an amazing place. The first time I came to Chichen Itza was with my guru on a yoga retreat many years ago. We entered with respect, and moved through the ancient site in a meditation. There is much to see here, and it is easy to get overwhelmed with the mass tourism and yes, unfortunately, the scam artists. Pay attention to your belongings. If you feel compelled to give something, be careful how you handle your money. Give of your heart if you feel like you should do so, but at the same time, be aware. When we move from place to place, take time to sit and meditate and feel the energy. There will be hordes of people walking around, children running and approaching you for money, teenagers on cell phones texting and snap-chatting, and adults using selfie-sticks, which they will no doubt hit you with because they aren't looking."

The group laughed with Nayana. She sure was painting a nice picture of tourists. Kristin was grateful that she did, because she would have most likely done some of these no-no's herself, being a relatively novice traveler.

Nayana continued. "I would like you to close your eyes for a moment. You can feel safe to close your eyes knowing that we are protected here in our circle and just come into your breath. Take a few moments to plant your feet and feel the sacred ground in which you stand. In a few moments one of the world's most striking pyramids will be before you. The Mayan culture flourished here at one time. Imagine yourself among the ancient ones, living a simple life here in the jungle. Respect the earth here. Respect the ancient structures. Treat it like your home. For it is. Welcome home."

Kristin smiled. She liked that: "Welcome home." It felt true.

The group opened their eyes, smiling, and began a slow walk towards the entrance. Nayana purchased their entry tickets and they received an official Mexican travel guide named Ramone to follow. Nayana alerted Ramone that they would be doing some meditations along the way, but that the group would also like to know what the different buildings used to be and any other interesting information that he could share. He smiled happily and encouraged everyone to follow him into the jungle path.

It seemed like quite a long road walking to the site. They passed through another small village area and kept going. The humidity was quite stifling. Kristin, not one to usually sweat so profusely, was already soaking through her blouse by the time they made it to the site. Her first reaction to the sprawling complex was one of awe. Her jaw did drop open and she heard herself mouth, *wow* out loud. The group expressed that same mutual feeling in unison. Among the awe-inspiring view, it seemed like hundreds of tourist scrambled about. They, as one, sounded like a swarm of bees buzzing in the background. Kristin was focused on the huge pyramid in the middle of the complex, standing tall, beckoning her to come.

Her thoughts were interrupted when Ramone began talking about the Chichen Itza, dating it, and giving some basic descriptions of the Maya and how they would have lived there. Kristin was barely listening to all of this. The stunning facility was too much to take in visually, let alone with verbal descriptions. Occasionally she looked his way and smiled, then turned back again to take in the view. Kristin imagined what it might have looked like to be here when this civilization had flourished. She wondered for a moment if she had been one of those Mayans who had lived here before. Perhaps in a previous lifetime she had!

The group began to walk farther along Chichen Itza to the left and stopped at a place the tour guide called the Temple of Jaguars and the ball court. Flanked by two tall game walls, the ball court was a game that was played using a ball, to most likely shoot through a small stone ring on each side. Not one to be interested in sports, Kristin started to tune out, until Ramone began discussing some of the sacred alignments of the walls to astronomical events in the sky, with the playing alley aligned north to south. What started to intrigue her as he spoke was about the various different patterns of things within the complex and how they aligned to stars or other celestial events. Didn't this ancient civilization have less knowledge than what they had today? How could they have known about some of these celestial patterns without having the equipment that we use now? Nayana intervened to discuss a theory that the Mayans had access to ancient knowledge that may have been quite superior to what was previously thought or taught by archeologists and in schools. This reminded her of the conversation that she and Jill had had the night before. As she took it all in, her perceptions of this ancient city started to change. She was now challenged by the idea that perhaps this ancient civilization was more advanced than that of even today's!

Nayana moved the group out of the ball court due to the massive number of people walking around. She found a less populated area where they could take a seat on the ground and do a short meditation. Nayana always began her meditations guiding them to their breath and the present moment. This time was no different, only meditating in the open and outside with many people walking around was difficult for Kristin to get into at first. She struggled with the outside noises, even though Nayana guided the group to release them. She continued to focus on her breath and just when she would get a glimpse of moving beyond that stuff, a kid would run by screeching; making that sound that only kids make! She wished only that she were more seasoned and able to more deeply without being distracted. Nayana would tell her that everything happens for a reason. So she tried to smile when she heard the children run by, and each time she did this she got a little closer to tuning in.

After the meditation, some folks shared their experiences. Kristin was embarrassed to share that she was unable to entirely let go of all the outside noises, but had caught herself from time to time beginning to feel something deeper — she just couldn't explain what it was. She listened intently as some of her fellow travelers described their experiences of feeling levitated or transported. Jill saw colors. Barbara described seeing a gigantic ball of white light with what looked like lightening inside of it on the top of the great pyramid. Kristin was envious. She noticed her new friend Jean was not saying anything either. She smiled, knowing that she and Jean were certainly two soul sisters.

The group continued around the perimeter. The great pyramid El Castillo was looming in the middle of everywhere that they went. There were many fascinating structures there. The impressive Temple of the Warriors was an interesting place to walk through. The columns would have at one time supported a larger roof structure. Today that was all gone, and these large stone piles stood in rows reaching up to the heavens and seemingly towards something vast and wonderful. The group was allowed some free time to walk around and through this area. Kristin found herself taking multiple pictures of the great pyramid through the column walls. She enjoyed the reference point of the column with the pyramid lurking in the background. And she kept saying to it, "I'll be there soon!"

During Kristin's picture shoot at the temple, Jean popped up from behind one of the pillars sticking her tongue out at Kristin. She took Jean's picture and the women had a few laughs taking some other funny shots together there too. She loved this woman. Just when she was diving in deep and getting serious, Jean was there to remind her that life was a joyous occasion! She started to think of Jean as a guardian angel of sorts. Jean reminded her a lot of her uncle.

When the time finally came to go to the center and see the pyramid, Kristin felt elated. She could hardly contain her excitement and started skipping across the complex, giggling like the staff at the resort. Soon, Barbara, Neil and Jean joined her and they skipped and laughed like all the other children who were running around. Once everyone reached the base; Ramone began his informational discussion. This time Kristin was listening intently.

"So, we call this El Castillo, which is castle in Spanish. This is the most well-known monument and what most people think of when they think of Chichen Itza. Historians believe it was built around the ninth century, and it has some very interesting markers of its own. First of all, the stairways on each of the four sides of the pyramid each contain exactly ninety-one steps. Ninety-one times four is 364. If you add the one step at the top, that is 365, the exact number of days in our solar calendar."

Stop it! Kristin thought. Again, she felt her jaw drop open and she was certain that she made an audible sound. But she didn't care. Ramone continued.

"Also this structure has fifty-two panels and nine terraces. Now, fifty-two is the number of years in the Toltec cycle. Each of the nine terrace steps can be then divided into two, which gives us eighteen for the months of the year in the Mayan calendar. But, that isn't the most interesting part of El Castillo…"

Kristin was holding her breath. Nayana would have not been pleased about that. She let it go.

"…On the autumn and the vernal equinoxes — the day of equal light between the summer and winter solstices, the sun shines on the platform edges and forms a series of shadows on the northern face that create a brief and amazing display that looks like a serpent appearing to move downward on the northern stairway. This is the embodiment of Kukulkan, the Feathered Serpent God!"

Kristin shook herself, feeling chills run down the back of her neck and arms.

"At one time you could climb the steps yourself, but we are no longer allowed to do this since too many tourists began to wear away the structure. To preserve it, we no longer allow anyone access to the top. So, you can take your time in walking around. Take some pictures and take in any sites that we did not visit together. This is the end of my tour with you. Have a very good day at Chichen Itza."

With that, Ramone smiled and waved good-bye to the group. They thanked him and Nayana shook his hand and walked a bit with him, before returning to the group. It looked as if she had given him a tip.

"Why so much attention to detail of the events in the sky?" someone in their group inquired.

Great question! Kristin thought.

Nayana's answer didn't reveal much: "Why, indeed!"

Nayana gathered the group around one of the less busy sides of the pyramid; one that appeared to be crumbling a lot more than the other; and asked the group to close their eyes and to tune back in to the energy of the place. She asked them to breathe deeply and tune in to the area above the crowns of their heads. She meticulously guided them in a meditation bringing up energy from below their feet, up through the body, and out above the head. To Kristin, time seemed to have stopped. Unbeknownst to her, all of the others in her group felt the same thing. They all felt a connection between worlds in some way, and to energy that was abundant and greater than that of the mind. Superfluous sounds faded off completely and the group felt as though they were hovering above the ground, suspended in time and space. In time, this feeling was simultaneously, forever and for just a brief moment. Knowing the truth of it didn't seem to matter. There was a feeling of connecting between the confines and dimensions of time and space. Kristin was able to move far past the distractions of her own mind's doing, and propelled herself to a place that she had never gone before.

When Nayana brought the group back and anchored them into the earth again, they erupted into applause and laughter, hugging each other and crying with joy. Kristin had never felt so connected and plugged in to energy before. The experience as a whole was indescribable, and yet they had all experienced it together. She hugged her new friend Jean long and full, both weeping and laughing at the same time. Jean snorted, of course, propelling them into an even deeper state of elation. Everyone was feeling this sensation of love. It was truly mind-blowing.

Nayana gave the group another hour to tour around the place and everyone was told where to exit and meet back up at the bus. Kristin stayed with Nayana and together they walked around, touching some of the wall stones and other areas to see what energy they felt. Kristin was most definitely drawn to this place. There was a familiar sense of something to her. She was starting to notice just how much she was having these feelings when with certain people or places. Nayana explained to her that when you are finally in the flow and on the right path that things start to line up in that way. This was another unexpected joy that Kristin was happy to have found.

Walking back to the bus Kristin finally found some time to share what had transpired for her the days before with the journaling and purging. She had realized how her father's death and the way she had been taught to handle emotions had contributed to her closing off her heart and not being fully there for anyone significant in her life. She realized how she had never allowed herself to have any real meaningful relationships, and that the few that she did have, she certainly hadn't given the right amount of love and energy to. As she outlined the chain of events leading up to her release, Nayana nodded and smiled, for she knew that there was always something more to physical issues than what most people would see. And she had been waiting for Kristin's walls to start coming down since she had met her. First a few pebbles may have fallen off. But now as she listened to Kristin, she could feel how much more had been removed. Kristin was opening up and blossoming, just like the lotus flower that comes up out of the mud.

On the way back to the resort, Jean fell fast asleep, as did many others. The bus was quiet. Kristin did not sleep, however. Her mind was full of thoughts about the sky, the universe, the interconnectedness of life and her part in all of it. She had broadened her perspective in some undeniable way over the past few days. And today she felt transformed by the incredible pyramid power of El Castillo.

* * *

Later that night, Kristin lay on the beach gazing up at the sky while her other friends slept. She was not tired. She felt energized. Something limiting within her had been released, allowing for something expansive to emerge. She imagined that she was an ancient one gazing up at the Yucatan sky. She wondered if there was something specific that they were looking for when they looked to the sky and if they had found it. Or, if they were just as thrilled with being alive as she was in that moment, and were perfectly content simply gazing. She hoped that one day she would know the answer to that question. Nayana would tell her that she already did.

Before heading to bed, Kristin gazed down at the digital watch she borrowed from Neil so that she could tell what time it was. It read 11:11. Chills ran down her back and arms and through her body. She had no idea what that meant, but felt mesmerized by the numbers. She stared at them, hypnotized, until it switched to 11:12. When it did, she blinked and took a deep breath, then headed in to bed.

Kristin would never forget the experience that she had in Mexico. Later she would refer to it as her "awakening."

Chapter 19

Opening the Door Wider

"Gratitude opens the door to...the power, the wisdom, the creativity of the universe. You open the door through gratitude."
~ Deepak Chopra

Four months after her experience on the yoga retreat in Mexico, Kristin found herself on a quest to understand more deeply the messages of the universe. There were so many ideas and philosophies swimming around in her head that she had never even thought of before. Kristin found herself thinking very profoundly about energy and the universe and it became increasingly difficult to discuss these things with some of her previous friends and family. Even Melissa would sometimes make fun of the way that she talked. Sandy hinted that perhaps she was losing her mind. But Kristin knew that she was just expanding it.

Kristin did not judge her friends who were on different paths from her and hoped that they also did not judge her. But she was also realizing that it didn't matter much what other people thought of her as long as she was being true to herself. This was an easy thing to say, but a little more difficult to manage. Kristin always tended to seek some sort of external approval in most matters. In fact, she argued that this course of action was usually approved of in her culture. She asked Joshua one night, "To not want to be validated by others usually implies a sense of selfishness, doesn't it?" His response? "What's wrong with focusing on yourself and not worrying about what others think?"

She attempted to have a meaningful discussion about karma with her mother one day. She thought that her new-age-loving mom would be open to it. But instead, she went directly on the defensive with Kristin, who was not attempting to point any fingers or wave any flags of blame at her mother, but trying only to discuss why certain things may have happened in her own life. Unfortunately, her mother just wasn't able to get to where Kristin had hoped she would. And any attempt to discuss anything about her father also fell on very defensive ears. So she had to let that go for now. Her mother just was not ready to discuss these things. She had to respect that. Again, easier to say than to do, since she had so many questions about her father and so much to still work through. And she knew that in the process she could also help her mother work through some of her own things. Unfortunately, her mother wasn't asking for any help or personal growth. Her mother seemed to be fine living in a fantasy world where puppy dogs and cupcakes loomed around every corner. She had the thought, *Who am I to mess that up for her?*

Joshua was incredibly supportive of her search for meaning. He had begun his own meditation practice and the two could often share what they were feeling through yoga and meditation. Their relationship deepened the more each of them dove into these esoteric teachings. To say that Kristin was in love with this man was an understatement. She was certain that she had found a soul mate or twin flame in him. She learned about these things in a workshop too! When Kristin was younger she had the idea that you had only one soul mate and if you didn't find him or her in this lifetime that you would be sad and lonely. Through this workshop she learned that each person has many soul mates. We each meet these soul mates at different stages in our life depending on what our lessons are. Twin flames was an even deeper connection than a soul mate. This was someone with whom your soul shared space with, and, to her understanding, a person feels incredibly drawn to another because they literally were the other half of your soul. That was deep. Kristin could easily say that she felt this way about Joshua. But one thing that she loved about their relationship was how they could have their own lives and experiences, and then come together and share in a deeper way in addition to the shared experiences that they had together. As Kristin watched some of her other acquaintances appear to be lost without their significant other, it seemed to her that the bond she felt with Joshua—which felt as though it spanned lifetimes—still allowed room for them to each be individuals. To her this was a perfect balance, and one that she deeply appreciated.

Kristin also found herself diving into books about energy, the chakra system, pyramids, ancient civilizations and more. She just couldn't seem to get enough and just when she finished one book, Jill, her roommate from Mexico, would message her recommending another one. It was easy to say that she was reading two to three books a week and she found herself starving for more information, ready to dive deeper all the time.

As for her body, Kristin always had to be mindful. That is the lesson that she was learning. She felt stronger and better because of the yoga practice, and most days felt no real pain. But she noticed that on the days when she pushed too hard or was not careful that she would sometimes be sore that evening. She knew very well that without her yoga practice she would be in greater discomfort so she was very grateful. But Kristin was realizing that the mindfulness component of the practice was the biggest and most important lesson that she had learned so far from yoga. It actually had crept into all the facets of her life too. In addition to everyday movements, Kristin realized that she was more conscious of her thoughts and her words and how she spoke to people as well. She tried very hard not to react quickly to anything or burst out into a knee-jerk comment or response. She listened better and responded appropriately to the situation. Yes, life had certainly changed a lot since Kristin had begun this yoga experiment...and all she could say was that it had changed her for the better!

One evening Kristin and Joshua took a long walk around a local park. They held hands and walked slowly, talking about daily events and engaging in lighthearted banter. Kristin noticed some time ago that Joshua had gotten very good at finishing her sentences. He did not do this in any annoying way, but rather an affirming way, as if he were acknowledging Kristin's own thoughts. He'd just done it again. She began to ask him about something simple at work and he completed the question with a full reply without skipping a beat.

"Do you realize we finish each other's sentences a lot?" she asked.

"I was wondering if it bothered you. Sometimes I just know what you're going to say and I get so excited that I see it so clearly that I blurt it out!" Joshua smiled at her and squeezed her hand.

Joshua found himself feeling elated. Sure, there were other moments in his life when he had felt this happiness: the birth of both of his children were at the top of that list, the time he had asked his ex-wife to marry him, and the day his father patted him on the shoulder and told him how proud he was of him. In fact, Joshua felt a sense of great gratitude for the many pure happy moments in his life that he had been given. He respected the universe for all that abundant love that it shared and he had a true sense of peace with his place in it. For that, he thanked his parents. His mother, a very spiritual woman herself, had always brought him up to be a kind and compassionate person. His father, a simple man, taught him what was truly important in life: love, family, integrity, and generosity.

"It's pretty awesome, isn't it?" she asked him, speaking of their connection.

They stopped under a beautiful tree and Joshua turned to her, taking both of her hands in his. "I've never felt this close to someone before. Sometimes I feel like we are one person, but not in a bad way. Do you get that?"

Of course she did. It was exactly how she felt too. Kristin smiled at him and replied simply, "I love you." There was no hint of fear when she spoke these words to him. Kristin's heart was wide open.

Joshua replied by holding her head gently with one hand and guiding her mouth to his for a long, full kiss. It was not a sloppy, sexy kiss. This was a firm, real kiss — the kind that stood time on its end. When they finally released their embrace, Kristin went in for a big hug and sighed gently into his chest.

"You know, I've been talking to the kids about you," he said softly, kissing the top of her head.

"You have?" she replied sweetly, not moving an inch, but rocking slowly with him in the hug.

"We've been discussing how it might feel if I asked you to move in with us."

Kristin smiled. "I know."

They pulled away enough to gaze into each other's eyes. They both knew that they were on the same page. A few months ago Kristin probably wouldn't have been ready to move in with Joshua and his kids. Heck, a year ago she would have not even given Joshua the time of day. She barely had when she met him that day at the party. Now, the thought of a couple of kids in the house sounded somehow comforting to her, in a weird way. They were good kids, after all. He had raised them right. Joshua was a good father and was very involved in their lives. He made it quite comfortable for her to be with them when she was. There was never any pressure to be anything more than what she was. The kids seemed well adjusted to their present living conditions between their mom and dad, and she was simply an added bonus when she was around. And now she was finally beginning to feel that they were also an added bonus in her life. How far she had come in opening up to that.

"Okay," Kristin said, smiling radiantly.

"You know, when I sat the kids down to talk about you moving in Gabriella was the first to ask why you didn't already live with us. She even said, 'Daddy, doesn't Kristin know that this is her house too?'"

Kristin felt her heart heave and her eyes welled up.

Joshua dropped another kiss on the top of her head, took her hand and they walked farther along in the park. The day couldn't have been any more perfect.

"Well, it's an open invitation at this point. The kids and I would welcome you to move in whenever you wanted to."

"Okay, I have some things to consider with my townhouse and my things. I really don't know what I should do or want to do. Can you let me sit with it and figure it all out? I know we don't have any rush."

"Absolutely."

"But I want to run another thing by you, as an idea," Kristin said teasingly.

"Ok..." He laughed. He knew it would most likely be good with him whatever it was. But he appreciated the fact that she wanted to run it by him first.

"What would you feel if I went to India to learn more about yoga and I was gone for a month or so?"

"I think that would be amazing, given you researched where you were going, maybe went with someone else who had been there before or knew a little about the area and I could reach you wherever you were."

Kristin thought about that before responding. It had been a thought in her head since the retreat. She wasn't actually sure if she knew anyone going in the near future, and she certainly hadn't looked into anything yet.

"I understand your concerns, and I absolutely would put in a lot of research before I went off to India," Kristin said.

She couldn't respond to going with anyone yet because she wasn't sure whom that might be or if it could be put together. She just felt this calling to travel and immerse herself deeper into the teachings of yoga. Since India was, in fact, the birthplace of yoga, that was her first natural thought. Kristin fell in love with Mexico on her yoga retreat and it was the first big trip of hers out of the country. Now she was ready to fly off to another land for another adventure. Kristin found herself wondering just who she was becoming. This new, fearless spiritual seeker certainly wasn't who she thought she had ever been. But perhaps she was finally just clearing off the dust that had covered her light for so long. She smiled at the thought. Kristin didn't share it with Joshua out loud, but somehow she felt that he heard her anyway.

Since she had begun to open up, Kristin had changed so much for the good. And her life had changed so much for the better in many ways. She had opened the door, reluctantly, but had been drawn through it in such a magical way that was unimaginable to her before. Kristin found herself full of life and hope as she considered opening that door more fully to embrace what was on the other side. And as she considered this, she wondered what might happen to her life when she finally took a step through all the way. The possibilities were endless!

Chapter 20

Living the Life of a Yogi — "Lite"

"Travel light, live light, spread the light, be the light."
~ Yogi Bhajan

Kristin had just returned from a short five-day stint at a yoga ashram in the Bahamas. Nayana and Annie both told her it was a slightly easier schedule from the ashrams in India and that it would give her an idea of what to expect should she chose to eventually go across the world on a spiritual quest of that nature. Kristin enjoyed the more comfortable approach to it through the Bahamas so that she could experiment. Not only was it much closer to home, but also she could go for a shorter period of time to check it out. She wrongfully assumed that this would also make it an easier, breezier ashram experience. Alas, it was still quite challenging for her.

Once there, she found herself rebelling immediately about the rules. The schedule was demanding, requiring one to awaken quite early in the morning for what they called "*Satsang*," which included meditation and chanting. After that, there was a morning yoga class to attend that included poses, breathing and relaxation. This was all to happen before eating breakfast. As she was not much of an early-morning riser, she didn't like the idea of getting up, not having anything to eat, and doing so much activity, not to mention that much of this activity was conducted seated in an uncomfortable position for what felt like an agonizingly long time. For although her hip and lower back were feeling much better, she still had to set up in a certain way to take the pressure off of it when in extended periods of sitting. Kristin also did not recognize any of the chants. They were very extensive and she was grateful to have a guidebook to them, but felt completely inadequate in the pronunciation, which she understood to be an important component of chanting.

Once she got through the morning rituals, brunch was on the horizon. The vegetarian meals; however did not provide her much comfort in the first few days as they had in Mexico. She did not enjoy the taste of yogurt. It was chalky and chunky and she just couldn't get it down. She ate plenty of fruit, but it was not very filling. Kristin found herself filling up on rice, mostly, since she wasn't sure what a lot of the other foods were that were being offered. And since she didn't want to have a repeat of her trip to Mexico and get sick her first day there, she decided to keep her diet as bland as possible and only eat what she could identify. Kristin was also very careful to drink bottled water only, even though the restrictions in the Bahamas didn't seem to be as much as they were in Mexico with regard to the water. Still, she was not making any mistakes this time!

There was open time after brunch, which was nice. Being in the Bahamas one could easily relax on the beach. You could book a massage or *Ayurvedic* treatment. Ayurveda is a scientific system of health from India that went along with yoga. Kristin had to research a little about each treatment before she scheduled any. She also heard you could consult with someone who would recommend what treatments you should have based on your "*dosha*," whatever that was! Around 4 p.m. there was another yoga class, followed by dinner at 6 p.m. Then at 8 p.m. there was another evening *Satsang,* which also included meditation, chanting, and either a talk or a performance of some kind. So basically if she were to break it down, she had to rise around 5:30 in the morning and didn't get to bed until after 10 p.m. Kristin wasn't used to keeping these long hours or doing this much yoga or activities in her normal everyday life, so the schedule was more than challenging for her. The first full day there was quite rough, actually, and she wondered how many more restrictions and schedules must be in place in order for Nayana and Annie to refer to the Bahamas as a lighter version of an Indian ashram!

At some point Kristin recalled her first full day at the yoga retreat in Mexico and remembered how much she had fought inner demons and created issues about all the aspects of the program, rooming with someone she didn't know, the food, and so on. Kristin was well aware that she needed to go through all of these things to push her buttons and lead her to illness so that she was forced to be alone with herself and work through her fears. Ultimately Mexico had changed her life. She knew that she was much more aware than she had been going into the last retreat. And yet Kristin found herself revisiting similar patterns here, albeit with a little less drama.

Kristin immediately set upon changing her outlook when she realized how much she was resisting here at this venue as well. She was learning about this pattern of fear and blaming and victimization that led to anger and resentment. Nayana told her this was one of the five *kleshas*, which means, troubles or afflictions of the mind. This one she exhibited as her pattern fell into the mindset of *Dvesha*, or aversion, although she also had other issues with attachment or *Ragas*. In fact, of all the five *kleshas*: ignorance (*avidya*), ego (*asmita*), attachment, aversion and fear of death (*abhinivesah*), Kristin had to admit that she had issues with each one. The more she learned about yoga, the more she learned about herself. And sometimes, these were not easy attributes to admit to.

On the first afternoon, she was standing by the water's edge contemplating all of these issues, when she heard a familiar voice.

"Hey, look who the sea churned up!"

She swirled around enthusiastically.

Could it be?

There she was before her, her fantastic yoga buddy from Mexico: Jean, the mysterious woman who came into her life, and then vanished, just as quickly as she had come into it.

"Jean!" she swooned, running up to her friend, as if she had known her forever instead of from a brief encounter from her trip to Mexico.

The women embraced and splashed in the water. What a joy to have a familiar face with her again serendipitously just as old wounds were beginning to open up again.

"What brings you here?" Kristin asked.

"A big plane!" Jean roared, slapping her leg with her own hand.

Kristin had to laugh. Jean's attitude was infectious and no matter how bad she might feel, she also had to laugh with her. Jean was that welcoming breath of fresh air on a hot, muggy day. How did she seem to show up just when Kristin needed that?

"Aw, I'm just kidding ya. You know, I woke up and said, 'Jean, it's time to fly again. Where do you want to go?' I didn't know where. I turned on my computer, logged into my email, and *BAM!* There's this message about the ashram here in the Bahamas. I figured, why not! I packed a little backpack, looked for the next ticket here and headed out. Here I am, ten hours later. Living the life!"

Kristin admired Jean's enthusiasm for life. Apparently even though Kristin had become a much more positive person, she still had a bit to go to rival Jean's vitality. And in the grand scheme of things, Jean had been through a lot more in her life than Kristin had in hers. Kristin was already feeling better seeing her friend.

"So what do you think about the food? The schedule here?" Kristin valued Jean's opinion, but knew that she would no doubt offer a different way of looking at things.

"I haven't seen it! Doesn't matter. I'll do what I can."

"It's pretty intense. I got up at 5:30 a.m. I haven't recovered yet," Kristin offered Jean, trying to pry her for more of a reply.

"Yeah? Huh. Well, you know what, I'm a grown woman. If I make it up, I'll be there. If I need to rest, I'll do that."

"I think they frown upon not being involved in the activities," Kristin replied, still trying to get Jean involved in her dilemma.

Jean splashed in the water, cleansing herself after her long plane-ride. She shook her head and then jumped into the sea. Kristin smiled as she watched Jean float, belly up, in the water. Kristin shook her head, jumped in and joined Jean floating belly up in the warm water. Why not?

The two women floated blissfully for several minutes in silence until Jean finally broke it.

"You know what your problem is?" Jean finally offered out of nowhere.

Kristin looked up. Jean was still floating on her back.

"You worry too much," Jean finished. "You're just in your head too much."

This was a given. Kristin knew it. Jean was not revealing anything new. She had gotten better at going with the flow. She thought about sharing that with Jean. Then she realized it probably didn't matter. Kristin still did worry too much. What was it that she worried so much about all the time? Was she concerned about someone not liking her? Getting in trouble? Conflict in general? Not being good enough? As Kristin threw all these ideas out there in her mind, she soon realized that they were all true. She thought again about the *kleshas*. They were written all over her "stuff." She was just about to ask Jean how she managed to not worry when Jean offered up her usual mantra:

"Life is too short."

Indeed, Kristin thought, having a sense of dèja vu.

They floated a bit more, peacefully in the water, before Jean lifted her head.

"Well, I should probably start drying off."

The women walked out of the water and sat down on some nearby chairs to dry off. Kristin told Jean about moving in with her boyfriend and how well the rest of her life was going. Jean was thrilled to hear it.

"Sounds like you found a good one," she said to Kristin.

Kristin nodded, telling Jean more about Joshua and just how wonderful he was. She shared with her the idea of going to India and why she had come to the ashram in the Bahamas first, based on her yoga teachers' recommendations. Supposedly this was a gentler approach to ashram life rather than heading to far off India. And although she thought that she was supposed to be having an easy experience, she shared with Jean that she was still finding it rather difficult. Jean thought that this was hilarious, and slapped her knee a couple more times, snorting. When she finally had finished with her good laugh she said, "Well, listen honey, it's the real deal. This is your ashram experience!" Jean said, throwing her arms in the air with a flair and looking as far to the left and to the right as she could. Then she stopped, slapped her hands onto her lap again and added, "Hey, I'll go to India with you!"

"You will?" Kristin jumped. "I'm still looking into it. I've got to get through this trip first!"

"Well, when you know, let me know. I'll go."

Jean was certainly easy to work with. But there was a little part of Kristin that wondered what she would be jumping into by traveling with Jean. She certainly was a brilliantly funny woman. She definitely didn't have any agendas. But would she be a careful and respectful travel companion? She wondered this. Jean must have read her mind.

"And I promise to be good."

Kristin chuckled. She knew she could be real with her. "I was just wondering how much trouble I would get into with you!" Kristin laughed at the thought. So did Jean.

"Aw, I know. I can be a loudmouth. But you know, I can be good when I need to."

The women vowed to meet up for yoga together and dinner afterwards, and the two set off to their rooms to prepare for the waning part of the day. Kristin's energy already had felt different than it had before she saw Jean. What a godsend this woman was.

* * *

As promised, Jean met Kristin just outside the yoga hall before class. They went in together and set up their mats towards the back of the room and lay down preparing for practice. Jean was lying down quietly with her hands on her chest, breathing and relaxing. Unlike Jean, Kristin pulled her knees into her chest and out, circled her knees about and took some deep letting-go breaths. Compared to Jean, she was the one presenting as restless and impatient. She kept taking those deep exhales through her mouth, in an effort to let go of her monkey-mind. It wasn't working too well. Kristin wondered if she was overtired from the early start to the day. She was beginning a familiar mental list of all the reasons why she was feeling so unsettled when the teacher walked into the room.

A sprite young girl with blond hair and a perky British accent welcomed the students and began to arrange everyone in a seated position. The class was strikingly similar to the morning one. At home, each yoga class was always so different and had a variety of themes, poses and breathing techniques. She did not realize that all of the classes here at the ashram would be of the same nature. There were beginner, intermediate and advanced variations on the schedule and she had decided to attend the beginner class first, since she was not sure of her level. Kristin was not sure how to assess herself with what she perceived to be such a particular routine. After some chanting and breathing exercises, they would warm up with sun salutations, and then perform several different postures. The class concluded with final relaxation and then a meditation.

Jean was immersed in the practice and seemed to almost be a totally different person on the yoga mat than outside. She was able to do all of the postures and hold them as long as they were taught. Kristin did pretty well but was feeling frustrated that she couldn't do more movement or attempt different postures than the ones they had done in the morning. She wondered why it was the same practice given that people often feel differently in the morning versus in the evening. This was something that Nayana and Annie both taught, and they changed up the way that they practiced based on the time of day. Kristin was in her head only half participating in the yoga class. She somewhat recognized this, yet did nothing about it.

After class, she and Jean headed to the hall for dinner, which they ate quietly, and then afterwards, the two women sat outside on a bench. Kristin was irritated. She was trying to understand why this was happening and why Jean seemed so content. Jean finally spoke up.

"You know, I'm not one to do what other people are all doing, normally. But there's something quite comforting about knowing what the practice is going to be and just tuning in to it."

Kristin looked up at Jean inquisitively. "You think?"

"Oh yeah. Look, I am not an advanced yogi person and there's a lot I don't even try to do. But at the end of the day, I do respect the tradition they have."

"You don't find the schedule and the classes a little monotonous and not conducive to particular needs?" Kristin asked.

"Well, if you're lookin' at it that way, you can find monotony in anything, really. I mean, getting up in the morning and breathing could be monotonous, right?" Jean laughed with a snort and slapped her leg. "Besides, they tell you right from the beginning to work at your own level. To me, that means, they're giving you recommendations, but you can do what your body needs."

Kristin shook her head approvingly at Jean. She had been coming at this ashram yoga from an entirely different perspective. As usual, it sure was nice to have Jean put it to her in another light.

"It seems like every time I go deeper into yoga, more and more of my stuff comes up. Like, I'm always dealing with unresolved emotions, judgments or negative feelings. It's becoming exhausting!"

Jean laughed and agreed.

"True," said Jean, "but you know, if we didn't have something like yoga to grow from, think about how messed up we would be!"

"Well, they do say ignorance is bliss!" Kristin replied with a smile.

"That must explain why my mother-in-law was always so happy!"

Jean and Kristin started laughing loudly. A few people walked by smiling at them. Jean had an infectious personality. Even the sound of her laugh made others smile.

"So, what's on your mind, jelly bean?" Jean asked Kristin. "What stuff is coming up for you now?"

"I'm not sure. I just find myself irritated with the schedule and all the rules. And then there's no variety in the yoga classes either. I like the idea of going deeper. I enjoy chanting and meditation and yoga. I do. But I'm not used to getting up this early and going and going and having to be on point so much. I'm tired. I kind of want a cigarette…and a hamburger…now I'm just complaining," Kristin realized.

"Well, heck, I would LOVE a hamburger too! Maybe we can sneak out and get one!" Jean was smiling, but Kristin was not taking it as a joke.

"Can we? Where would we go?" Kristin said brightly.

The women decided to look into those options tomorrow. As it was getting late and there was another early morning the next day, they both decided to call it a night and meet at the morning programs. Kristin went off to bed silently, smiling with the potential of sneaking out of the ashram and grabbing a hamburger! Something about that idea delighted her to no end. She fell fast asleep that night with a smile on her face.

* * *

The morning came too soon. Kristin was not ready to get up. In fact, she was pretty annoyed about it. The only reason she decided to get out of bed was to find Jean. If it weren't for her little Minnesotan guardian angel, she knew that she would have stayed in bed that morning and slept in. Kristin yawned wide as she walked into the meditation hall that morning. Many people were already seated quietly. A quick glance did not produce sight of Jean, so she chose a place to sit near the back so that she could watch people come in and leave.

After the morning session, she still hadn't seen Jean. But as she was getting onto her yoga mat to prepare for class, Jean's familiar face plopped down next to her.

"Hey!" Kristin said, smiling. "I was looking for you this morning."

"Yea?" Jean sounded puzzled. "I decided to sleep in. I was pretty tired from yesterday's traveling and the late night. I'm feeling ready now!"

Kristin found herself annoyed, but not with Jean. She was annoyed with herself for not sleeping in too because the reality was she could have used it. She did not share this with Jean. She did not want her friend to know how she felt. So Kristin pushed it in and waited for the teacher to arrive and begin class. She felt her back starting to lock up, and realized her old pattern had fully returned. She was holding in her emotions, and her body was talking to her. She knew that she would have to remedy that on the mat.

There were no surprises in class. The sequence of the postures, breathing exercises, chants and meditations went off exactly the same way as it had the day before, except that the teacher was now a tall, skinny kid from the Ukraine. Kristin was starting to learn some of the script now and even found it somewhat enjoyable when she knew what was coming. She even found herself smiling once. She took a lot of exhales through her mouth during class. She allowed herself to rest more often and come out of the poses. She even allowed herself to move more and do other things within the postures if she felt that she needed to. She found the class to be much more enjoyable, and at one point the Ukrainian teacher came by and offered her an even different variation of something that she was doing. At the end, she was more than ready for brunch. She felt like she had really worked up an appetite.

Again, they ate in silence, but after the meal Kristin told Jean she would catch up with her later and decided to find a nice, quiet place to sit and relax. She soon dozed off, getting the extra sleep that she had desperately needed. When she awoke, Kristin felt refreshed. She had no idea what time it was, so she decided to go find out and was surprised to know that the evening session was about to begin in twenty minutes. She mulled it over for a few minutes, wondering if she wanted to attend or not. Part of her wanted to go to her room and hide. Another part of her wanted to do the class. Kristin had to really sit and figure out if doing the class was for her or if she just wanted to see Jean. Ultimately, she decided it might have been a little of both.

Since she was feeling more energized, Kristin began heading to the beginner's class, when a group of people with yoga mats walking in another direction caught her attention. She interrupted one of them to inquire which class they were attending and when they said the intermediate, Kristin decided to turn around and join them. Kristin didn't know why she had made this sudden decision, but she went with it, feeling content and ready.

The class began similar to the beginner class, with sections feeling a little longer, perhaps. Since she wasn't watching the clock, she couldn't be sure. Once the postures began, Kristin noticed that more advanced variations were being given, with slight deviations from the basic postures. She liked this. And although she was given the variations to do the postures differently, Kristin held back and still conducted them from the basic and beginner perspective. This seemed ironic, since her main annoyance had been the structure, yet here she was, doing it the same way anyway.

She found her thoughts drifting back to her previous job. Kristin remembered being hidden in a cubicle, unhappy with her life, physically ill, and mentally a mess. She thought of Jeff. She remembered how unhealthy her life was and her lack of any understanding of how disturbingly negative she was. She thought about the deadlines and working weekends when she hadn't finished reports. Kristin remembered what it felt like during the cuts and watching some of her work friends get fired, wondering if she would be next on the chopping block. She remembered how confined her life had felt back then — how hopeless. And right then, in the middle of the pose and the class, she began to cry. Were they tears of sadness or tears of joy? She wasn't quite sure.

Coming gently out of the posture, Kristin came into child's pose and continued to cry. She tried not to wail loudly, but she didn't hold back. She allowed the tears to stream down her face and onto her mat. She felt her back heaving up and down as she wept, but she allowed it to happen. And for once, she really didn't care who knew it. And the thing was, nobody else seemed to notice anyway.

After a good cry, Kristin lay down on her back for final relaxation. The rest of the class would be there soon, for that she knew. She decided to arrive early and let herself rest and integrate what had just happened. She felt lighter. Again, she had released something.

The rest of the trip at the ashram went more effortlessly for Kristin. She allowed herself to go with the flow. She didn't worry about the schedule and she also didn't push herself if she felt she needed to rest or pull back. Sometimes Kristin attended beginner and other times intermediate classes. She chose not to attend any advanced classes because she felt like she was right where she needed to be, that lesson learned back in the good old U.S.-of-A a while back!

She and Jean found each other here and there. But she also did not find herself needing to search Jean out like earlier. When they did meet up it felt natural and right. And when

Kristin was on her own she would often meet another interesting person from a different country or state. She even enjoyed her alone time too. Kristin personally enjoyed eating quietly during mealtimes. She noticed that she enjoyed the food more when she focused on chewing and what she was eating. She found herself praying in gratitude for each beautifully prepared meal, and not worrying if she would like anything that was made. Kristin always had enough, and she and Jean never did sneak out for that hamburger.

When the day came for her to leave and travel home, Kristin felt like she could have stayed even longer. But at the same time, she welcomed going home to a familiar bed with Joshua. She was even looking forward to seeing her co-workers at the bank on Monday. This time she and Jean exchanged phone numbers. She was not going to let this woman float out of her life again. And with an open travel buddy to India, who knew when they could take up and take flight!

Kristin had a sense that the trip to India would not be happening any time soon, however. This "lite" version of living the life of a yogi had been challenging enough for her. And although she enjoyed growing, changing and becoming a better person, that didn't mean that she was ready to go to India to find herself — like the stories of many others doing so that she had been reading in yoga magazines. She was coming to realize that her journey was hers and hers alone. And her journey would be different from everyone else's. After all, there was still a lot of good inside her. And she decided with clarity that she would focus more on how she could use those good qualities within her to help others right at home.

Excited to get home, Kristin put out to the universe to show her a sign of just how she could do that.

Chapter 21

Integration

"Yoga is an interior penetration leading to integration of being, senses, breath, mind, intelligence, consciousness, and Self. It is definitely an inward journey, evolution through involution, toward the Soul, which in turn desires to emerge and embrace you in its glory." ~ B.K.S. Iyengar

Kristin had just finished her first batch of homemade hummus. She was quite proud of herself. She had soaked the chickpeas overnight, gathered the garlic, olive oil, tahini and other ingredients, and began a slow process of blending it all together to make a healthy protein-rich snack to share at their picnic the next day. Joshua came by and enthusiastically stuck his finger into the hummus, then into his mouth.

"Hey!" Kristin smiled. "This is for people!"

"Well, I'm people!" he said jokingly, swinging her around and dipping her back for a kiss.

She giggled like a little girl, kissing him sweetly. They shared a loving smile, and then she pointed to the hummus and softly asked, "So, what do you think?"

Joshua squished his tongue around in his mouth, bounced his head from side to side, and made unsure faces. She slapped him on the arm for teasing her.

"It's good!" he said, pretending that her slap on the arm actually hurt. "Maybe some more salt?"

She took a sample for herself. Perhaps he was right. It needed a little something else.

"The consistency is good though," Joshua finished. "It's almost there!"

"That should be the story of my life, *Almost There.*" Kristin laughed, grabbing the salt to add a few pinches and remix the hummus. As she swirled the spoon around the bowl, Joshua sat down on a chair in the kitchen, suddenly remembering something.

"Hey, there's a *kirtan* event next Saturday at Universal Yoga, do you want to go? I can get us tickets. Neil came into the bank today and said he had some extra."

Kristin nodded positively to his question. She hadn't seen Neil since he had finished his yoga teacher training and started working at a nearby studio. She loved the idea of seeing her old yoga buddy and chanting, so the *kirtan* sounded great.

"I was thinking we could bring the kids," Joshua said.

Kristin beamed with delight. This would be their first official yoga-related event. With how much yoga had helped her with her life, she only wished that she had known about it at their age. Perhaps it would have spared her a lot of undue aggravation and helped her move more smoothly through life's challenges. She had secretly wanted Joshua to involve the kids in it in some way, but she didn't want to push. She had been sending him the vibes about it, knowing that he was getting them on some level.

"They will love it. Especially if they can clap and dance," she said.

"I was thinking that too," Joshua said warmly. He had been looking for such an event to bring the kids to that had positive energy and the type of lively fun that would keep them entertained. *Kirtan* seemed perfect. He knew it would mean a lot to Kristin, and would be another great bonding experience for them all. Besides, she had been secretly sending him messages to do something with them through yoga. He had heard her loud and clear.

As in all divine timing, the kids bounced into the kitchen just at that moment and Joshua presented them with the idea of going to the event.

"So, it's singing?" said Michael, confused.

"Well, kind of," Kristin said. "You are singing, but someone sings a line first, and then the rest of us repeat it. And the beat and the tempo changes and gets faster as we chant. Some people even stand up, clap and dance around."

"I love to dance!" cried Gabriella.

"We know!" Michael said, very big brotherly.

"I love to sing too," she said hopping onto Joshua's lap. "I want to go, Daddy."

Joshua nodded to his little girl, then turned to his inquisitive son. "Michael, what do you think?"

Michael moved his mouth around a bit, considering it. Kristin watched him mimic the same faces that Joshua had made moments ago when questioned about the hummus. Michael was a little "mini-me" version of him. She found it adorable.

After some deliberation, Michael smiled and with a smirk on his face inquired, "Can we go out to dinner after, too?"

This was another trait that Michael had learned from his father: how to work both sides or as her uncle would say, "Kill two birds with one stone." Kristin never quite liked that idiom. She wondered often why birds needed to be killed in that scenario. Somewhere in one of her spiritual books she'd read, "feed two birds with one seed" and liked that much more. But back to the current situation — Kristin often thought that Joshua would have made an excellent lawyer. Perhaps that was in Michael's future. It was a little early for those declarations, however. For now, she could only hope he would find something that showcased his skills.

In response to the dinner question, in unison Kristin said, "Yes" and Joshua said, "No." The two then looked at each other inquisitively. The kids seemed shocked too. Normally they finished each other's sentences and were on the same page. What was up with this? Everyone was looking around wondering the same thing.

Joshua laughed. He loved to get them all thinking. He went on to explain further, "Well, the *Kirtan* is at 7:30, so we should probably go out to dinner *before* it."

"Daddy! You are so funny!" Gabriella said, planting a big kiss on her father's cheek, and bouncing up and down on his lap. She was a truly happy kid, the infectious happiness kind that you like to be around. Of course, she was only five, or "five and a half!" as Gabrielle liked to remind everyone, daily. Everyone hoped that she would remain this happy and carefree as she aged. Kristin had planned on supporting that in any way that she could. She knew all too well how easy it was to lose your sense of self and forget to enjoy life. If she had her druthers, that was not going to happen to Joshua's children.

"What's that?" Michael asked, abruptly changing the subject and pointing to the hummus. The look on his face seemed to say he was not too keen about the looks of it.

"It's hummus," Kristin said, "want to try it?"

Michael tilted the right side of his mouth up towards his nose and shook his head no.

"Are we ever going to have chicken nuggets again?" the boy finally replied in defiance, no doubt to Kristin's recent interest in vegetarianism. She was aware that this diet was not for everyone. Kristin had tried to keep a good balance for Joshua and the kids and to not press it upon them, unless they were interested in trying it themselves. For her own self, she was enjoying the newfound energy that she had now that she was eating mostly organic, whole foods. But she understood that even a few months ago she would have wanted some meat too. In fact, there were some days where she also thought about it.

But after learning more about the meat industry in the country and the inhumane treatment of animals, Kristin just had a very difficult time actually putting it into her mouth anymore and enjoying it. As long as she didn't smell any bacon cooking, she was pretty good at sticking to the vegetarian way of life. If she did, however, all bets were off and she was eating the bacon!

"We will have hamburgers and turkey burgers tomorrow at the picnic," Kristin replied. She understood it was not the same as chicken nuggets, but she had to draw the line somewhere. She and Joshua had agreed that they were not going to be eating processed foods. While they couldn't control what the children ate when they were at their mother's house, at theirs, they were going to eat as healthy as they could. And truthfully, their mother was also trying to keep them to a healthier diet.

"I'll try it," said Gabriella. "Is it healthy?"

Kristin laughed and told her that she had tried to make it as healthy as possible. If Michael was Joshua's mini-me, Gabriella was her shadow. She had taken to liking pretty much anything that Kristin did. Surprisingly, Kristin enjoyed her little shadow. She loved the feeling she got when Gabriella smiled and twinkled those little eyes at her. She loved watching Michael mimic his father, unknowingly. Kristin thoroughly enjoyed having these two in her life. Enjoying children surely was a new concept for her. Previously, children presented as more of a sticky, dirty nuisance. With her new life path of living more like a yogi by eating better, meditating, practicing yoga, living more mindfully and opening her heart, she had transformed into a totally different person. Everyone in her life had commented on the positive changes Kristin had made and how much happier and healthier she looked. And it was true. She was content, even. And it felt good.

Kristin put a tiny bit of hummus on a spoon and handed it to Gabriella. She licked it like peanut butter and made funny movements with her tongue assessing the texture and taste. She was trying to be like her brother. Kristin could see a little bit of Joshua in there too when she made the faces. She smiled, awaiting the response.

"May I please have some more? I am not sure if I like it," she finally said.

Joshua held back a laugh as Kristin put some more hummus on the spoon and "airplaned" it into Gabriella's mouth. She giggled and grabbed her stomach as she ate the hummus. She nodded and said, "I think it needs some salt."

Kristin and Joshua both laughed. *How could this kid know it needs salt?* Kristin thought. She must have been listening in on their conversation before she came into the kitchen. Kristin had caught her watching the two of them many times before. She commented to Joshua that it was a good thing they were always on good behavior, lest the little ones see something that their little eyes shouldn't!

"Why don't you kids go wash up and get ready for bed? We have a big day here tomorrow," Joshua instructed the children.

"Huh?" asked Michael.

"The picnic, remember, silly?" Gabriella told her brother, as she shook her head disapprovingly and folded her arms in front of her chest. That was a move she learned from her mother. Kristin had seen it several times by now. It was sort of their mother's signature move. Thankfully Joshua's ex was a good woman and a nice person, but in knowing her more she was starting to see why she and Joshua's marriage had not worked out. Kristin's ego liked to remind her that she was much better suited for Joshua than his wife was. But others had commented as much to her as well. In any event, keeping an amicable relationship with each other surely meant that her relationship with Joshua and the children would have one less hurtle to maneuver through. And for that, she was quite grateful. Gratitude was another thing that Joshua had taught her about. For no matter what the situation, he always seemed to find something about it to be grateful for. She learned something from that man every day. Kristin only hoped that she was giving him as much in their relationship as she was getting. She sure was trying.

"Right..." Michael said, nodding in affirmation. "Hey, will there be anyone my age to play with?"

"Yes, my niece is coming. And I think also some other friends are bringing their kids too. Trust me, we'll have games to play and there'll be a lot to do. You won't be bored," Kristin assured Michael.

He smiled and skipped out of the room. Joshua gently tossed little Gabriella off his lap and patted her bottom so that she would go along after her brother. She knew the drill and followed happily along.

Joshua got up and walked behind Kristin, folding his hands around her waist and resting his head on her shoulder. She reached up and patted his head. They rocked a little from side to side, and she put a little more salted hummus on a spoon and fed it to him.

"Mmm, you got it!" he said, kissing her neck. "So, what else do I need to get for tomorrow?"

"Just the ice. Everything else is ready. Everyone is bringing a dish to share. There's not much else to do, really."

"Good, so once the kids are in bed, we can sit down and relax!" He was certainly looking forward to putting his feet up and unwinding. Life was good, but it was even better when he could plop on the couch at home with his best friend.

"Yes!" Kristin was certainly ready to sit down and rest after a week of work and an evening of preparing things for the picnic. She had even taken off work today to get everything ready so that she could chill out and enjoy the day with her friends and relatives tomorrow. But even though there was so much going on, she wasn't tired. She was excited, kind of like a kid on Christmas morning. This was her and Joshua's first official party together since they had moved in together. They had both invited an assortment of friends. Kristin would be seeing old work colleagues, new yoga friends, buddies of Joshua's, and family on both sides. For the first time, all the people that she loved would be together in the same place — their place — their home. She couldn't have asked for more. She was in the full-cup-runneth-over mode!

Kristin sighed and began to put away the hummus as Joshua went upstairs to start squaring away the kids for bed.

Gabriella was already in bed waiting for her story. Michael, of course, was still in the bathroom, doing whatever boys do to avoid going to bed. He did not feel the need to disturb his son. Instead, Joshua lay down with his little girl and prepared to read her a story.

"Daddy, I want you to read this one to me. It's the one Kristin gave me for my birthday," she said sweetly.

"Are you sure you don't want Kristin to read it to you?" he asked.

"Daddy, *you* read my stories," she reminded him, grabbing his arm and thrusting the book into his hands. She then fluffed up her pillow and threw her head back on it. "Whenever you're ready, Daddy," she ordered.

Joshua laughed. She was too much, that kid. He looked down at the book: Shel Silverstein's classic *The Giving Tree*. He read the sad, but comforting story to his little girl and she often paused his hand to gaze at the pictures a little longer before she let him turn the pages. The truth was that she could have probably read the book to him, for she had memorized most of its passages. But she still wanted Daddy to read to her, and every other night, she chose this book, probably because it was something Kristin had given her. This little book and what it meant to his daughter made his heart swoon.

When he finished reading the book, he closed it and kissed his little girl's head. She clasped her hands in front of her belly and sighed.

"So, the tree and the boy are happy again," she continued, "because they still have each other and they are not lonely."

"That's right," Joshua replied, kissing her one more time.

Gabriella reached around to hug her father, and then said goodnight to him. That was his cue to leave. She always decided when she was ready to go to bed.

"Do you want me to send Kristin in to say goodnight to you?" he asked, just about to turn off her light.

His daughter bolted upright and gave him a stern look.

"Of course!" she replied, annoyed that he even had to ask. Then plopped her head back down on the pillow and pretended that she was already asleep.

Enough said.

He shut off her light, and went on to find his son.

Moments later Kristin came in to tuck Gabriella into bed and kiss her goodnight. Kristin always gave her butterfly kisses by gently touching their eyelashes together and blinking. It was their little thing. After a quick hug, she moved on and after peeking into Michael's room to say goodnight, she headed downstairs to sit with Joshua on the couch.

He had lit a candle. She lit a little incense. It was Nag Champa she had gotten from the yoga studio. Then they cuddled together in the quiet living room. Although there were many times when they finished each other's sentences, they also were able to sit quietly together. They did this for some time before either spoke, enjoying the fragrant incense wafting about and the soothing flickering of the candle and the designs it made as the light danced around the room. Neither of them had any idea how long it had been since they sat quietly and relaxed. Both were completely content.

"Gabriella is excited about *kirtan* next week," Kristin finally said, softly, indicating what she was thinking about.

He smiled and replied, "Gabriella would be excited about jumping out of a plane if you did it too."

She let out a soft laugh and replied, "Well, good thing I don't do that!"

"Hey, don't knock it until you try it!" he teased her. "I think your mother's boyfriend did that just last week!"

They laughed and Kristin reached for the throw blanket and pulled it up over her legs. She lay back against Joshua and sighed. With the blanket, she felt even comfier, if that were even possible.

"What time is everyone coming over again?" he asked. Joshua knew the answer to that question. She wasn't quite sure why he had asked.
"Around one. Why are you asking?"

"Just wondering how long I can lie around in my underwear."

"Hah!" Kristin laughed exuberantly, "as if Gabriella isn't going to have you up at seven anyway."

"True." he said. "Should I let you sleep in?"

She shook her head, "No, I'm still getting up to meditate and do a light yoga practice. I'll do that when you guys get up."

"Meditate? Hmm, maybe she'll sleep in and I can join you," he said.

"Well, you don't need me to meditate. It's not a partner sport," she teased him back. Joshua tickled her on her ribs and she jumped up. He quickly pulled her back to him. This time he sighed. And they were quiet again for a little while before he broke the silence.

"Are you meditating now?" he teased.

"Stop it!" she laughed. "I'm just relaxing, like you."

"Isn't that meditation…or final relaxation? It's like the same thing," he responded to her comment, again in a teasing fashion.

Kristin let out a disapproving sound. Joshua reacted by shrugging his shoulders.

"Maybe you're right. I don't know. You can ask Nayana tomorrow — or Annie. One of them will have a better answer for you. I'm still learning this stuff, you know. I am a novice."

Kristin was not kidding about feeling like a newcomer either. The more she learned about the practice of yoga and meditation, the more she realized how much more there was to understand and just how little she actually knew about it in the first place. It was quite humbling, actually. This thousands-year-old practice seemed never-ending and she often wondered how the ancients came to realize all of this so long ago, at a time when there were no technologies to help them figure anything out. Or maybe that was the key to it, that all they had was time to reflect, and with patience and consistency, they mastered the answers to all of life's questions and to enlightenment. She wasn't about to get into yoga philosophy with Joshua that night, for he was in a teasing mood. Teasing was okay too. Although yoga had become a very important part of her life, it wasn't the only thing in it either. She had found something even more important: love. Not just love of a man, but love of life. Kristin had found a true sense of peace and happiness in the present moment, perhaps what she truly thought the goal, if there were one, to yoga. Then again, she could be terribly wrong and way off base. She was still integrating all that she had learned over the past year through these practices. But boy, look how far she had already come! If she could change so much in just a year, she wondered where she would be in another year, or five, or more. Kristin smiled thinking about how much better life could be.

As Kristin lay her head down on her pillow that evening, her last thoughts before falling asleep were that of complete gratitude. She felt grateful for her injuries and her issues that had led her, albeit kicking and screaming, to her first yoga class. She was grateful to have family and friends who had not given up on her when she was at her lowest. The gratitude she felt for her amazing teachers whom she continued to learn from every day was also particularly important to her. Kristin realized how urgently she had needed their patient guidance. And, of course, had it not been for all of that, while she still may have met Joshua through her sister, she certainly wouldn't have been able to open up to loving him and his children as she had. Gratitude seemed to overwhelm her emotionally, and a tiny tear of joy escaped her eye. How lucky she was, indeed.

As Kristin bathed in that energy of love and appreciation for all of the challenges that had gotten her to that point, she felt a warmth surround her that she had never felt before. She could only describe it later as angel wings wrapping around her body, in a soft, comforting embrace. She felt her heart center expand energetically wider than she had felt it go before as it reached beyond her body and opened like a beautiful lotus flower. She was drawn to open her eyes and, when she did, the face of the digital clock immediately clicked to 11:11.

Kristin smiled and closed her eyes. As she fell off to sleep, she knew without hesitation, that she had just had another energetic awakening like that time in Mexico near El Castillo. She was certain that the master number eleven was confirming that she was expanding to greater love and true oneness. And she understood how fortunate she was to now be integrating it into her entire life.

Chapter 22

The Yogini Emerges

"Who you are is what you love, not what loves you."
~ Baron Baptiste

With the picnic in full swing and being gifted a beautiful day, Kristin floated about the yard between friends and family. While the kids played, the adults laughed and talked for hours. A lively game of horseshoes sprouted up in the latter part of the day when Joshua and Neil challenged Sam and Brian to a game. Just the thought of those four people together playing horseshoes tickled Kristin to no end! What an eclectic crew they were! Those four men, certainly, on the surface, seemed to have a world of difference between each of them, but watching them together, Kristin realized just how much they also had in common. They were all really good men who didn't need much around them but love, and maybe a cold brew, in order to enjoy themselves.

Sandy and Kristin happened to be watching the match at the moment, when Sandy gently nudged her sister in the arm.

"There's your boyfriend," Sandy said in a teasing way as she nodded towards Joshua.

Kristin nudged her sister and responded in same, "So what, there's yours."

The two women giggled. Kristin hadn't felt this close to her sister in a very long time. She was happy about that too.

"So, any talk of you two getting engaged anytime soon?" Sandy said to her sister teasingly.

Kristin quickly pushed her sister.

"No, stop it. We are perfectly happy the way things are right now. I don't need a ring or to be engaged to change how I feel. And I know how he feels," replied Kristin.

Sandy seemed unconvinced as she simply replied sarcastically, "Uh-huh…"

Kristin gave her sister a look — the disapproving kind of sister look.

"Sandy, things are different from when you and Sam got married, you know. People don't necessarily even get married anymore. Lots of people live happily together without needing a piece of paper saying it is more sacred."

Now Sandy returned her sister's disapproving look.

"See, you just said, 'sacred,' as if marriage was not a solemn and sacred vow that you take. It is just that. It does mean something more than living together."

Kristin rolled her eyes. Even with her newfound enlightenment, she still didn't like when her sister was right. She decided to let it go without another remark. Instead she went about cheering on the guys.

"Get 'em, honey. Watch out for Brian, he used to win horseshoes at the company picnics! He's a ringer!"

Brian threw his hands up in the air, and yelled back, "Why you giving away my secrets?"

She laughed, he laughed, and the guys continued to throw their shoes. Just then Kristin's mom came walking up with Joshua's mother, who was in town for a visit.

"Kristin, Eleanor was just telling me that you're vegetarian now! I am so glad that you're finally taking care of what you are putting inside your body."

Kristin rolled her eyes again, wondering, *Why is it so much harder to let things go around your own family?* Then she remembered a famous Ram Das quote, "If you think you're so enlightened, go spend a week with your family." This was certainly true. These people knew exactly how to push her buttons. It was comforting to know that a well-known yogi like Ram Das also acknowledged this to be true. To her chagrin, her mother continued:

"Eleanor," she said, tugging at Joshua's mother's arm, "this girl used to be the worst eater. When she was little I would tell her she couldn't leave the table until she ate all her vegetables. Kristin would sit there all night. She was so patient. She would wait me out until I finally told her to go to bed. Then when she lived by herself she would eat macaroni and cheese or those horrible canned noodles, what are they called?"

Without skipping a beat, Sandy chimed in, "Spaghetti-os."

This wasn't the story as Kristin had remembered it. Of course her mother and her sister were finding something to team up against her about.

"Thanks, Sandy," she said, slapping her sister's arm. There was a feeling of relief that the children were out of hearing range about the canned spaghetti, lest that fuel more fire for Michael's desire to eat chicken fingers.

"Oh, Spaghetti-os, that's right. Those horrid, fake meals in a can! She wouldn't cook, this girl. She wouldn't eat anything good for her. She was a real mess."

Kristin's mother finished the comments by folding her hands in front of herself and shaking her head. Joshua's mother, Eleanor, simply laughed, and then graciously replied, "Well, you could have fooled me. Look at this healthy spread she put out today for us." Eleanor smiled, and then leaned towards Kristin. "It's all very lovely, dear."

"Thank you, Eleanor," Kristin said, then she stuck her tongue out at her mother and sister. Sandy stuck her tongue back out at Kristin. Her mother simply shook her head. For all the personal growth that she had done, Kristin still acted six years old around her family.

"I'll tell you what else," Eleanor continued, "my grandchildren certainly are looking healthy since she has been taking care of them. And I know that Gabriella just thinks the world about you! You should hear the way she talks about you, Kristin."

Kristin felt herself start to sparkle like a star. It truly filled her with joy to know that she was being a positive influence on the life of the kids. Not that they didn't already have wonderful influences in their life, but now she was also contributing to the enhancement of their growth as little spiritual beings. This made her very happy.

Kristin looked around to see just where that little minion, Gabriella, was and what she was up to. She found her sitting on Melissa's lap talking quite expressively with her hands. She tried to figure out just what was being discussed. She watched Melissa laugh and reply with her hands, but she couldn't make it out. It could have been anything knowing those two. And if you couldn't tell their ages apart by looking, you would probably think that they were very close in age by the way they got along. Kristin smiled.

She moved her gaze from Melissa and Gabriella because Michael and Brenda went running past them. Kristin watched them run around the table, grab a cookie, and keep going. She wondered just how many times they might have done that today and nobody noticed. *Everyone deserves some cookies*, she thought. Besides, unbeknownst to them, they were vegan cookies. Kristin smiled devilishly knowing she had fooled them into eating healthy snacks, and they would never know it.

As she moved her gaze to the table, she noticed past and present co-workers mingling and talking. They too seemed quite happy, but you could see and feel the difference in the business discourse happening at that table, versus the lively upbeat one transpiring between Gabriella and Melissa. She had thought to invite her old boss, Tom and secretary, Betty. Betty, as it turned out, had retired and moved to Florida with her husband, but Tom happily made the picnic with his wife. They were currently discussing something with Shea and Lynn from the bank where she currently worked. She rarely talked work outside the bank. Working there was a fine job and it afforded her many comforts, but at the end of the day, Kristin was clear that it was not her life's purpose to open new checking or retirement accounts for people. But she was grateful for it nonetheless.

Kristin thought about going over to see what they were talking about and mingle, but they seemed to be getting along just fine without her. She wondered if she was looking for a reason to get away from her family or not. She figured she would drop back in on them a little later. She should probably be with her family a little longer and work on that gratitude.

As Kristin glanced back towards the horseshoe pits, she noticed her yoga friends having fun playing with some acrobatic yoga or "Acro" yoga poses, near the sunny side of the yard. Annie's girlfriend was lying on the ground with her legs in the air, while Annie lay backwards from her feet, reaching her arms down to her girlfriend in a backbend. Nayana and some others stood around encouraging the play, and providing potential support in the event that something went awry. When Annie started to fall to the side, Nayana went in to hold her, and managed to fall into a big pile with the other two women. Everyone applauded as the three women laughed and rolled in the grass. Now that was something Kristin could easily get involved in. Well, the lying in the grass part, anyway. She had decided to stick to more conservative yoga practices rather than to push herself in some strange way. Kristin understood now the importance of knowing your own edge, which was that place of comfort and ease, yet with effort, in the practice. She knew that she still had a little ways to go for the ease part to come, but she also knew that she had to acknowledge and honor her limitations too. After all, she had certainly come a long way in creating a more healthy life for herself, even if she hadn't started out that way as her mother had so nicely reminded everyone just moments ago. Yes, while she was looking about the yard and watching all her friends mingling and playing, she was also somewhat aware that her mother was still rambling on and on about her previous ways.

"Kristin," her mother broke into her chain of thoughts, "I was talking to Neil. Why don't you enroll in the yoga teacher training?"

"Huh?" Kristin replied to her mother. This wasn't just in response to half listening to her, but also because she didn't think she had any right to apply to yoga training.

"Yoga teacher training. I mean, you love it so much, you work at the desk at the studio twice a week and you do all these fancy retreats. Why don't you become a yoga teacher?"

Her mother, sister, and Eleanor waited patiently for her response. The thing was, she didn't really have one.

"I really hadn't given that any thought. I mean, I am still just learning about yoga," she finally said.

"Well, isn't that a way to learn more?" her mother retorted.

She looked at her mother and smiled.

"Yes, Mom. I suppose it is."

Her mother smiled back, pleased at herself for bringing it up. She then took Eleanor by the hand and led her away talking about a new herbalist that had moved into town. With a positive-thinking mother like hers, Kristin wondered how she had gotten so off track for such a long time. If she had only listened to her mother years ago instead of fighting her every step of the way, perhaps she would have been a healthier person back then. She both acknowledged that, and knew that she would never reveal the fact that she acknowledged it to her mother. Instead she just smiled as her mother and Eleanor walked away, gossiping about all things healthy.

Gabriella ran up to her, holding Melissa's hand.

"Kristin, Kristin, did you hear the news? It's AMAZE-BALLS!" Gabriella screeched in delight.

Melissa was smiling ear to ear. Gabriella covered her hands over her mouth to contain the new information, but nothing was forthcoming.

Impatiently, Sandy spoke up, "What is it?"

That's when Kristin noticed Melissa holding her hands over her stomach. Her jaw fell open, and as she was about to say it, Gabriella belted it out: "Melissa is having a baby!" She quickly threw her hands back over her mouth, as if the cat wasn't already out of the bag.

Sandy went for Melissa, "Oh, My God!!! This is so awesome! Congratulations!"

Gabriella screeched and jumped up and down. Kristin took her hand and joined her. Sandy and Melissa all jumped up and down too. Soon everyone was gathering to hear the news. When Melissa shared that she was three and a half months pregnant, everyone cheered regardless if they knew Melissa or not. Joshua proposed a toast to the happy soon-to-be parents, and gushed about the joy that they would soon find. Eleanor grabbed her son's face and told everyone what happiness he had brought to their family and how she wished the same for Melissa and Bob. One by one, many of the picnic goers gave their own blessings for the parents. There certainly was something about baby news that seemed to really bring people together. Kristin found herself crying with joy, along with Melissa and many of the others. She was no longer afraid to show her emotions in public. In fact, she was often proud to.

Kristin felt a little tugging at her shirt. Looking down, Gabriella was gazing up at her, lovingly.

"Why are you crying?" she asked Kristin.

Kristin leaned down and picked up the little munchkin. "I'm crying because I'm so happy for my friend."

"Oh, I thought maybe you were crying because you don't have a baby," replied Gabriella. But before Kristin could reply, she brightened up. "Maybe you and Daddy can have a baby!"

Kristin laughed and gave her a little kiss, "I don't need to have a baby. I have you and Michael in my life, my niece and now Melissa's soon-to-be baby. I feel so full already."

Gabriella threw her arms around Kristin. She wiped her eyes and caught Joshua smiling at them. Kristin couldn't be sure if he had heard the conversation or not, but she didn't care. She wasn't looking to have a baby, and he knew it. They were both perfectly happy with the current situation.

Kristin's mother interrupted all the good news with her newest and most brilliant idea.

"Kristin, you should teach children's yoga!"

The attention shifted abruptly from Melissa's happy news to what appeared to be Kristin's. She was not comfortable with that. Kristin gave her mother a disapproving look.

"Can we be happy about the new baby just for a minute, Mom!?" Kristin yelled sternly.

But Melissa had no qualms about shifting the attention. "Kris, you have a couple of years to get a certification in kid's yoga before mine is old enough to teach. You should totally do it! I'll preregister him, or her now!"

Gabriella started to bounce up and down in her arms. "I will be your first student! And I will be the best student," she told her.

Michael and Brenda started to move organically into yoga poses. They pressed their hands together at their heart and balanced on one leg.

"Look, Aunt Kristin!" Brenda bellowed, then fell over.

"See, you already have students," Kristin's mother announced matter-of-factly.

Kristin thought to herself, *Hmm, that woman is probably right again,* but decided not to share the thought out loud. She simply nodded and smiled.

* * *

Later that evening, once the picnic had ended and the kids were in bed, Joshua and Kristin finally had a chance to relax right where they had the previous night in preparation for the picnic. As the last of the party was cleared up, she plopped down on the couch and took a resounding sigh, or surrender breath as they called it in yoga. It never ceased to make her laugh when she did one of those, considering how silly it sounded when she first had heard this breathing technique. Well, it still was quite funny sounding, but she got it and thoroughly enjoyed the release that it gave her when she did it. Joshua took one as well. For as much fun as gatherings were, they were still a lot of work. Both were quiet for some time after the long sighs, enjoying the silence and relaxation. Well, Kristin was just enjoying the silence. Joshua was too, but he also had other things on his mind. He finally opened up the conversation, after considering it for some time.

"So, what do you think about what your mother said?"

There were so many possible answers to that question. But because she wasn't quite sure which comment he was referring to, she asked for further clarification. Kristin didn't want to assume it was one of the embarrassing remarks that her mother had made.

"Becoming a kids' yoga teacher," he clarified.

"I don't know. I honestly hadn't thought about it before she brought it up today. What do you think about it?"

Without skipping a beat he answered, "I think you'd be an amazing kids' yoga teacher. I see how you are with kids and they love you! And you love yoga. I think it's a great fit."

Kristin nodded her head. She was still assessing the idea. Something in her lit up after her mother had brought up the idea, and she wasn't sure why. She still questioned if she was ready to be a yoga teacher, however the thought of teaching children a practice that they could use to help them throughout their life seemed more than worthwhile. Nowadays, she heard about so many issues that kids were dealing with, that she and her friends never had when they were younger. It was a new time that they were living in. Information was coming fast and furiously and it seemed like children never had any down time to just play and be free anymore. There were certainly different stressors today. Kristin remembered being young and getting home from school and anticipating seeing her friends the next day to find out what they had done the previous evening or over the weekend. Kids today were in touch with each other every second of the day in this digital era, so there is nothing to wait for. They don't even have to go to the library to discover things. If they have a question, they can Google it and in seconds have the answer.

While Kristin found some of these technologies to be beneficial, she had a feeling that it was causing so many of these other issues to occur for children. In an effort to make progress, she wondered if society hadn't forgotten about the things that were more important in life; namely, connecting to nature, natural energies, and each other as human beings. It was kind of sad, really. She just knew how much the practices of yoga had helped her reconnect body, mind and soul. Why wouldn't this be a good tool for children? She added the thought, *before it's too late and they become unhappy adults.*

"What are you thinking?" Joshua asked her, recognizing that she was deep in thought.

"I guess I am wondering if that's what I am supposed to do. I mean, that's a big responsibility, isn't it? I don't have my own kids so this is asking people to trust me with their own children's well-being. And I mean, I have only been practicing yoga for a short time now."

Joshua didn't see what the big deal was. He thought she would be a terrific yoga teacher in general. He had watched her grow from the practice in wonderful ways. She had a smile in her heart that lightened a room. She honestly cared for others without any hidden agendas. She was always striving to better herself and her understanding of the practice and the world. And he saw how she was with his children. They may have not been ones that she created, but she certainly was a mother to them now.

"I think that it just keeps going, ya know?" Joshua continued. "I think you just keep learning and deepening your connection to things. I think if you are waiting to be an enlightened being to start teaching, you are going to miss out on some incredible experiences helping others find their peace. I understand your integrity to the tradition. But what about how it can help people? After all, if we get to kids while they are young, we may save them a lot of pain and stress as they get older."

"True," she agreed. It was exactly what she had been thinking.

Kristin was not sure why she was second-guessing what she knew was right.

"So you don't think it's bad that I am still just beginning to learn about yoga, and I would then attempt to teach it to kids?"

"Nope. I think they would benefit from your knowledge and honesty," he answered, and then kissed the top of her head. Kristin smiled and reached back for his arm and pulled it around her.

"I'm going to look into it," she said, smiling. Kristin knew that the first thing tomorrow morning she would be on the dreaded computer machine looking things up. *See, technology does have some good points*, she thought. She realized that all that was needed was to blend it all together. To be able to use technology to society's advantage and still keep connections to others, and our self, that was the trick. That's exactly what she would want to teach to kids.

She pictured Gabriella or Brenda and Michael or their friends giggling and laughing during yoga poses, but then finding calmness and stillness too. She thought about how yoga would help them focus mentally and also to keep fit physically. Kristin imagined their grown-up lives so much better due to their knowledge of it. She pictured all of the children that she knew fully immersed in their own yoga practices and she could see exactly how it would benefit them. It was like a whole movie was playing out in her head as she thought it through.

Kristin knew that she had to do it. She had to teach yoga to kids!

Kristin sighed again and had to admit to Joshua that this just might be her calling in life. She just had that much confirmation about it within her.

"Look at you, my little yoga girl," said Joshua, teasing her, of course.

"I think the term is '*yogini*,' she corrected him. Then she thought for a moment if she was indeed correct or not. Honestly, she wasn't sure. She admitted again that she still had a lot to learn. Not knowing everything was okay with her. It helped keep her humble, a quality that she felt a good yoga practitioner should have.

Sometime soon after their conversation, Joshua fell asleep on the couch. His head fell back and his mouth fell open, snoring — just a little. Kristin took a few rounds of deep breaths, and then a surrender breath again. He was out, "like a light" — another saying of her uncle's. He would say it, and then flip off the light switch, cracking Kristin up. She wondered what her uncle would think about her being a yoga teacher. She wondered what her father would think about it too. As she thought about these important men in her life and took deep breaths, the same feeling that overcame her the previous night came back again: angelic support wrapping around her and her heart-center expanding exponentially beyond her body. She had to look and see. The clock on the cable box confirmed that it was, indeed, 11:11. She quickly closed her eyes to come back to her visions.

She immediately saw her father. Kristin shivered and the hairs on her back and arms stood up. She saw her father smile. She knew that he was with her. He had probably always been with her. Maybe he was her guardian angel, and he was always guiding her. Maybe he had guided her to this very moment. Kristin cried for a moment, missing the time they could have had together, and then grateful that she could see him now in this way. She stayed here with him for as long as she could and found no desire to sleep right away after the special experience.

She knew that she would not be able to discuss this with her mother, and maybe not even her sister. Then she realized that this was for her and her alone. As the angelic support enveloped her, Kristin knew, without doubt, that she was on the right path. Not that long ago she was a lost soul. She had worked very hard at finding her true self, and yet it wasn't until today that she thought she finally had.

She mused at the thought of once thinking that yoga was like a cult. She shook her head about many things that she used to think. She certainly couldn't see much of a trace of her old self now. This was most certainly a good thing!

This gave rise again to the concept of being a *yogi* or *yogini*. If yoga was a practice of bridging body, mind and soul together, she certainly felt like she was pretty darn close to that. At the very least, much closer than she ever was. She was more connected to her body and less in her erratic mind. And now that she was having these energetic awakenings, she knew that the only way to describe them was being in the divine presence of God.

Kristin had to admit to herself, *I AM a yogini*!

How had that happened?

When had it happened?

Kristin was excited to see where this next phase of her life was going to take her. She took another surrender breath, and as she exhaled, she let go of any fear about not being good enough, and as she inhaled, she breathed in all the beautiful and amazing possibilities ahead of her. Kristin decided not to try to figure all of those things out. Instead she would simply allow the universe to guide her on this path and go with its natural flow. She mused that she had become a *yogini*, albeit unintentionally, but a *yogini* nonetheless. This was indeed a part of her life path. And she was ready to embrace it with all of her being…

...well, Kristin would certainly embrace it all, after reconciling how she was going to admit to her mother that she had been right — again.

Made in the USA
Columbia, SC
21 March 2018